DARK HARVEST

DARK HARVEST

Love, Hate & Coffee

Andrew Fewtrell

Andrew Fewtrell is a first-time author, who
was inspired (by a dream) to write this debut novel.
He was born, educated and raised in the industrial city of
Birmingham in central England. He now lives in the Gold Coast
region of sub-tropical, Queensland in Australia, after migrating
from the UK in 1980. Andrew is married to his wife, Louise,
with three grown up children and two grandchildren.
After a lifetime of working on the sales and management
side of a diverse range of industries, Andrew – or Andy to
his mates, had the urge to indulge in his passion of writing.
Now in his early 60's, he plans to expand on this calling.

Edited by Melanie Scott
Book design by Adam Hay Studio

Published with the assistance of
Publicious Book Publishing
www.publicious.com.au

ISBN: 978-0-6452856-0-4 (pbk)
ISBN: 978-0-6452856-1-1 (ebk)

Dedications

I would like to dedicate this book to my beautiful family. Both in England and here in Australia. Firstly, my parents Alf and Betty, who always encouraged me to be the best person I could be. They both gave abundant love and opportunities to my sisters, Eleanor and Liz, and myself even though the family's finances weren't always the best.

My beautiful wife, Louise and my three children James, Blake and Emily – along with their lovely partners – have been a constant encouragement to me in completing my first novel. Their love and support have been vital and gratefully received by me during the long process of producing this book and I love them all dearly for it. Their inspiration and input were a source of joy for me throughout the process and also I used their traits and peculiarities to form many of the characters in the book.

I also had a team of dedicated friends and family, mainly female, who read my initial writing and storyline efforts, and gave me invaluable feedback and offered ideas. These lovely ladies will know who they are, so thank you to my two sisters in England, Susan (my cousin), Mandy, Lee and Helen (The Witches) and Janette (the Aston Villa fan!). I could not have developed the characters and finished the book without the help and support of two great friends, Helen Cardow and her partner John. Thank you, from the bottom of my heart to all my helpers.

Finally, a mention for both my editor, Melanie Scott and my book designer, Adam Hay. Both these exceptional and talented professionals helped me give life to this novel and gave me immeasurable gems of knowledge from their years of experience. Thank you both.

Contents

Brazil Family Tree

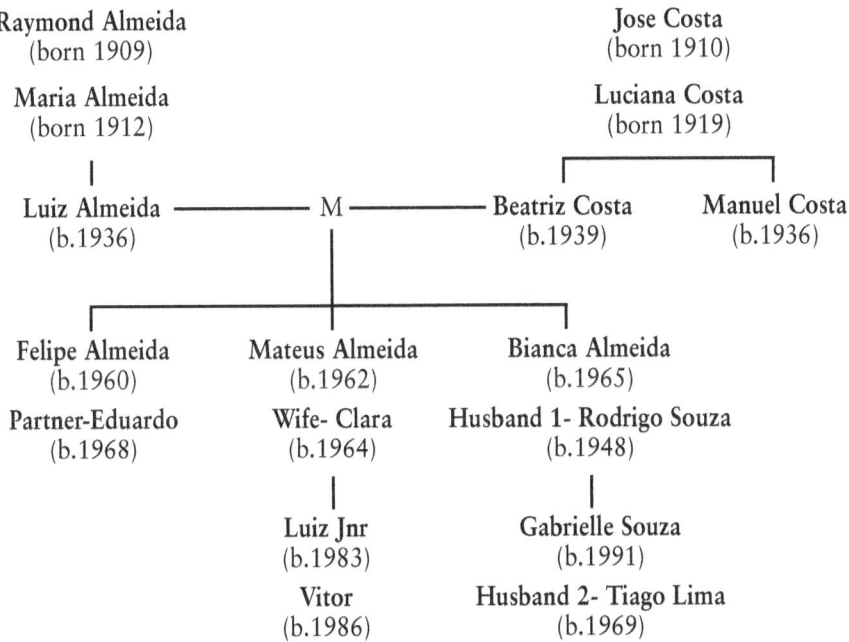

Raymond Almeida
(born 1909)

Jose Costa
(born 1910)

Maria Almeida
(born 1912)

Luciana Costa
(born 1919)

Luiz Almeida ————— M ————— Beatriz Costa
(b.1936)   (b.1939)

Manuel Costa
(b.1936)

Felipe Almeida
(b.1960)

Mateus Almeida
(b.1962)

Bianca Almeida
(b.1965)

Partner-Eduardo
(b.1968)

Wife- Clara
(b.1964)

Husband 1- Rodrigo Souza
(b.1948)

Luiz Jnr
(b.1983)

Gabrielle Souza
(b.1991)

Vitor
(b.1986)

Husband 2- Tiago Lima
(b.1969)

Vietnam Family Tree

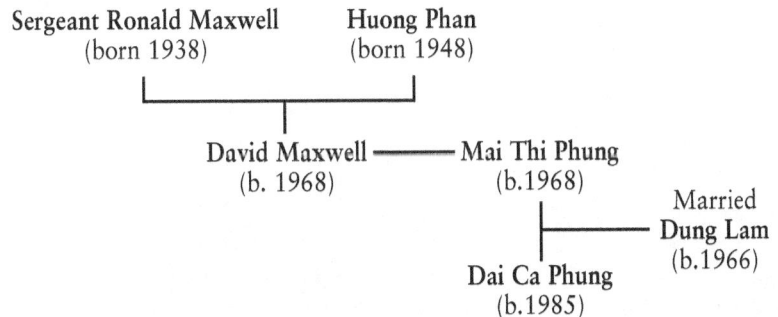

Sergeant Ronald Maxwell
(born 1938)

Huong Phan
(born 1948)

David Maxwell ——— Mai Thi Phung
(b. 1968)   (b.1968)

Married
Dung Lam
(b.1966)

Dai Ca Phung
(b.1985)

Other main characters who are not family members
Mi Ling (b.1938) – Dai's adopted grandmother.
Dr. Phan Chien (b.1946) – Dai's elder nemesis.

Brazil, 2014

Luiz Almeida sat in his comfortable armchair on the back balcony overlooking the lush, green valley below his rambling homestead. A warm, haphazard breeze swept through and moved the trees in a rhythmic pattern. The massive coffee plantation, which had sustained his family's wealth and happiness over many generations, was spread up and down the valleys surrounding his beloved home. As he sat and watched, the seventy-eight-year-old wondered whether the tragic news he had just received from his youngest son would, indeed, signal the end of his family's coffee dynasty and maybe even the end of his own life.

Vietnam, 2014

Dai Ca Phung was a young man in his late twenties, currently employed within the coffee business at the burgeoning Lam Dong Company. This fast-emerging enterprise, based in the town of Buon Ma Thuot in the Central West Highlands area of the country, was a specialised subsidiary of one of the largest coffee-producing and exporting companies in Vietnam, Highlands Coffee.

The Lam Dong Company had successfully developed and cultivated the higher quality arabica-style coffee bean. Dai Ca Phung, now an enterprising executive, had been instrumental in the successful propagation of this new style of coffee, aided by the ultra-suitable climate of his local Highlands region. He had further aspirations to take on the might of Brazil and win, by whatever means necessary. His endgame was to wreak havoc on anything linked to America. His reasons were more than financial. They were very, very personal.

The rise and rise of Vietnam

During the 1990s, Vietnam had surged from being a small-time player in the coffee-producing industry to become the major producer of the robusta-style beans across the world. By the end of 1999 Vietnam had earned the mantle of second largest coffee producer in the world after Brazil.

In the process they had usurped another South American producer, Columbia, but at a huge cost. The intense methods of production and low level of wages paid to growers and pickers alike in Vietnam had forced down the price of green robusta beans to below $1 per pound. By 2001 the price had dived to 50 cents a pound, far below the sustainable cost of production, and a glut of coffee had been dumped onto the world market. The world coffee price crisis at this time was finally resolved when, because of the number of growers leaving the industry due to low returns, the prices started to increase as production slowed. By the beginning of 2005, the price of robusta green beans had gradually eased back up to $1 per pound. But it was clear to see that, by engineering vast overproduction and then a downturn in supply of the world's favourite caffeine hit, the price could be manipulated with great effect. One person, currently working in the Highlands region of Vietnam, was fully aware of the ever-fluctuating market price of the humble coffee bean. This man was Dai Ca Phung.

In the beginning

The Almeida family business was positioned on the northern outskirts of the town of Nova Serrana in the southern Minas Gerais region of Brazil. The town was situated around one hundred kilometres west of the region's capital city, Belo Horizonte, amongst the rolling hills of the Brazilian Highlands, to the north-east of São Paulo. This area is considered the heart of Brazil's coffee country and spawned many family-based enterprises from the early eighteenth century, when the humble coffee bean was first introduced by the colonising Portuguese to South America's largest country. Its temperate climate averages seventy degrees Fahrenheit year-round and, mixed with the region's moderate sunshine and rain, it is ideal for the propagation and growing of the top-quality arabica and the hardier, but less popular, robusta coffee beans. Even though the conditions seem perfect, many a fortune has been won and lost in this lush and verdant landscape in Brazil's coffee-growing history.

Luiz Almeida's family had been involved in the coffee industry since the late 1800s, when his grandparents had started up the plantation. By the time his parents, Raymond and Maria, had established themselves as the owners of the business in the middle of the twentieth century, Brazil boasted the lion's share of the burgeoning world coffee export market. Raymond Almeida had raised his only child to be a hard-working young man and Luiz's mother, Maria, was a loving wife who ensured that there was always food on the table for her beloved husband and son. She was also a strong believer in the Christian faith, which she often called upon to help the family through some of the leaner times in their life on the plantation. She instilled this faith into her son, although Luiz was never as zealous in his beliefs.

Luiz adored his father, who had not only been a strong and loving figurehead to his only son, but also someone who Luiz could model himself on. Raymond had been raised and had developed his coffee-growing skills with the help of his own father on the family *fazenda*, as the plantations were called back then. Raymond was keen to carry on this tradition with his own son and ensured that Luiz knew all the rudiments of the trade by the time he was in his mid-teens. This included horse-riding, which Luiz loved and at which he became extremely skilful. Raymond and Maria had fervently hoped for more children in their marriage, but unfortunately this was not meant to be. Maria consoled herself with the thought that this was God's will, so they poured all their love into their only son.

Luiz had spent all his working life in the vibrant cash cow of the Brazilian economy, which had had its fair share of ups and downs during the 50s and 60s and he had risen to take over the reins of his parents' successful venture by the time he had turned twenty-eight years old. The company had concentrated on developing the best quality arabica coffee beans under the brand label of Nova, named after its local town. The Brazilian government had offered great incentive payments to encourage the growth of both the coffee and the beef industries in the quickly-developing nation. Luiz's wily business acumen took full advantage of these favourable trading conditions. By the mid-1960s the Nova brand had developed export markets all around the world, predominantly in the huge North American market, and was going forward in leaps and bounds. The Nova Coffee Company employed over two hundred and fifty staff at this time, spread across the areas of cultivation, harvesting crops, processing, transportation and storage. The fledging Scientific and Chemical Department was also established in that decade, helping to develop better and more productive ways of growing the crop and protecting the precious coffee beans from the menace of disease and parasites.

By this time Luiz had also met, wooed and married the beautiful Beatriz, only daughter of the famous Costa family. Her family's claim to fame was the ownership of a thriving import and export shipping business based in Santos, the bustling waterside precinct just south of São Paulo. So, the marriage was not only rooted in a deep and passionate love, but also a very handy economic alliance.

Luiz and Beatriz

Luiz and Beatriz had met in October 1956. Luiz was a handsome twenty-year-old, with more than his share of female admirers; Beatriz was a strikingly beautiful, dark-haired teenager approaching eighteen years of age when their paths crossed for the first time.

Beatriz's father, José Costa, was the current President - and therefore an influential figure - at the local Santos football club and had asked his daughter to accompany him to one of the famous team's numerous social events. His wife, Luciana, had taken ill that night and had begrudgingly decided not to attend the gala evening. The ever-confident Beatriz had jumped at the chance to be amongst the social elite of the São Paulo region who attended such prestigious events. She was also spurred on by the fact that she could be introduced to some of the adored soccer players who had become legends at the club. None shone brighter than the enigmatic Pelé – or Edson Arantes do Nascimento, to give him his full name. Pelé, as a mere sixteen-year-old, was setting Santos football circles alight with his brilliant skills and was heading for greatness in Brazil's national sport.

José Costa's daughter had always loved football. Partly because her father was involved in the game, but also because of Brazil's great passion for the national side that was on the verge of immortality at the time. Her elder brother, Manuel, was also a fervent fan of the game and the siblings had often played football, which was like a religion in their country, together as youngsters. But Beatriz could never be described as a tomboy. She also loved to be in the limelight and attending events such as this would ensure she would be noticed.

Luiz Almeida's reasons for being there were different. His passion for Santos had been born out of a football-mad family and he had been religiously spurred on by his father. Luiz had regularly attended the Vila Belmiro, Santos' home ground, since he was a young boy of six. His father, Raymond, had long looked forward to introducing his only son to the 'beautiful game'.

As Beatriz entered the near-full ballroom where the charity event was being held, a dozen or so admiring, well-heeled young men turned their gaze to look upon her beauty as she passed by. Her shy glances at her father could not hide the fact that Beatriz was distinctly aware of the attention being afforded to her. She wore a full-length, crimson dress, delicately embroidered around the neckline, complimenting the colour of her deep jade eyes. The silver necklace sparkling against her olive skin was borrowed from her mother's collection, and further enhanced her beauty. The carefully chosen dark red colour of her lipstick belied her young age and accentuated her full lips as she smiled at her many admirers. As she was seated at the head table, she was greeted by the guests who were lucky enough – or who had paid enough money – to have been invited to share such a prized position at the event.

José was visibly proud of his young daughter as he introduced her to the other eight occupants of the elegantly dressed table, on which sparkling, long-stemmed wine glasses, fine silver cutlery and stiff, white cotton serviettes were arranged artfully on a jet-black tablecloth. An arrangement of radiantly coloured local flowers, mainly sempre-vivas, freesias and begonias, constituted the centrepiece and lit up the table. Besides Beatriz, all the guests at the table were male, save for one. The only lady, wife of one of the club directors, had been the centre of attention prior to Beatriz's arrival. She seemed uncomfortable with the introduction of such a vivacious young guest, as all the men's gazes were averted from her towards José Costa's beautiful daughter.

Some fifty metres from Beatriz's prime position, at the back of the room, Luiz took his seat at a table of ten die-hard fans. Each of them had proffered a sizeable amount of their hard-earned cruzeiros – a currency that has since been replaced by the Brazilian real – to attend this sparkling social event. Luiz was a popular member of this group of old school friends and workers from his family's business. He may not have had brothers and sisters to grow up with, but his magnetic persona and natural empathy had brought him many solid friendships.

His dark, tailored jacket and eye-catching black and gold tie suitably enhanced the well-built physique of the handsome coffee-grower's son from Nova Serrana. Luiz's fashionable, white, starched dress shirt contrasted with his heavily tanned skin, deep chocolate eyes and shock of dark brown hair. His father, Raymond, sat next to him. He was filled with pride at the fact that his only son had grown into such a fine young man, not only respected by the workers at his coffee plantation, but also admired by a throng of young female beauties amongst the São Paulo in-crowd, many of whom had already noted Luiz as a potentially good catch.

The night was a remarkably successful and boisterous affair, with lots of joking and slapping of backs amongst the mostly male attendees. Many doctors, lawyers, politicians and businessmen had put hands into their considerably deep pockets to raise money for a local charity supporting homeless children in the favelas. The room was energetically entertained by a well-known local band, featuring a quartet of nimble-footed trumpet players and an exotically dressed female lead singer. Their rhythmic steps as they blasted out their tunes encouraged the big crowd to get up onto the dance-floor and enjoy themselves enthusiastically well into the night. There were some elegant and exuberant versions of the local samba, carimbó and forró styles of dance on display amongst the thronging couples and singles.

Large amounts of Brazilian wines and spirits, specially chosen by José Costa, had been consumed during the night. These included sparkling white wines made in the champagne style; Jose's favourite the Casa Valduga "Maria Valduga" Brut Chardonnay-Pinot Noir from the famous Serra Gaucha region, close to the border with Uruguay. It was also a firm favourite of the ladies of Brazil and had been appreciated by many of them during the dinner. For most of the men present, an array of popular local beers such as Bohemia, Brahms and Antarctica were on offer. The draft "Chopp" version of Brahms beer was the most consumed, especially by Luiz and his table. All these beers were of the favoured Pilsner lager variety – light-colored, mid-strength beers served icy cold to quench the thirst of the partying menfolk. To finish off the night, José had ensured that there was enough Cachaça available for the many revellers. Brazil's most consumed alcoholic beverage was made sweet and strong from fresh local sugarcane juice, which was fermented, distilled and then drunk with muddled lime wedges over crushed ice. Multiple bottles of the "Cabare Cachaça Extra Premium" were emptied on this happy and eventful night. All the alcohol that night had been happily supplied, free of charge, by José's ever-willing band of southern Brazilian wine and spirit manufacturers. They exclusively used his services to export their products to their many overseas clients and, consequently, were often afforded prized tickets to FC Santos' key matches at the Vila Belmiro.

By 11.30pm the room was beginning to empty. The manager of the Santos first team had been the keynote speaker at the event earlier in the night. As well as a fleeting appearance by the youthful Pelé, some of the lesser lights of the team had also turned up, lured by the chance to have a free feed and mingle with the crowd of Santos supporters to have their egos stroked.

José Costa sat with a fat Cohiba cigar wedged between his teeth as he chatted with the guests at his table. He had been pleased by the turnout and by the amount of money raised for the grateful charity. At that moment, he glanced away from his table and spotted an old friend and business associate standing at the nearby bar. He recognised the craggy features of the man in his late fifties, talking to a younger man. Many years of arduous work amongst the coffee trees of his plantation had etched a rugged texture into the face of Raymond Almeida. However, he was a strapping, healthy looking man for his age, and José knew that he also had a great head for business. He was also a particularly important client of the Costa Exporting Company.

"Hey, Raymond!" boomed out José's deep voice across the now quite empty ballroom. Luiz's father cocked his head to see his old friend shuffling towards him.

"Good evening, José," said Raymond. "What a wonderful night it has been, *meu amigo*!" José took Raymond's strong hand and shook it with vigor. "This is my little boy, Luiz. Do you remember him?" asked Raymond, nodding in the direction of his tall son.

"Wow, he has filled out since I last saw him! Is he playing football still?"

Luiz smiled politely as he was introduced to his father's friend. "I'm afraid to say that my level of skills will never allow me to play for the mighty Santos, Señor Costa. But I still have the odd game with the boys at the plantation. It is an honour to meet you again," replied Luiz.

At that very moment, Luiz noticed a vision of loveliness nestling close to José. Her father put his arm around Beatriz's slender shoulders and introduced her, firstly to Raymond, and then to an awestruck Luiz.

"So very nice to meet you, Señor Almeida," started Beatriz, her stunning jade green eyes lowering as she spoke. She then turned and extended an elegant hand towards Raymond's besotted son. "And, also to meet you, Señor Almeida junior. I do admire your necktie!"

"The pleasure is all mine, Señorita Costa, and please... call me Luiz. I borrowed the tie from my father's collection... It is not that often that I wear one." Their eyes remained transfixed on each other and Luiz realised that he had held onto Beatriz's delicate hand for a moment too long. He retracted his hand sharply. "Well, perhaps you could take me shopping one day and help me buy a selection of ties. I may need my own one day," added an emboldened Luiz, with a glint in his eye.

Raymond gave his son a quizzical look and winked knowingly at his old friend. "Oh, these young ones, José, always wanting to spend our hard-earned money!" The comment was acknowledged by José with a quick smile and a nod of his head. The Costas made their farewells and retreated to a waiting taxi. As Beatriz made her way to the exit of the ballroom she slowed and looked back towards Mr Almeida and his handsome son. Luiz's gaze had never left her as she accompanied José Costa out of the venue.

A smile rippled over their faces, as their eyes met across the emptied dance-floor again. The moment that the Costas had disappeared through the door, Luiz turned to his father, gave him a loving hug, and blurted, "What a fantastic night, Papa!"

Luiz Almeida and Beatriz were inseparable following that magic night at the Santos Club. Beatriz went home that evening with a flutter in her heart and, the very next day, took up Luiz's offer to escort him shopping for a range of fashionable clothes and accessories... Any excuse to see him again.

The chemistry between the handsome couple had been instant. Much to his father's pleasure, Luiz had accepted Beatriz's phone call and a plan was made to visit the newly emerging retail suburbs of São Paulo. This was the first of many outings for the couple – a multitude of lunches, dinners, theatre visits followed. Beatriz shared Luiz's passion for horse riding, and this resulted in multiple visits to the Almeida homestead so that they could enjoy time together riding through the lush green pastures and tree-lined fields that surrounded Luiz's home. Beatriz's engaging personality helped her instantly bond with Luiz's parents, especially Maria, who was thankful for some female company. If any pair of lovers where meant to be partners for life, it was the coffee-grower's son from Nova Serrana and the charming daughter of the Santos Football Club's President.

Ever the romantic, Luiz, now a well-heeled young gentleman of twenty-two years, had chosen to propose marriage to Beatriz whilst on an overseas trip to Sweden, which was hosting the football World Cup Finals in the summer of 1958. José Costa's connections within the Brazilian football fraternity had its benefits, including airfares to the host country for himself, along with his son Manuel, Beatriz and her boyfriend, Luiz. Not surprisingly, Luiz chose the final game of the tournament – where his heroes of the Brazilian national side had solidly beaten the host nation, 5-2, with Pelé scoring twice – to drop to his knees and ask Beatriz to marry him. The previous night he had secretly asked José Costa for the hand of his daughter in marriage. Her father was delighted and immediately agreed to Luiz's request. That mighty Brazilian team, including the seventeen-year-old Pelé, Mário Zagallo at centre forward and the irrepressible Garrincha on the wing, were now the best football team in the world. The timing could not have been any better and, with a nod from her father and a whoop of glee from Beatriz, she squealed an excited "Yes!" in reply. The union of the Costa and Almeida families was cemented. To top it off, Brazil were the World Champions and a huge grin exploded across Luiz's handsome face.

They were married in late 1958 and within seven wondrous years their lives had been blessed by the arrival of three children. Now the family of five was complete, and Luiz had also taken over the reins of his retiring parents' successful coffee business. The world seemed to be as perfect as it could ever be.

The Almeida Family

March 20th 1960 was an immensely proud date for Luiz and Beatriz Almeida. Their first child, Felipe, was born after a short labour at the São Paulo General Hospital, a mere two kilometres from Beatriz's parents' home. Her father, José, had great plans for his first grandson – maybe he would be the next Pelé when he grew up? Baby Felipe was a healthy eight-and-a-half pounds at birth and grew into the most beautiful toddler, with a smile that would melt the hearts of his adoring family members. He had striking jade green eyes, mirroring his mother's, and a dark complexion inherited from his father's side. The handsome little boy seemed to have it all, but expectations of the first-born are often carried like lead weights around their small shoulders. Indeed, Felipe would have many burdens to bear in his troubled life ahead. He was the "little prince" to his two doting sets of grandparents, the heir to his father's growing business and the pride and joy of his adoring mother.

The coffee business was rolling along very successfully for Luiz, and young Felipe wanted for nothing in his developing years. Two years later a little brother came along as playmate for the "little prince". Second son Mateus was born on August 15th 1962. It was a further occasion to celebrate in that year, after their beloved Brazilian football team – now known as the *Seleção* or the chosen ones – had won a second consecutive World Cup in Chile in June. The mighty Brazilians had beaten Czechoslovakia 3-1 in the final and, of course, José Costa, Manuel Costa, Luiz and his soccer-mad father, Raymond, had travelled across South America to witness the tournament. Although

Beatriz also wanted to go, her husband and father convinced her that, at seven months' pregnant, it was probably a better idea to stay at home and watch the tournament on the brand-new television set, recently purchased for the family. She begrudgingly agreed. The joy of Mateus' birth in August was tempered by the fact that José Costa, Beatriz's father, had been diagnosed with terminal throat cancer on his return from Chile. Although his doctor had informed him of his situation in early July, José had kept the news quiet and had only told his distressed wife, Luciana, the awful truth after the birth of their second grandchild. Beatriz had always been remarkably close to her father and she took the news very badly. As the months went by and her father's health visibly deteriorated, she became very withdrawn and depressed. Luiz struggled to deal with his wife's swinging moods, caused by the strain she felt from trying to handle her father's demise and looking after her two young boys. Felipe had noticeably been affected by the tension abundant in the home and his increasingly outward show of jealousy towards his young brother was cause for concern for Luiz. Thankfully, the solid support from his own parents, Raymond and Maria, along with Beatriz's mother Luciana's surprisingly strong help, meant that Luiz was able to cope during this very torrid time of their lives.

Alas, José Costa would not live to see either of his grandsons play football for the great Brazilian national football team, as he had fantasied. The pain that he endured until his death in January 1963 was tempered by the knowledge that he had lived to see his beautiful Beatriz become happily married and the mother of two wonderful boys.

In late January Beatriz's famed jade-coloured eyes were full of tears as she bravely read a touching eulogy for her beloved father at his funeral, which attracted nearly one thousand souls. It took place at the massive São Paulo Cathedral, only recently built in 1954, a fitting location for the devout Roman Catholic José Costa to be farewelled. Its soaring Gothic architecture, topped by a huge Renaissance-style dome, added the appropriate splendour for a man who had been a big part of the city's commercial success throughout his life. People from all walks of life attended the event to pay their respects, even the great Pelé.

José, businesslike as ever, had left the running of the Costa Import and Export enterprise to his son, Manuel, in his will. Beatriz's brother had worked within the business since leaving school as a sixteen-year-old and had grown into his position gradually with his father as his great mentor. By now in his late twenties, Manuel was more than able to take on the challenge and his father had told his mother that their son would be the heir to his throne. Beatriz had never shown any interest in being a part of the family business. Indeed, she had also never shown the desire to be part of Luiz's company Nova either, other than in a quasi-PR role. She loved being a mother and a wife to her family, therefore Manuel's elevation within the Costa company was of little consequence to her and she supported her brother's progress. Luciana was also happy that her late husband had placed his confidence in their only son.

Young Felipe seemed to carry the sadness from his grandfather's loss a lot longer than any other member of his family, even his mother. Beatriz would often find him crying in his bedroom for no apparent reason, other than that the "little prince" missed his grandad.

As the years progressed, Mateus grew into an incredibly happy, outgoing boy, whilst his elder brother was often broody and sad; even though Felipe was highly intelligent and academically bright.

October 4th 1965 saw the birth of the daughter that Beatriz had dreamed of. In stark contrast to the happiness of his personal life, Luiz had recently been through hard times with the Nova Coffee business, but now things were changing for the better. He had managed to diversify his business by adding a scientific department to the company. Luiz had always seen a future for this part of their business. For many decades Nova Coffee had bought pesticides and chemicals from American or European conglomerates. The mighty multinationals had developed and sold their products to many agricultural concerns around the world, to help control the various pests that hindered productive growth of their precious coffee trees. Luiz thought that locally produced pesticides would be much more cost-effective and specifically relevant to the Brazilian and South American strains of the various diseases. Along with some local Nova Serrana businessmen who understood and had some experience in these matters, he skilfully put together a mix of scientists and technically able associates to bring the project to fruition. It was an investment that Luiz could barely afford, but the savings that this development would bring to Nova could help him with the company's cashflow eventually. It was to be one of the best decisions that he had ever made as head of Nova Coffee.

With the birth of his daughter, whom they had named Bianca, Luiz thought that happier times were due to him and were maybe just around the corner. Beatriz was back to her charming, lovable self and the wide smile that had typified the younger, confident Luiz was evident once again on his handsome face. Luiz had discussed with Beatriz the benefits of employing a full-time nanny to help her manage the three children. Although initially Beatriz, along with her mother and in-laws, had put up some resistance to this idea, within a month of Bianca joining the growing family, it became apparent that the antics and energy of both Felipe and Mateus were becoming harder to cope with for all the ageing grandparents and Beatriz herself. Luiz talked with his staff and the wife of one of his most trusted employees was taken on as a full-time nanny for the Almeida children. Her name was Esmeralda and her hiring proved to be yet another very astute decision by Luiz Almeida.

As the Almeida family grew together through the late sixties and the early seventies, the children's characters developed in truly diverse ways. Felipe was increasingly becoming confused about his place in the world. By his fourteenth birthday he was struggling to find his way in life, although very astute at school and excelling in the subjects of English, history and art. He had a very fertile imagination and could create the most amazing pieces of artwork or make up stories full of intricate details and brilliant description. Felipe had never taken to the physical world of sport, unlike his younger brother, who had developed his sporting prowess with ease. Mateus seemed to always win the sprints and long jumps at the local school athletic carnivals and was a standout in the swimming pool and especially on the football field. Even though he was only twelve years old, Mateus had already been identified by the famous Santos FC Youth Academy as a possible future star. His late grandfather would have been enormously proud of him.

Bianca had lived most of her first eight years as a spoiled "princess". Although Luiz did not approve, Beatriz would often give in to their daughter's whims. With the considerable wealth that the Nova Coffee Company was reaping for the Almeida family, nothing was too expensive for Beatriz and her little treasure. After all, José Costa, the father of his only daughter Beatriz, had showered all sorts of luxury on her as a young child, so why shouldn't she do the same?

New Year's Eve 1974 was an exceptionally joyous occasion. An excellent coffee market during the year had seen Nova jump into being one of the top ten performers, amongst the coffee companies in Brazil. All Luiz's children, his wife and even his ageing parents were healthy and happy and the future, financially, seemed to be secure. The New Year was celebrated with a huge party at the newly renovated Almeida house with more than a hundred guests, made up of family, business associates and friends. For the 38-year-old Luiz, the world was his oyster. He was proud of the fact that he had been successful in his chosen business and had raised a beautiful family. 1974 had started so wonderfully... but it was to end in the worst possible way.

The Vietnam War

In January 1968, early in the Vietnam War, North Vietnamese and Viet Cong forces swept down upon several key cities and provinces in South Vietnam, including its capital, Saigon. The surge became known as the Tet Offensive, named after the famous Tet holiday, when all Vietnamese celebrate their various religious beliefs. This show of military might had caught the US military and its Vietnamese allies off guard and was a huge blow struck by the communists against the South. However, within days American forces turned back the onslaught to recapture most of the areas lost to the marauding invaders. From a military point of view, Tet was a huge defeat for the North Vietnamese Army, but it turned out to be a political and psychological victory for the communists.

In February 1968, the Battle for Huê went on for twenty-six days as the Allied forces battled to recapture most of the lost areas, one of which was the former religious retreat of Huê. The town was almost totally levelled in the battle and left nearly all the population homeless. Following the so-called American "victory", mass graves containing the bodies of thousands of South Vietnamese citizens, who had been executed during the communist occupation, were discovered. The rising resentment against the vilified Viet Cong had reached fever pitch by mid-March 1968. Conversely, demonstrations from anti-war protesters back home in the USA were also portraying their own forces as heavy-handed killers. Many of the young men of the US military were getting confused and scared because of the mounting atrocities that they were becoming involved in.

On March 16th 1968, Sergeant Ronald Maxwell, a thirty-year-old veteran Marine, along with the rest of the increasingly angry and frustrated men of Charlie Company, 11th Brigade and other US forces entered the small village of My Lai. "This is what you have been waiting for. Search and destroy. Go for it, boys!" urged their superior officers. Fuelled by vengeance, sheer terror and copious amounts of narcotics, a short time later the killings began. The My Lai massacre was to become a watershed moment in the Vietnam War.

Ronald had no idea what he was doing. Visions of previous traumatic experiences in his sorry life came flooding into his head. The worst moment of his life thus far had been when he was a young teenager, and it had transformed his life. As he waited to disembark from the landing helicopter in My Lai he was lost in his thoughts.

Whilst playing with his younger sister, on his father's farm outside of his Midwest home in Ohio, Ronald had playfully pushed twelve-year-old Judy as they enjoyed a game of tag in the farmyard. She fell awkwardly, striking her head on the metal wheel arch of one of their father's old tractors. "Get up, you little wuss!" shouted Ronald to his sister as she lay motionless in the mud. With no response coming from Judy, the scared young man squatted down next to her. A single flow of fresh, red blood trickled from her nose; her eyes still open in a look of frozen shock – she was dead. Ronald couldn't move. He could not believe what had happened; he began to frantically shout out.

"Mom, Dad, come quickly, come quickly! Mom, Dad, please!" he screamed in the general direction of the house, where his parents were eating lunch. His father, Ronald Senior, was the first to react, followed closely by his wife. As his father reached the scene of the incident, Ronald Junior stood up slowly, turned towards his parents and blurted out.

"I am so sorry, Mom, Dad... it was an accident. I didn't mean it!" Tears cascading from his eyes, he fell into the embrace of his mother, who instinctively hugged him, until she saw the awful consequence of what had just happened. She looked with horror at her shaking son and quickly pushed him away. Immediately she fell sobbing in a heap next to the lifeless body of her daughter.

"How could you do this to your sister?" the distraught mother demanded of her shaken son. Ronald Senior looked at his son with rage. No words were forthcoming. Young Ronald had never forgotten the looks on his parents' faces or the agonising shame in his stomach at what he had done.

This memory was fresh in his mind as Ronald hit the ground amongst the burning mayhem of the small Vietnamese village, the throbbing sound of the helicopter rotors thudding and echoing inside his confused head. The tragic accident with his sister had not only affected his relationship with his parents, but also had led to a young and immature Ronald leaving home as a sixteen-year-old, banished to join the army. His parents had never spoken to him again after he had signed up with the military and his sorry tale had been completed by the brutal training of the American war machine, which had led to him seeing action in Korea, before the disaster that was Vietnam.

The My Lai villagers were slain in the manic Marine attack, firstly from helicopter gunships and then in hand-to-hand combat. Some of the cocky Americans saw it as their right to rape, as well as murder, the terrified village women and children who got in their way. Huong Phan, a young village girl, had thought the worst was over after she awoke from the initial bomb blast and automatic gunfire that had killed her family. The twenty-year-old found herself pinned on the floor of her burning house by the frantic ravages of a deranged soldier ripping at her clothes. He then forced his hand across her screaming mouth, as he let his frustration out on the diminutive village girl. The savage rape was almost over when Huong noticed the soldier's embroidered name badge emblazoned on his uniform. As Sergeant Maxwell pressed himself against her small frame and came to his climax, in an amazing show of strength, she grasped at his fatigues and ripped the name badge from his clothing. He responded by slapping her across the face and forcing himself away from her trembling body. As Maxwell stood up and adjusted his clothing he looked down through glazed eyes to where she lay and said, "I am so sorry, ma'am, I am so, so sorry." Huong looked up, expecting to be finished off with the military man's bullet, yet, as their eyes met, she noticed a genuine look of remorse on the crazed soldier's face. To the relief of the petrified young girl he turned and ran off towards the continuing battle, as flames continued to lick the once peaceful home of Huong Phan. She lay, incredulous, on the bamboo floor with tears streaming down her face. In her hand was a tattered scrap of material bearing embroidered letters she could not understand – but was determined to keep.

The My Lai massacre proved to be a turning point in the war. When news of the atrocities eventually surfaced, it sent shockwaves through the US political establishment, the military's chain of command and an already divided American public.

By August 1968, Sergeant Ronald Maxwell had been ferried back to his homeland, away from the war, due to his psychological problems. Issues from his past had been awakened during his tour of duty in Vietnam. They had been infused into his unbalanced psyche, ever since his sister's tragic death. As he found his way home to America, he had no way of knowing the chain of events his rabid antics in My Lai would unleash. Ronald would silence the ghosts of his past with a deadly overdose of sleeping pills six years later, but the legacy of his actions would play out over many decades to come.

By April 30th 1975, South Vietnamese President Duong Van Minh had delivered an unconditional surrender to the communists and the last remnants of the defeated US forces were evacuated as Saigon fell to the North Vietnamese. The communist victors accepted Minh's surrender and assured the Vietnamese people that "only the Americans have been beaten. If you are patriots, consider this a moment of joy."

Huong Phan, David and Mai Thi

By the time that South Vietnam surrendered, Huong Phan's illegitimate son, born in December 1968, was almost seven years old. Six months after his birth an impoverished and sickly Huong Phan had given her traumatically conceived baby up for adoption. She had travelled back to Saigon after the My Lai massacre, struggling with the issue of abortion after discovering her forced pregnancy. The ailing twenty-year-old had decided, because of her strict religious beliefs, to have the child and try to raise it. She talked to the staff at the hospital where her son was born about the meaning of the wording she had ripped from her rapist's chest. Huong discovered that the name of the child's father was Maxwell. For reasons known only to herself, she named her baby boy David Maxwell, perhaps thinking that the American moniker might help him in his future life. This was at a stage of the war when the South Vietnamese were still hopeful of a victory, along with their American allies. Huong Phan, now a broken woman, left Saigon a month after giving David up for adoption. Although racked with grief by this decision, she had realised that her child would have always been a constant reminder of that terrible ordeal she had suffered in My Lai. Huong's future was to become even darker as the nightmares remained from her experiences during the war, leading to a life of self-abuse and loneliness. Her poverty and ill-health hampered her at every turn, resulting in the young woman falling prey to the menacing lawlessness that had gripped the troubled nation in the years after the war. She died from a drug overdose before she had even turned thirty years old – another anonymous victim of the war that had ravaged the country so deeply.

Her son, with the American name, but very Asian-looking features, including his mother's dark almond-shaped eyes, remained in a Buddhist orphanage in Saigon from 1969 until 1983, looked after and raised by the dedicated monks. The orphanage housed around 850 orphans of the war and was a loving, yet strict, environment for the unfortunate children to be brought up in.

By 1983, David Maxwell, although enriched by his Buddhist upbringing, was a troubled young man, haunted by his background. The orphanage system in Vietnam after the war harboured thousands of children with similar horrific stories to be told. The fact that he was one of many mattered little to David. As his physical features developed with age, his appearance grew more western, especially the tint of red in his hair. But the telltale dark, almond-shaped eyes guaranteed that his half-caste status was set for life. A curse carried by the many unfortunate and cruelly named "bastards of the war".

As a physically well-developed fifteen-year-old, David had decided, after many futile attempts, that he would never be one of the lucky ones, those who were blessed with a willing middle-class family to take them away, mainly overseas, to be adopted. He knew his advanced age was against him, as well as appearing to be too much trouble for any kind-hearted prospective foster parents. He had realised by now that he had to forge a life on his own. He was a truly angry young man, but he had made his decision.

By the middle of 1984 David Maxwell had absconded from the only place that he knew as home and headed for the bright lights of downtown Ho Chi Minh City. The former capital city of South Vietnam, Saigon, had now been renamed by the conquering communists in honour of the Great Chinese Patriarch. As an enterprising street urchin, the young redhead was soon enmeshed in the seedy underworld of inner-city crime. To survive, eat, drink and to buy the necessary uppers and downers that kept his sorry life going, he lapsed into the inevitable life of petty crime and self-depredation.

Luckily for him, an angel appeared to light his way, an angel in the shape of Mai Thi Phung. Mai was a sixteen-year-old runaway from Hanoi, the former capital city of North Vietnam, who had lost both of her parents in the war and was an only child. She had sought out the inviting lure of Ho Chi Minh City, much as David had done, to be her saviour. From the moment they had met at the small Tong's Café in the District 1 area of the city, they had clicked.

Mai had secured a job at the café as an underpaid and badly treated waitress, working for an over-bearing boss, Mr Van Tong. On first meeting David, she initially had been fascinated by the odd-looking redhead, then warmed to his surprisingly mature view of life for an almost sixteen-year-old. The young couple began to spend most of their spare time together and an awkward love developed between the two. Following one balmy afternoon that turned into a long night, the two spent their time getting high on stolen alcohol and LSD – a drug that had been introduced to the youth of Vietnam by the Americans during the war – procured by David from one of his many street contacts. They had ended up sexually entangled at Mai's rundown bedsit above the café. Their inexperience soon evaporated and gave way to a sense of joy as they engaged, for the first time, in sex between two people who genuinely cared for each other, erupting into the most amazing feeling that neither of them had ever imagined or experienced before.

The next few weeks seemed like a fairytale for David and Mai as their bond grew. Even in the midst of the lonely, seedy existence that the two lovers had been a part of, the prospect of hope that had ignited their lives seemed to offer a strange sustenance for a fleeting moment. That moment was shattered by a cruel twist of fate on a hot and steamy evening in January 1985.

Mai had not been feeling well for a few days. She had asked her fat-bellied, evil-smelling boss if she could have a couple of days off work to sort herself out. Tong had begrudgingly agreed, but insisted that she go straight to bed after seeing the local doctor, so that she would be ready to waitress at the weekend. Arriving at the medical centre, she quickly entered one of the dingy cubicles that passed as a doctor's clinic. After a few simple examinations from the local nurse, her worst fears were confirmed – she was pregnant by David. Mai strode out of the doctor's rooms, headed straight for the Milk Bar next door, and poured some of her remaining coins into the payphone.

"Can I speak to David, please?" she pleaded, as the phone call was answered at the pool hall where Mai knew that David would be that afternoon. "Sorry, miss, David is out on an errand right now. I can give him a message when he gets back if you like," came the reply.

"Please tell him that Mai called and can he come as soon as possible to my room at the café – it's urgent... Please tell him to hurry!" The phone clunked down at the pool room end, and Mai desperately hoped that the message would get through to her young lover – she needed to see David.

As she returned to her modest room above the café, Mr Van Tong spied her entering and followed a distracted Mai upstairs. "Are you okay, little girl?" he asked.

"What?" responded Mai in a startled voice.

"I have got something for you, Mai," said Tong.

By this time, the pushy café owner had followed her into the bedsit. He had been excessively drinking his usual cheap whiskey and had a wild glint in his eye. "Please, Mr Tong, leave me alone, I am not well," she pleaded.

"You owe me for everything you have, little Mai – it is time that you showed me some overdue appreciation," slurred the fat man. He lurched towards the frightened girl and pushed her onto the bed. Mai let out a loud scream.

David had indeed been given the message from Mai, via his friend at the pool hall. He was quickly making his way to the café to see his true love. He was just entering the café downstairs when he was startled by Mai's scream from above, prompting him to bolt up the stairs to see what was happening. David noticed that most of the customers in the café seemed to have heard the noise as well but had decided not to intervene. As he pushed open the door, he saw Mai struggling with her frenzied boss, who was spreadeagled on top of her resisting, small frame. David's rage soared as he grabbed a statue of Buddha from Mai's sideboard and crashed it down, with all the force he could muster, onto the back of Tong's skull. The small stone statue shattered, ripping a wide gash in Tong's balding head. Tong let out a shriek and his body involuntarily lurched off Mai, as she struggled to push him away. The blow was deadly. Tong's body slid to the floor and was motionless, save for the trickle of blood exiting the head wound and starting to spread like a pool of red wine around the dead café owner's head. David grabbed Mai in a bear hug and she hugged him back.

"Are you okay, Mai?" he blurted. "What the hell happened?"

"The fat bastard tried to attack me David, and you... you've killed him... Oh my God, what are we going to do?"

"No-one is going to believe it was self-defence, Mai, we have got to get out of here, and quick!" David wailed.

"You go, David, the police could be here shortly with all the noise – I will contact you soon. Go, go, please go, David... Now!"

David's eyes met Mai's. The couple kissed each other desperately, and he fled down the stairs, trying to avoid the glances of the few inquisitive people at street level who had been drawn by the commotion. He disappeared into the busy street, not looking back, running frantically with his heart almost beating out of his chest.

Mai Thi knew she had to think on her feet; the situation was clear in her mind. A very dead business owner in her bedroom did not give her much of a chance against Vietnamese justice. She threw together her few belongings into her tattered old canvas bag and headed out of the building's rear exit. No-one saw her go. No-one would see her in Ho Chi Minh City again – not even David.

The Lovers' Journeys

Mai Thi Phung's escape from Ho Chi Minh City had led her deep into the Vietnamese countryside via a train trip, various local bus rides and finally by foot. She had caught the first train that was heading out of the city's main station, not thinking of where it might take her. A very exhausted Mai ended up 320 kilometres north-west from the scene of her boss' death, in the province of Dak Lak, situated in the Central West Highlands of Vietnam, closely bordering neighbouring Cambodia. She had shuddered every time a policeman or a soldier had ventured near her during her escape. This fear was to stay with her for many months after her distressing trek away from Ho Chi Minh City, not knowing if the authorities would put any effort into finding the killer of such a worthless person as Tong.

The energy-sapping, humid tropical air filled her lungs as she entered the capital city of the region, Buon Ma Thuot, one day late in February 1985. The few remaining coins and notes she had carried with her allowed her to seek refuge in a rundown hostel nestled within the outer suburbs.

There she collapsed onto a grubby pillow on a shaky old bed and let sleep consume her tired body. The baby she carried, David's baby, was still safe and growing inside her. It suddenly hit her that she had not actually told David of the pregnancy. However, Mai was determined to keep the child and make a new life for herself and her soon-to-be born baby. She fell into a deep sleep, still thinking of David, not knowing of his fate, and wondering how life would turn out for the quirky redhead she had briefly known and loved.

David Maxwell, the troubled Vietnamese-American war baby, was now, at least in his own opinion, a fully grown man. Half a world away from Mai's existence, he had fled the country of his miserable birth and had put considerable distance physically and mentally between himself and that frightening day in Ho Chi Minh City.

Fearing for his life, David had stowed away on a large commercial container vessel in the big shipping port on the south side of Ho Chi Minh City. After escaping the capital on the night of the incident with Mai's boss, he had found himself at the docks and had got onto the first vessel he could board. His only thought was to flee as fast as he could. Before he knew what was happening the ship was heading out to sea, destination unknown to him. By befriending some of the low-paid Vietnamese and Filipino below-deck staff on the ship, David managed to remain unnoticed by the hierarchy by joining in with the everyday labours of the savagely underpaid and overworked crew. He eked out a terrible existence by grabbing food and water whenever he could and keeping his head down. A couple of months later, the destination turned out to be the third busiest port in America, the Port of New York and New Jersey. When he disembarked, the skills he had honed on the tough streets of Ho Chi Minh City served him well. He managed to dodge all the levels of authority that were pitted against him to find his way out of the bustling port area unnoticed, setting out for an alternative life in a vastly different land. He was not sure where he was going, only that he needed to survive.

In Buon Ma Thuot

On awaking the morning after arriving in Buon Ma Thuot, Mai Thi felt amazingly refreshed. A walk through the crowded, yet friendly streets of the city enlightened her senses further. It gave her hope and sent her mind racing with all the possibilities that could be open to her in a pleasant place such as this.

Over a third of Dak Lak Province is rich in basalt, producing a precious type of earth and allowing the region to develop the coffee, rubber and pepper industries that it has become famous for. In fact, the city of Buon Ma Thuot was at that time slowly becoming known as the producer of the best coffee in South-East Asia.

Within days of her arrival, Mai Thi had secured work in the local Lam Dong coffee plantation, one of the largest of the newly emerging Vietnamese coffee growers and roasters in the Western Highlands region. The company had only been established two years earlier with the help of government grants and had grown rapidly to become a huge consumer of labour in the locality. In fact, many families were moving out of the bigger Vietnamese cities, still struggling in the aftermath of the communist victory a decade earlier, to seek a new life and regular employment in areas such as Dak Lak.

Mai's admirable work ethic and charming manner, mixed with a knowledge of life well beyond her seventeen years, enabled her to gain employment with ease. Even in her developing maternal state, she was a hardworking and reliable member of staff at Lam Dong and became well-liked by all her work colleagues. By the time her son was born in early August 1985, she had established a tight circle of friends and confidantes that would help her survive the demanding early years of motherhood. She had named the baby boy Dai Ca Phung – Dai in deference to his father, David, and Ca meaning "firstborn" in Vietnamese. The extremely healthy and well-proportioned Dai came screaming into the world on August 4th. Cradled in the arms of his loving mother, he was a very blessed individual with a solid home life, set up by the doting Mai Thi Phung.

As the years passed and Dai grew bigger and stronger, Mai made a lasting bond with an older fellow worker at the plantation, Mi Ling. Although in her late fifties, Mi Ling was notably young in spirit and had adored Dai Ca from the moment she had set eyes on him. She would often babysit her "little angel", as she referred to him, to allow his mother a period of freedom from her work and home life.

In her early twenties Mai had developed into a beautiful young lady, well appreciated by the throng of young men at her workplace. She often thought of her young son's father, David Maxwell. Where did he go to? Would he attempt to try and contact her in the future? She had resolved that her feelings for him had been just puppy love and not the true and never-ending love that she yearned for. The fact that she had an illegitimate child was not an issue for her where future relationships were concerned. The war years had spawned many of her ilk, although many had suffered like her, the sheer number of them made their existence less taboo in this vibrant, re-emerging country. However, Mai's requirements of a future beau were already ingrained in her mind. She knew that she wanted to be romanced by a gentleman who could show her, and her little Dai, a side of life that she yearned for. A life free of struggle, full of safety and, if she was lucky, also full of love and contentment. None of the cheeky, good-looking twenty-somethings who often competed for her attention came close to fitting the bill. That is, not until she caught a glimpse of a young man called Dung Lam, a man that she had seen around the factory, but had not yet met. She had, by now, convinced herself that she would never see Dai's father again, and so had inwardly planned for a future in search of the next love of her life.

Dung Lam's Story

Born in the middle of the Vietnamese War, Dung Lam, son of farmer parents in the Dak Lak province of the Western Highlands, had more than outstripped his poor parents' aspirations for him. The second youngest of four brothers, Dung had shone brightly at his local school and started working at the Lam Dong Coffee plantation and factory, along with two of his siblings, as a sixteen-year-old. His family had emerged from the war years relatively unscathed compared to many Vietnamese. His father had not served in the war, as he was deemed too old to join the South Vietnamese army. He continued his rice farming in the Dak Lak region with Dung's mother. His youngest brother stayed working with his parents when his elder siblings joined the Lam Dong Coffee company.

After his initial training period, Dung's wily skills in the roasting of coffee beans to perfection had been noted early by the management team. Although his two brothers left the coffee factory to take up higher-paid work in Ho Chi Minh City as they got older, Dung persevered and quickly rose through the ranks of workers to attain the position of manager in his Roasting section and then to Factory Manager by the time he was only twenty-two years old, a rare feat in a country that lauded age and experience as the ultimate yardstick of achievement. This fact initially made his meteoric advancement within the company a source of envy and resentment for some of the more aspirational older men on the same career path. However, Dung's methods of inclusive management and the consultative approach he took with all the decisions he made ensured that his doubters soon saw that he was an impressive leader, and their respect was gradually gained. The results he engineered at Lam Dong Coffee ensured that the product they were making was always of the highest quality, and this helped gain a reputation for the company, ranking the fledgling subsidiary amongst the elite in the Highlands Coffee parent company's massive nationwide network.

Like Mai Thi, Dung Lam was very knowing and wise for his tender age. One April morning he strode into the section of the factory where Mai Thi had now been employed for just on five years. She had worked hard to become a leading hand in the Roasting Department and was admired and respected by her fellow workers.

A visit by the overall Factory Manager was always an honourable occasion, and this time was even more so as he was touring the whole plantation with the Senior Vice-President of the Highlands Coffee Company, the owner of Lam Dong. HCC was one of the largest growers, roasters and exporters of the humble green bean, which had catapulted Vietnam to worldwide significance in the coffee market.

Dung Lam's rise through the ranks of the smaller coffee concern had not gone unnoticed by the Senior Vice-President of the parent company. He was most impressed by the methods, checks and balances that the local farmer's son had put into place to produce a premium product, which enhanced the HCC brand both nationally and in their growing export markets.

Dung Lam had been experimenting with the propagation of the higher quality arabica-style coffee bean in the very fertile earth of the Dak Lak Province. He replicated the ingredients and the temperate conditions that had made Brazil's Highlands region so capable of raising its world-renowned crops. His experiments had created a potential challenger to Brazil's hold on the world coffee market. He knew that, if he could get the backing of HCC's considerable cash reserves, his little company could grow even higher in stature amongst Vietnam's coffee elite.

The factory visit was a special occasion for most of the production staff. As Dung Lam and his high-ranking guest neared the immaculately kept Roasting Department, overseen by Mai Thi, a sense of pride was instilled in the diminutive young mother. The steely-eyed SVP was quick to pick up on this mood and openly congratulated Mai on her attention to detail and, of course, the exceptional end product that her section steadily and continually produced. Her eyes shyly lowered as the important group accompanying Dung Lam passed by. The factory boss was well pleased with the reactions he was receiving from his eminent visitor and a warm, wide smile beamed from his face as his eyes met Mai Thi's. The girl had already caught his eye from afar in his Manager's office, situated one storey above the Roasting section. This girl now viewed the extraordinarily talented young manager as someone whom she would very much like to get to know better. The intense chemistry that she had only known once in her young life had finally been reawakened. Destiny had brought them together, but neither of them knew that yet.

Dung Lam, Mai Thi, Mi Ling and Dai Ca Phung

Dung Lam was becoming a rising star of the coffee industry in Vietnam. The Lam Dong Company had become the leader in arabica bean production in Vietnam and the Highland Coffee Company had rewarded Dung Lam by offering him a place on the board of directors of the Vietnamese coffee giant. As well as bestowing great honour on his family and the local area, the position came with financial rewards and made him a very wealthy young man.

By this time, he had also made great strides forward in his personal life. He had plucked up enough courage to ask Mai Thi to accompany him on several social occasions and their relationship had become the main topic of conversation amongst the Lam Dong staff and the social scene in Dak Lak Province.

Mai Thi had called on her dear friend, Mi Ling, to look after her son Dai Ca on many occasions during her courtship. The bond between Dai, now aged seven, and the woman who had become his de facto grandmother, had grown strong. Mi Ling had lost her own husband in the Vietnamese war, before they had managed to have children, and the love she showered on her "little angel" Dai was more than just friendship. She had mentored his mother through some tough times in the early years of Mai Thi's introduction to her adopted hometown of Buon Ma Thuot and had certainly become part of the family over the ensuing seven years. Her deeply felt love for Dai and his appreciative mother was cherished by all three of them. Young Dai had naturally bonded with Mi Ling, and his hard-working mother had encouraged the strong link whenever she could. She had known the loneliness of being an only child and an orphan. She desperately wanted to create a loving, family atmosphere in which to rear her child and Mi Ling, now in her mid-sixties, had helped her tremendously in that quest. Now that Mai had eventually found the potential of a loving relationship for herself with Dung Lam, Mi Ling was the first to encourage the possibility. Dung and Mai were both in their late twenties. The company that they worked for was experiencing huge growth as Vietnamese coffee went from strength to strength in the world market.

Over the next decade, work-wise and personally, the positives just kept happening. In 1994 Mai and Dung finally married. However, on the negative side, their failed efforts to fall pregnant caused constant heartache for them both. Dung Lam longed for a child of his own and Mai was keen to add a little brother or sister for her big boy, Dai. Eventually, after many efforts and subsequent medical testing to confirm the reason, the Lams discovered that Dung Lam was unable to father any children. Although a matter of huge disappointment initially, they resolved to put all their efforts and love into Dai Ca Phung and their working life.

Dai continued to grow into a very solid and capable young man. Much of the credit for this was due to his mother, and his ever-doting grandmother figure Mi Ling, as well as the new influence of his stepfather, Dung Lam. As a well-educated and intelligent boy, Dai was fascinated by the machinations of the coffee industry that his family was a big part of. So much so, in fact, that from the age of twelve he had worked part-time in the business, both after school and during the summer vacation periods. This enabled him to learn all he could about how the industry worked, and the processes involved – from growing to roasting, packaging to selling – to ensure that Lam Dong Coffee was maintained at its elevated level. Mai and Dung Lam were overjoyed that the industry that had been their passion, and had brought them together, was now being adopted by young Dai. He went on to study Chemistry at university and finished in 2007 with excellent results before being offered a full-time position with his stepfather's company.

Dai always kept himself neat and tidy in his university days. His hair was not long and unkempt like most of his student cohort. He made regular visits to the local barber's shop, situated in the commercial section of his university, to have his jet-black hair maintained at the manageable length that he preferred. He shaved daily to ensure that the odd red stubble which sprouted during his holiday periods away from the university was kept at bay. He was unsure why his facial hair had developed with an odd section of red around the bottom of his chin. He disliked this part of his appearance, so kept up the constant shaving to abate the problem. He dressed fashionably and was a keen member of many sporting clubs, keeping his body fit and strong by attending the university gym regularly. This activity helped Dai to become a successful and popular team member in the local football, baseball and tennis teams. His sporting prowess also had the bonus of helping him get the attention of a growing throng of female admirers. His mixed-race bloodline had developed him into a striking-looking young man with a fit and appealing body, and so he was never short of partners for the many social occasions that occurred on campus. He also became regularly active in the various debating events, highlighting his natural talent as a compelling orator. From these occasions he developed a keen interest in Vietnamese politics and student platforms, which again seemed to boost his popularity amongst his peers.

Throughout his whole childhood, through his teenage years of angst, and now that he had grown into a young man, his mainstay, confidante, and loving backup had always been Mi Ling. Her love and support had been there for him for as long as he could remember. He had often spent weekend "sleepovers" at his Ba's homely little cottage, situated close to the centre of Buon Ma Thuot. Mi Ling had taught him all manner of interesting life skills and interesting facts, such as gardening, birdwatching and how to cook basic meals. He would offer to mow her beautifully kept garden lawn once he had developed physically enough to manage the task, and she was so grateful for Dai's help around her home, especially as she grew older.

Not long after his graduation, his mother pulled him aside one day to explain his heritage. Mai Thi had never really spoken about his bloodline before, but she felt it was time for Dai to know where he came from. She had only ever divulged this information to Mi Ling in the past and, more recently, to Dung Lam following their marriage. Both had accepted it as being a part of their generation's ordeal, which did not, as far as they were concerned, reflect badly on Mai Thi's character. As Dai sipped on a cool iced tea in the luxury of his mother's new family home, he listened incredulously to the story that had begun with the My Lai massacre in 1968, his birth father's upbringing and the events that led to his mother's arrival in Dak Lak Province all those years ago. However, his mother spared him the part about the café owner's gruesome demise, as she had also done with Mi Ling and Dung Lam. Dai had seen his mother work so hard to raise him from the early days in Buon Ma Thuot and had been amazed at her strength and dogged determination to find work and excel at her duties. He loved her deeply for all of her selfless devotion to him, her only son. Yet he was taken aback by her story, his link to the Vietnamese war and his American blood. The information shook him to the core. He needed time to absorb what he had just been told... he needed to talk to his Ba, his grandma.

Mi Ling answered her ringing telephone at home. "Hello, who is this?"

"Hello Ba, it's Dai," came the reply.

"How is my little angel today?"

"I need to talk to you, Ba, can we meet?" replied Dai.

"Yes, of course, I could do with a bit of exercise. Let's meet at the Central Teahouse... Is 2pm okay for you?" offered Mi Ling.

"That is great, thank you Ba. See you then... I will buy the tea. I know what you like," was Dai's response.

A smile came to the wrinkled face of his adopted grandma as she thought of the many, many times he had sought her advice. He was always so polite, so gracious and he always – always –listened. Even though Mi Ling was now in her seventies, she was still spritely and energetic for her age. A long life full of hard work, a sensible diet, and an existence free from the evil clutches of drugs and alcohol, had led Mi Ling to believe that hers was a fortunate life. This was a hugely different story to many of her generation. Her devoted Buddhist faith had also supported her greatly and she loved her daily visits to the local temple to pray and make offerings. She looked at the wall clock in her small kitchen. It was 1.15pm and the Central Tea House was only a measured ten-minute stroll from her comfortable home in downtown Buon Ma Thuot. She needed the exercise and it was a beautiful day outside. As ever, the thought of seeing and spending precious time with her young Dai filled Mi Ling with joy, and she hummed a happy tune as she let herself out of the back door a few minutes later.

Being the thoughtful and well-mannered young man that he was, Dai had arrived slightly early for his meeting to ensure a good table at the Tea House. It had always been a very popular meeting place amongst the locals and he knew that Mi Ling loved to be seated on the ornately furnished balcony area, facing the impressive stand of pine trees, thoughtfully planted by the colonising French in the nineteenth century. Never a lover of the imperialist occupation of his homeland all those years ago, Dai viewed the now-mature set of trees from his balcony vantage point and whispered under his breath, "Bloody French Imperialists!"

He took his seat on the sun-drenched balcony of the magnificent Tea House, smiled at the very accommodating waiter – a man he had known well since he had been introduced to him by Mi Ling as a ten-year-old - and awaited the arrival of his "Ba". His mind was still racing since the earlier conversation with his mother... what would Mi Ling think of his sullied family history? He drew a long breath, surveyed the Tea House menu, and waited.

Mi Ling had almost completed her steady but slow walk from her house. Her eyesight was still very good for a lady of her vintage and she could make out the young man seated on the first floor balcony of her favourite Tea House She was excited to be seeing her "little angel' and, full of anticipation, she stepped off the pavement to cross the road.

Peter Collins, an American student, was on a long-awaited vacation in Vietnam after completing a degree at Yale University. He had hired the classic sports car after arriving at the local airport from Ho Chi Minh City, and was on his way to meet his Vietnamese girlfriend, who he had met in the States. Her family home was only a few minutes away. Full of anticipation, he rounded the corner into Buon Ma Thuot's main street a little too quickly. He did not see the old lady who had stepped into the street in front of him until it was too late. Mi Ling's concentration was fixed on her grandson, waving at her from the Tea House balcony as she ambled across the roadway. As the hideous screech of car brakes filled the air, Dai jumped up from his seat to try to warn his precious Ba as the awful event played out in front of his unbelieving eyes.

All went silent for a few moments after the terrible collision. His beautiful grandma lay motionless on the hot tarmac. The American student had done his best to avoid the accident, but control of the car, hindered by excessive speed and the narrowness of the street, was far beyond him. Dai had screamed at the top of his voice, but to no avail. Mi Ling did not hear him.

Dai raced down the old wooden staircase and, as he approached the scene of the tragedy, saw Peter Collins kneeling next to the clearly deceased old lady, sobbing uncontrollably and professing how sorry he was. Dai hugged his Ba in his strong, young arms and, as well as the flow of tears, an innate anger consumed his body. He kissed the face of Mi Ling and noticed that, apart from a single trickle of blood coming from her right ear, there didn't seem to be any bruising, no dis-figuring injuries visible. In fact, she looked quite serene and peaceful, as if in a slumber. Dai consoled himself with the thought that the end would have been quick and painless. As he held her tight his gaze drifted to the driver, still racked with despair.

"You have killed my Mi Ling... my Ba!" Dai blurted out, venom and hate dripping from his words.

"Oh my God, I am so, so sorry... I just didn't see her, she stepped out in front of me and..." muttered the American, breaking off as he was pulled to his feet by police officers arriving on the scene.

"You Americans have ruined my life, my country... everything. I hate you!" shouted Dai.

By now a crowd had gathered. Dai was taken to one side by a paramedic, who had quickly arrived on the scene in an ambulance, as Mi Ling's body was respectfully attended to by his colleagues. All Dai could do was stare at the person that had ripped so much love from his life. "I hate you Yankees, I hate you all!"

Love and Loss

1974 had started brightly for Luiz, his family, and the whole Nova Coffee Company. The now thirty-eight-year-old Luiz Almeida was at the top of his game. He had risen to become the regional Vice-President of the Southern Highlands Coffee Growers' Association and regularly represented the region in export talks with their major trading partners in North America. The quality of the Nova Coffee arabica beans had been recognised as the best in the world and its high selling price reflected this, as shares in the company recorded all-time highs, making the Almeida family rich beyond their wildest dreams.

Beatriz had become the queen of the local São Paulo social scene and was the centrepiece at most charity fundraisers that were held in the region. She had become exceedingly popular on local TV chat shows and had blossomed into a wonderful ambassador for the Nova Coffee Company by her mid-thirties. Her high profile ensured that she was always one of the first personalities to be invited to any grand social event in the São Paulo area. She was living the dream.

Luiz's parents, Raymond and Maria, were now living in their own new house, built for them by their son, on the family property overlooking the coffee plantations that were the basis of all their wealth. Both were still active and healthy in their mid-sixties and were great role models, as well as occasional babysitters, for their grandchildren Felipe, Mateus and Bianca – when Esmerelda, the much-loved nanny, was not available.

Young Mateus, now twelve years old, was progressing well with his sporting prowess and doing superbly with the Santos youth soccer team. He had watched on TV in June 1974 as the Brazilian World Cup team had yielded to the emerging powers of West Germany and Holland to finish a disappointing fourth place in the tournament, held in Germany. By now the great Pelé had retired and the team was no longer seen as the best in the world. Maybe Mateus could make it all the way to the top in football and become an idol to Brazilians, as Pelé was to his father.

As the southern hemisphere was idling out of spring, heading towards the heat of the summer, the month of November was turning out to be a terribly busy time for the Almeida family. Luiz and Beatriz's daughter Bianca had just turned nine years old and had thankfully developed into less of a brat than Luiz had feared she would. She had grown exceptionally beautiful, much like Beatriz in her looks, and she seemed to be smitten with the same socialising bug that her lovely mother had developed earlier. Happily for Luiz, his young daughter had also become an enterprising student at school. She had developed a marvellous aptitude for numbers and was excelling at mathematics and even some of the science subjects that she had recently been introduced to at the local Nova Serrana school. Maybe Bianca would grow up into the intelligent young lady that he had always hoped for. The coffee plantation was in full swing and Luiz had just conducted successful negotiations with the mighty coffee buyers of America that would yield a huge amount of business for not only the Nova Coffee Company, but also the general Southern Highlands coffee community.

Beatriz had just taken possession of a beautiful new sports car – the Mercedes 450SL convertible – in the first week of November and was keen to take it on a trip to São Paulo to pick up her second son Mateus from his soccer academy training camp in the region's capital city.

Elder brother Felipe, now fourteen years old, was also keen to have a ride in the new, bright red convertible. He had begged his mother to take him along on the trip, even though he hated the thought of watching his talented younger brother playing the game that Filipe abhorred. He dreamed of having a flash sports car when he was older and the drive down to São Paulo would be something that he could brag about to his schoolmates – especially those in his beloved drama classes. He also relished the fact that his annoying younger brother would be relegated to the cramped jump seat in the rear of the car on the long trip back home, whilst Felipe would ensure that he enjoyed the comfort of riding up front, alongside his mother.

Luiz caressed his beautiful wife before she left. "I love you, honey. The car looks so beautiful, but you are a lot lovelier, my darling," said Luiz as they parted with a passionate kiss and a ruffle of the hair for his eldest son. Luiz added a last quip, "Don't let Filipe drive, honey – not yet anyway!" He gave a knowing wink to his son and a blown kiss to his Beatriz.

She was looking radiant in a charcoal and red jumpsuit, her raven hair covered by a fashionable headscarf, and in response she blew a kiss to her handsome beau. "I love you darling!" she mouthed as she jumped into the waiting Mercedes. Felipe certainly was not the happiest of children, but Luiz would always try to put a smile on his face whenever the opportunity arose.

"Adiós, Papa!" belted out Filipe as he jumped into the passenger seat next to his mother and snapped on the gleaming seatbelt, adorned with a custom-made sheepskin covering. He loved the feeling of luxury. There was a smile on his face and a glint in his eye as the powerful 4520cc, V90 engine pulled the magnificent Mercedes down the long meandering driveway, through the Nova Coffee property gates and into the distance: destination São Paulo. Luiz waved them goodbye with a huge grin on his face. He adored the fact that he could make his beautiful wife and his troubled young son so happy. Oh, how he loved his family – he was so blessed.

More than six hours later the phone rang out in the Almeida family home. "Hey, Mama, can you get that please? I am out on the back veranda," shouted Luiz to Maria.

Luiz sucked on the fat Cohiba cigar that he had just lit, as he surveyed the coffee trees down below from the balcony of his home, a contented look on his tanned face.

"Luiz, the call is for you, darling, can you take it in the office, please?" replied his ever-helpful mother after she had answered the phone.

On the other end of the line a very sombre police inspector awaited Luiz. The news he had was not good. Luiz had picked up the receiver and greeted the caller in his customary happy and positive manner. "Hello, Luiz Almeida at your service, how can I help you?" A few seconds later, his face dropped and he slumped into his office chair as the caller told him the awful news. Just north of São Paulo, Beatriz's sports car had failed to successfully overtake a huge truck carrying cattle and had collided at high speed with another oncoming car. At this stage details were vague, but both Beatriz and Felipe were in hospital and the owner of the other car in the accident had been killed instantly. Both Beatriz and his son were in a critical situation and it was imperative that Luiz travel to the hospital in São Paulo urgently.

Tears streamed from Luiz's eyes, as his mother hugged him and called out in a screaming shout to Luiz's driver, Paulo, to come quickly. Luiz sat motionless in his office chair; an unbelieving look on his face.

"No, Mama, it can't be... it is not true... not Beatriz, not Felipe. Why?"

By this time Luiz's father, Raymond, having heard his wife's scream, had strode quickly into his son's office where he had taken the fateful phone call. "Oh, my son, what has happened?" he pleaded when he saw the agony on Luiz's face.

"Papa, it is Beatriz and Felipe – in a road accident, what am I going to do?"

"Are they... okay?" Raymond enquired.

"No, Papa, they are both in a bad way in hospital. I must go quickly!"

Paulo, Luiz's ever reliable driver and general assistant, had read the situation, as always, and had driven the big four-wheel-drive Toyota to the front door. He was a trusted aide and was always on hand to help the family when needed. Raymond and Maria ushered their distraught son to the waiting car, tears streaming from their eyes.

"Go quickly, my son, and be careful Paulo, take it easy please," Raymond urged.

"Papa, Mama... look after Bianca, please," replied Luiz.

"Don't tell her anything until I call you. Also, can you please ask Esmerelda to call the football academy and talk to Mateus' coach, Miguel. Ask her to ask him to look after my son, until I ring him later."

Paulo prised the Toyota into first gear with a strong hand, then released the handbrake and hurtled down the driveway and through the property gates, heading south from Nova Serrana. Luiz sat slumped in the passenger seat, his eyes, moistened by tears, set in an eerie glaze. When he closed them he could see, in his mind's eye, the picture of beauty that was his gorgeous wife Beatriz and the face of his young boy, Felipe... Would they survive?

Six and a half hours later Paulo pulled the Toyota into the entrance of the Intensive Care department at São Paulo Hospital. He had driven the powerful motor quickly but expertly, ever mindful of his boss' mental state. Each time Luiz had enquired "How long now?" Paulo had calmly replied "Not long now, Señor, not long."

As they arrived, Paulo parked the big vehicle and pulled on the handbrake. Luiz was away and out of the car at top speed into the near-empty reception area, a wild look in his eyes.

"My name is Almeida, Luiz Almeida. I must see my wife and son; they are in intensive care. Quickly, quickly, please!" he pleaded as he approached the stern-looking woman at the reception desk.

Chief Inspector Manuel Delvaz had been waiting for Luiz, and he strode quickly across to the reception desk. He was well aware of the Almeida family and of their standing in the local community.

"Good afternoon, Mr Almeida. I am Chief Inspector Manuel Delvaz – I spoke to you on the phone earlier. Please come with me. I will take you to where your wife and son are… I need to say that you must be prepared for the worst. It is not looking good, I am very sorry to say," the slightly overweight policeman spluttered, as Luiz looked into his eyes in sheer disbelief.

"Take me to them please!" pleaded Luiz.

Chief Inspector Delvaz led Luiz to the end of a long corridor, where two doctors were in close consultation with each other.

"Dr Ramon, this is Luiz Almeida, the husband and father of the patients…"

Dr Ramon had met Luiz and Beatriz socially at a recent São Paulo event, and he now looked into Luiz's eyes with great sadness as he approached.

"Senior Almeida… Luiz… I am deeply sorry to meet you again in such sad circumstances. Please follow me to your wife's room – you need to see her now. We will then visit your son, who is in a better situation."

Luiz's eyes widened in amazement as he heard the doctor's words… was she gone? How bad was Felipe?

"Is she…?" he began, but he could not bring himself to say the word.

"Please follow me, Señor," repeated the non-committal medic.

"And what of my son, Felipe?" pleaded the distraught Luiz.

"Your son is resting at the moment and he is out of imminent danger, we will see him soon."

He led Luiz to a darkened room, where Beatriz lay motionless in the bed, eyes closed, with the innocuous beeps of an array of medical equipment the only sounds to be heard. Her head was heavily bandaged and her face was badly bruised, but the tell-tale long eyelashes and shapely brows told Luiz that this was indeed his beautiful wife. A tube taped into her mouth was taking air into and out of her slim frame. Luiz's shoulders visibly lowered as he stood next to the bed and carefully stooped to kiss his beloved Beatriz.

"My darling, oh, my darling... why, why?" he sobbed.

Dr Ramon respectfully touched his shoulder and spoke in a low voice. "Señor, I am afraid it is only the breathing apparatus that is keeping your wife's body going. The injuries Beatriz received in the accident were very, very major. The vital signs we can detect are rapidly failing, especially in the last 30 minutes, and the trauma she suffered to the head and brain was, well... exceedingly heavy. Luiz, I fear the worst. I am so sorry to be the one to tell you this. I will leave you alone together for a few moments."

"Can she hear me if I speak to her?" asked Luiz.

"I would say, with the extent of her injuries, the answer most probably is... no. But I cannot say that for sure... I will leave that for your heart to decide," Ramon responded.

With that the doctor retreated from the room to talk to the waiting Chief Inspector. Luiz sat in the chair next to Beatriz's bed. He took her left hand in his and kissed it tenderly.

"My darling Beatriz, how can I say goodbye to you like this? I have loved you ever since that night we met in São Paulo. My love for you will never fade, my darling, you will always be in my heart." A tear formed in Luiz's eye and slipped down his cheek and, as if in slow motion, landed on the tanned, smooth skin of Beatriz's left shoulder. Just as the salty liquid touched and exploded onto his wife's skin, Luiz thought that he saw an involuntary flicker of Beatriz's eyelids... and then nothing. He knew that the love of his life was gone, even though the rhythmic mechanics of the breathing apparatus were artificially showing signs of life.

Dr Ramon reentered the room and subtly caught the attention of the distraught husband.

"We need to talk, Luiz," the doctor told him very softly.

Luiz nodded as he turned his head to acknowledge the doctor and rose very carefully from the chair, tenderly unclasping his hand from Beatriz's.

He placed a delicate kiss on his wife's forehead as he got to his feet and walked slowly to the door, not looking back.

"My son Felipe, doctor, where is he? Can I see him now, please?" asked Luiz.

"Certainly, Luiz, follow me."

They walked together in silence, past Chief Inspector Delvaz. Luiz's eyes met the policeman's gaze, but nothing was said. Dr Ramon led him to the next ward and ushered Luiz into the room, three doors down on the left-hand side of the darkened corridor. Inside, the single bed that Felipe was occupying seemed more homely and less sterile than that of his mother. Luiz's eldest son lay still, breathing steadily, eyes closed, with a bandaged head and his right arm in plaster. He was in a peaceful sleep. Luiz bowed down and kissed the bandaged forehead of Felipe, whispered, "I love you, my boy," and placed a warm, tender hand on his shoulder. He turned to Dr Ramon, who had followed him into the room, and enquired, "What news of Filipe, doctor?"

"Better news, I am pleased to say, Señor. Although he has some head trauma, it seems he is responding well to treatment and the scans show that there is no long-term physical damage to the brain. Slight swelling, originally, but that is now receding. He does, however, have a severely broken arm and a dislocated shoulder, and Felipe also suffered a blow to the ankle and lower leg area that will require further surgery. We will know more in the morning when he awakens. I have given him pain relief to help him sleep and all his internal organs seem to be functioning at this stage. I have booked him into surgery for his lower right leg and ankle tomorrow afternoon."

Luiz's face bore a puzzled look; he was clearly shocked by the events of the last few hours. His son Felipe, so fragile in his life to date, had now been given more problems to cope with. How would he deal with the imminent loss of his mother and the possibility of future physical and emotional scars?

"Can we go somewhere to talk, doctor?" asked Luiz.

"Yes, of course, we'll go to my office."

Inspector Delvaz once again rose from his seated position as Luiz and the doctor approached.

"I understand your situation, Mr Almeida, but we need to talk about the accident. But only when you feel able, señor."

"I know, Inspector. Please give me a few moments to collect myself and talk with Dr Ramon," said Luiz wearily.

The policeman raised his hand in acknowledgment without saying a word, forcing a smile onto his tired face.

Luiz followed Dr Ramon into his office and gently closed the door behind him.

"So, doctor, where do we stand?" enquired the grief-stricken husband.

Dr Ramon looked at him with a pained expression as he took his seat.

"Please sit down, Luiz," he replied, gesturing to the seat opposite.

"Can you please give me your informed opinion of Beatriz's situation, doctor?"

Dr Ramon was well-known to the Almeida family and was a highly respected and skilled practitioner. Luiz did not want to hear the opinion the doctor was about to offer, but he knew that it would be well thought out and truthful.

"It is now entirely a matter for you, Luiz... but it is only a matter of time I am afraid. The internal injuries are too massive to operate on, in fact, but for the machines, Beatriz is already lost to us," lamented the surgeon.

Luiz took a deep, audible breath and looked directly into the doctor's eyes, tears streaming down his tanned cheeks.

"I will need to talk to her mother, Luciana, and my own parents before I give my consent to..."

With this, his grief overtook him, and he let out a gasp before the tears fell harder and he held his head in his hands. The doctor rose from his chair and placed a caring arm around the shattered man's shoulders.

"Take a moment, my friend. I am so sorry for your loss... please use my phone to make the necessary calls, if you need to," offered Dr Ramon, gesturing to the black phone on his office desk.

"I will leave you alone for a while," he added as he exited the room, carefully closing the door behind him.

After a short while Luiz had gathered his thoughts together and decided to visit his wife one last time, before he made the phone calls to his family and then made the awful decision that he knew he had to make.

As he passed the police officer sitting patiently in the corridor, again their eyes met, but again nothing was said.

The inspector stood up and placed a consoling hand on Luiz's shoulder, understanding the gravity of the situation. Words were not needed. Inspector Delvaz took his seat again and Luiz made his way slowly to the room where Beatriz lay.

A nurse was checking his wife's condition as he entered the room. With a concerned look on her face, and a clear recognition of the position he was in, she offered a weak smile and excused herself from the room.

Luiz sat down beside the love of his life and a wry smile appeared on his face as he surveyed Beatriz and said in a whisper, "My darling, even in this hopeless moment, you look so beautiful to me. If you can hear me, I want to thank you for all the love you have given me and for the three beautiful children we have created together. I will miss you every single second for the remainder of my life, but I will never, ever forget you or stop loving you. Forgive me for making the decision to turn off these noisy machines that are keeping your body alive, but you are too beautiful and proud to be left in this lifeless position. I don't know why God has done this to you, but I will let you go as the gorgeous woman that I was so proud to call my wife, my love... my Beatriz."

At that moment Dr. Ramon appeared at the doorway and stepped inside. Luiz turned from his seated position and looked up at him.

"Let her go, Dr Ramon. Let her go. Beatriz was a practicing Catholic, so can you please organise for a local priest to administer the last rites to my beautiful wife? Thank you, doctor."

After Beatriz

The next few months were cold and lonely for Luiz, even though it was a ridiculously hot summer. After the awful realisation had hit the whole family; after the lavish, but stressful funeral had been and gone; even though his eldest son's physical injuries had thankfully healed, the pain in Luiz was evident for all to see. Although he had been raised in a strictly Catholic household and had grown up surrounded by intensely religious people on the plantation, his own beliefs were nowhere near as strong as the average Brazilian. However, this did not dissuade him from believing that, after his life was over, he would be united with Beatriz once again.

Although Luiz was devastated, it was Felipe, again, who seemed to be the member of the family who grieved his mother's loss most intensely. Added to this trauma was the fact that the leg injuries he had suffered in the car accident had left him with a slight limp. Another knock to his fragile self-confidence.

A legal battle also ensued from the family of the man who had been killed in Beatriz's accident. After a lengthy process, the court found that Beatriz Almeida was culpable for the accident and the Almeida family were ordered to pay financial recompense to the aggrieved family. Luiz did not argue with the result and dutifully paid up.

As the years passed, Luiz's heavy heart became lighter. He knew that Beatriz could not be replaced by anybody, but that did not stop the many unmarried ladies of the district attempting to pry his heart out of retirement.

The children all grew and developed in their own ways. The youngest, Bianca, became the new darling of the São Paulo social scene – her mother would have been proud. The middle child, Mateus, forever the sporting star, fell in love with and married a local tennis professional, Clara, in 1983. Almost immediately Luiz's first grandchild, Luiz Junior, came along, followed by a second, Vitor, three years later. By the time young Vitor had arrived on the scene, Mateus had made the painful decision to retire from FC Santos as a player. Luiz had been so proud of the fact that Mateus had the ability to attain a professional contract from such a prestigious club when he was only a 16 year old. As well as being a skilfull and dynamic midfield player, his leadership qualities were also recognised by the club. They had made him captain of a very successful youth team in the late 70s and he had broken into the first team by the time he was only twenty two. A big future looked imminent for the talented player. However, a nasty Achilles tendon injury had hampered his football career for several months in early 1986 and he had been advised by the medical team at the club that his best days were over as a professional player. His father happily employed him within the production area of the Nova business, and he flourished in the role. His no-nonsense attitude served him well as he put all his focus into learning his trade. More importantly, in his father's eyes at least, he used his strong leadership skills, honed on the football field, to get the best out of all the young men that worked with him on the plantation.

Also in 1986, Bianca finally succumbed to marriage with Rodrigo Souza, a rich banker nine years her senior. She had been wooed by the affluent and elegant older man after a chance meeting at one of her many social events in São Paulo. After six years of travelling around the world and socialising with Rodrigo, Bianca finally settled down, and Luiz's first and only granddaughter was born – Gabrielle, who came into the world in 1991. Bianca's husband had felt trapped and hampered by the prospect of fatherhood and had been caught out by his wife on several occasions entertaining other women, during and after the pregnancy. This blew over and he came back into line; however, it did not bode well for the future of their relationship.

By then Luiz was 55 years old and had still not remarried. Although he had flirted with the fairer sex on many occasions, no long-lasting relationships developed – he could never replace his Beatriz.

The eldest boy, Felipe, had come out of his shell eventually, and by his mid-twenties was working within his father's business, heading up the Marketing department. He had also come out of the closet a few years earlier.

Felipe's father was incredibly supportive of his son, although initially shocked to discover that his son's sexuality was different to his own. Luiz, nevertheless, was an extremely compassionate human being on many levels. Felipe had noticeably grown much closer to Luiz after the death of his mother, which pleased his father immensely. The timing of Felipe's coming out – on his 21st birthday – did not really come as a surprise to Luiz, his family and those that knew him well. His younger brother, Mateus, had often accused his sibling of being a "bloody fairy" during the late teenage years. But when the dust settled, the whole family, especially Bianca, rallied around the troubled Felipe. The relief of coming out changed his persona for the better and, even though his grandparents, now all in their seventies, were quite disturbed and confused about the situation, the love that they gave to all of their grandchildren never diminished. Their generation had tended to push the subject of homosexuality firmly into the closet, where they believed it should remain shut away. Their strong Roman Catholic upbringing had always forced them to believe it a mortal sin. In total contrast to this, Luiz's rather lacklustre adhesion to a religious pathway meant that the fierce and strong support he displayed for his son encouraged Felipe to excel in his marketing position at the family business, which again warmed Luiz's heart.

Sadly, the 1990s saw a downturn in the financial fortunes of both the Nova Coffee Company and the Almeida family. It also heralded the passing of both Luiz's parents, Raymond and Maria, within months of each other. Beatriz's mother, Luciana, lived into her nineties and survived to see three great-grandchildren get to their 21st birthdays. She also lived to see her granddaughter, Bianca, divorce her first husband Rodrigo after a twenty-year marriage, in favour of a man four years her junior. His name was Tiago Lima, a B-grade actor from Brasilia. This marriage only lasted two years and came to an acrimonious end in 2009, with Tiago not managing to stay faithful to his new bride for even eighteen months, blaming the numerous "distractions" in his industry for the failure of the marriage. Luiz and the rest of the family were noticeably relieved when this unfortunate union was finally ended, having never been great admirers of Bianca's choice. Bianca, to her credit, had thankfully seen the error of her ways and decided that she would dedicate her immediate future to her daughter and the Nova Coffee Company. This resulted in her re-educating herself with the acquisition of a Diploma in Business Management at the local Nova Serrana College of Business. Her excellent aptitude for figures and her self-belief helped Luiz's only daughter become a very welcome new member of the Nova Coffee Company. Over the years ahead she grew into a very competent manager of the financial and administration departments within the family business. Now more settled and enjoying her time working from home, Bianca was also developing into a great support for her young daughter, Gabrielle, and their relationship blossomed in a pleasing way.

Two years later, in 2011, Bianca and Rodrigo's daughter, Gabrielle, was heading towards the end of her Bachelor of Chemistry degree at the University of São Paulo, when her great grandmother Luciana died from a stroke at the grand old age of 92. This left Luiz as the eldest of the Almeida clan, a fact that was not lost on him, but a role at which he excelled. His children had now grown up and were a huge support to him personally, as well as within his beloved business.

The Nova Coffee Company had ridden through, and survived, the tough economic times of the late 1990s and the early 2000s. It certainly seemed that things were looking up for the coffee industry once more as the first decade of the 21st century drew to a close. Luiz was now the Grand Old Man of the Brazilian coffee trade, yet still played a major role in exporting the region's coffee products to the vast caffeine-supping giant to the north, the USA. But even at the ripe old age of seventy-six he was still running his family company with great aplomb and making money for its shareholders, including his family.

His two sons were both working at a high level within the Nova Coffee Company. Felipe, now the Chief Marketing Officer, was in his early fifties and, joyfully, now had a strong and loving partner in his life, Eduardo Ramírez. Felipe had met the slightly younger Eduardo in his late thirties, after many fruitless years of playing the field in the São Paulo gay scene and struggling to commit to any worthwhile relationships. He finally realised that Eduardo was the one when, over a bottle of vintage Argentinian Malbec, he asked him to move into his house, the residence originally built for his grandparents on the massive Almeida compound, and Eduardo happily agreed. Their relationship was solidified by the purchase of their beloved pet, a white Pomeranian puppy, which they named Olive. Felipe was still troubled by the leg injury that he had received in the car accident all those years ago and walked with a very slight limp, a fact that did not trouble the loyal Eduardo at all. The couple were well suited, and Eduardo was immensely popular with the Almeida family clan, especially young Gabrielle, who adored him. Felipe was by now, outwardly, a lot happier in general with his life. However, he still suffered from a lack of confidence compared to his brother and father.

Mateus, was still playing competitive social tennis at a local level. After his budding football career had come to a premature end, he had concentrated on his working life at Nova and then decided to delve into tennis and golf. Even at fifty years of age, he was still fit and well able to beat some of the younger men who dared to challenge his sporting abilities. He was also doing an excellent job of running the production side of the Nova Coffee business for his father. Between his two sons and Bianca – who now headed up the administration and financial department – Luiz felt that Nova Coffee was in good hands. This was a comforting thought to him, and it came to his mind again one afternoon in summer 2012 as he contemplated a visit to the clinic two days prior.

Sudden severe headaches had been bothering him for weeks. Eventually Luiz had decided to see his lifelong friend and doctor, David Alma, to get a checkup. Subsequent tests had revealed a small tumour close to his brain. Dr Alma had reassured him that, although it was operable, there would be risks and had prescribed medication to help with the pain. Luiz had chosen not to inform his offspring about these medical developments. He had also decided not to go forward with the operation just yet. This was with the knowledge that any undue stress or tension in his life might cause an instant reaction, potentially leaving him severely disabled or even killing him.

"Well," he thought to himself. "I have had a good life, the company is in good hands and I am nearly 80 years old... not a bad life, really."

Back in Vietnam –
The Beginning of Hate

Dai Ca Phung had endured a very harrowing week. He had insisted on arranging the funeral of Mi Ling, his precious Ba, and, of course, the ceremony was well organised, beautifully executed and was a fitting tribute to the lady whom he called Grandmother. His grief had stirred up the knot in his stomach caused by the story of his family tree that his mother had told him, which now intertwined with the senseless killing of his wonderful Ba by that stupid American. He longed to enact a fitting revenge on the country that had, in his eyes at least, brought torment to his country and to him personally.

On the brighter side, Dai's career at the Lam Dong establishment was going exceedingly well. His groundbreaking work on virus strains in the coffee plantation environment had produced amazing results. He and his team had successfully managed to isolate the genes within the virus that often caused outbreaks of fungal infection in coffee bean trees. By extracting these genes from the fungus, *Hemileia vastatrix*, which discolours and eventually dries up the foliage on coffee trees, the disease can be held at bay or even eradicated. This strain of fungus is spread by parasites and eventually will strip the trees of their leaves, leaving the precious coffee bean open to the elements, which in turn ruins the crop.

The fungus is generally referred to as Roya or Leaf Rust by the industry. The preventative measures that coffee growers have used, historically, to keep the fungus at bay, in the form of chemical agents, had become less and less effective due to climate change and the higher temperatures it brought. Producers worldwide continued to look for even stronger strains of chemical herbicides that could eradicate the parasites that spread the diseases.

During their research Dai's laboratory team had stumbled on the gene that caused the activation within the fungus. By deleting this gene from the process, it rendered the disease impotent and no damage was inflicted on the coffee tree leaves. Conversely, Dai had found a way to extract and cultivate the radical gene and produce, if required, potentially super-aggressive strains of the fungus containing more of this "super-bad" gene.

If introduced, this fungus could wipe out whole crops of coffee trees and absolutely devastate the coffee industry of any given region. Dai's thought processes were now spinning at ever-increasing rates, fuelled by his hatred of all things American and his desire to inflict appropriate revenge on them. The USA's major partner in supplying coffee beans into its huge market was Brazil. If Dai could somehow introduce the "super-bad" gene into the crops of the world's biggest exporter of coffee to North America, then the world's second biggest exporter of coffee beans, currently Vietnam, could take over the mantle and charge excessive prices. The old "supply and demand" adage had the potential to create previously unthought-of wealth for his country, his company and for Dai Ca Phung personally.

Could it really be that simple? Ruin Brazil's coffee economy and at the same time exact exorbitant prices out of the USA for its caffeine habit?

Dai's next move was to perfect the evil gene and then plan a visit to Brazil. If his plan was to succeed, then he would have to find a coffee grower that was significant to the USA market. One whose quality was renowned as the best, the market leader in sales of arabica beans to good old Uncle Sam. His research led him to what seemed to be the perfect target. A brand that he had only heard a little about, but one that filled his criteria to the letter – the Nova Coffee Company, in the Southern Highlands of Brazil.

Gabrielle's Story

Gabrielle Souza, only child of Luiz's daughter Bianca, had finished her degree at the São Paulo University on a high. Her results in her Chemistry major in late 2012 had set new records for the local university. After this result she gained her Honours degree, and Gabrielle had then decided to pursue a Master's degree in Science and Biochemistry at a prestigious overseas university, the University of California in Berkeley. This seat of learning was the pinnacle of biochemistry education in the whole of the USA. Her proud grandfather, Luiz, had naturally told all who would listen that, "Of course, she obtained her beautiful looks from her mother, but her brains are from the paternal side of the Almeida family." Maybe Gabrielle's father, Rodrigo Souza, would have had something to say about that. But he was currently working in Switzerland and had kept his distance from Bianca and his daughter in the years following the divorce, preferring an existence dating young heiresses in Europe.

Whatever the gene pool had created, however, had gifted the world with an intelligent and creative young woman with an instinctive flair for the sciences. A young Gabrielle had worked in the chemical laboratory of the Nova Coffee Company during many school holidays through her teenage years and this had fired her enthusiasm for that line of work in the future. She had nurtured a unique understanding of how biochemical interactions between the precious coffee bean and its environment affected its development, and how they helped the growth and quality of the end product. Her time there had taught her that the key to the success of the coffee-growing system at Nova was a delicate mixture of the rich earth, the recently developed water rationing system which ensured adequate moisture even during unusually dry periods, the thick local foliage, and the wonderful temperate weather. Added to this was the scientifically developed use of the most appropriate chemical herbicides, to help keep the ever-present scourge of parasites at bay. Gabrielle had learnt the system and varied the components to produce the best possible outcomes and was a revered contributor to the wellbeing of the plantation, even gaining accolades from the experienced team of Nova scientists who had worked there for decades. She loved the work with a passion and learnt very quickly, mopping up all the pearls of wisdom she extruded from her willing mentors. Gabrielle's beautiful nature was also very well received by all the Nova staff. Even though she was the boss' granddaughter, she was treated just like any other employee and was never precious in her attitude. She always showed great respect to her grandfather's long-serving staff and knew her place, always. Her uncles Felipe and Mateus, as well as her mother, had also kept her in line throughout her youth and she loved them dearly for it.

Although she had a marvellous intellect, looks to match and a wicked sense of humour, Gabrielle had never found that "special" boyfriend, even though her social life was hectic. She was not too bothered about this fact, preferring to study hard to cement her future in the industry that she loved. She had been to many wild parties on the São Paulo University campus during her four years studying there. The lure of alcoholic drink and the occasional puff on the easily available marijuana had inevitably led her up some dark alleys, and her lessons in the physical side of love had played out in a very casual and unfulfilling manner. But deep down, she hoped that true romance, and all its wonderful consequences, would follow later in life.

Her time spent away from her homeland at Berkeley would gift her with some new and interesting life skills. Her experiences there would also develop a side of her character that would help her in her future life. They acted as a catalyst to force a young and trusting Gabbie into the mature, wiser young lady that her adoring grandfather had hoped for.

San Francisco

Being offered the chance to study for a Master's degree at the University of California in Berkeley, a city on the east side of San Francisco, was an opportunity that Gabrielle Souza was never going to pass up. Her science lecturers and her Head of Faculty at São Paulo University had implored Gabrielle to add postgraduate education to her list of excellent achievements, after she had finalised her four years of study there. She had strolled through her Bachelor of Science degree and had added an Honours degree to this the following year, majoring in Biochemistry. Her plan now was to apply for a position at the prestigious Californian institution to complete a Master's degree, majoring in Agricultural Biochemistry, within a timescale of twelve months, if that was possible. This university, and its Molecular and Cell Biology (MCB) faculty in particular, had been lauded for many decades as one of the best possible establishments in America, and indeed the world, to earn a Master's degree in her chosen area of expertise.

Her family, urged on and supported financially by her proud grandfather, had agreed to fund the expense of this venture. Bianca and Luiz saw the benefits of all the skills and knowledge that young Gabrielle could receive from such a quality education in a place of learning so esteemed in the subjects she had chosen. It would be a clever and wise investment by Nova Coffee, according to Luiz's thinking, one which, he was sure, would reap financial positives in future years for the growing Brazilian business. The opportunity would also give Gabrielle a great chance to experience a culture outside of her own country. Her time abroad would also help her understand the American character, practice her English-speaking skills, and maybe help her to mature quicker than would be the case at home in Brazil. More importantly, she would learn how the biggest and most influential customers of her family's coffee business viewed the world.

The relevant glowing "letters of recommendation" from São Paulo University, the money from her grandfather's company and the blessing of her mother were all in place by the fall of 2012 for Gabrielle to start her Master's at Berkeley the next year. The official application had needed to be made twelve months before her starting date, as the admission programme was an exceedingly stringent one. Having gone through all the processes, form-filling, checks and balances, the high level of her graduation results had clinched her a place amongst the International Student brigade of Berkeley. An excellent achievement, as less than 14 per cent of students were allowed into this section of the prestigious university from overseas aspirants. It was a proud moment for the Almeida/Souza family when the acceptance letter arrived in late March 2013.

Bianca escorted Gabrielle to the Californian establishment in early August 2013. All the Almeida family had congregated at Luiz's house the night before for a dinner to bid farewell to their most educated member, as she spread her wings and travelled to Berkeley. It was an extremely happy event, even though the thought of not seeing Gabrielle's smiling face around the Nova compound for a year had left her grandfather rather melancholy.

An early-morning flight from Nova Serrana airport to Rio had landed Bianca and her daughter in Brazil's most glamorous city before noon. They were booked on an American Airlines flight out of Rio De Janeiro international airport. The girls were afforded business-class tickets by Luiz and their Boeing 767 flew out at 4pm, local time. The flight was just over seventeen hours, including a two-hour stopover in Dallas, Texas. After clearing US customs, their connecting internal South West Airlines flight was on a Boeing 737 through to Oakland International Airport, San Francisco, again.

Both Bianca and Gabrielle were disappointed that they did not get a clear view of the iconic Art-Deco Golden Gate Bridge as the plane lowered its altitude in preparation for landing. As they approached the west coast, their flight path had taken them over the lesser known, Oakland Bay Bridge that joined the mainland to the downtown city area of San Francisco. The city itself was set on land jutting out northwards from San José in the south, with San Francisco Bay to its east and only the mass of the Pacific Ocean on its western flank. On this sunny August day, it was a beautiful sight to behold, as their plane descended towards the airport. Bianca pointed excitedly out of their cabin window when she spied the historic and very famous Alcatraz Prison Island sitting just behind Treasure Island in the bay's sparkling, calm waters. There was a slight smog haze floating north from the city, which unfortunately only served to mask a decent view of the Golden Gate Bridge.

"I'm sure that I'll get plenty of opportunities to see the bridge over the next few months, Mum," said Gabrielle, as the plane glided effortlessly across the bay to land at the airport, situated on the eastern edge of the water.

The taxi journey from the airport to the university took a long time, due to the heavy afternoon traffic. Their driver, an elegant man called Giovani, explained that the trip normally took only 20 minutes at quiet times, but today it was busy, so they could expect to spend at least an hour in the back of his car. They headed north on the Nimitz Highway, through the charmingly named suburb of Jingletown, then through the city's Chinatown, bypassing the slip road onto the westward entry of the Oakland Bay Bridge to the city's downtown area, continuing to head north along the 580 Highway, through Emeryville. The women were greeted with a view of the massed, mainly white-painted sailing yachts bobbing in the water to their left, with their multitude of bare masts rising from their decks, silhouetted against the bright blue sky. There were hundreds of leisure boats anchored at the marina of the McLaughlin State Park, awaiting their well-heeled owners to motor them out onto the sparkling bay, before hoisting their spinnakers and flying across the water when a timely wind filled them with sufficient power.

"I think I am going to enjoy myself in San Francisco!" called out Gabrielle to her mother, an excited smile beaming across her face as they both gawked out of the taxi windows at the passing scenery. As Giovani guided his taxi further north, they approached a big junction, the green and white sign above the highway indicating "University Avenue".

"Almost there!" shouted Giovani as the lights changed to green and he motored into the right lane, his indicator flashing. As the car turned, heading inland towards Berkeley, Gabrielle looked to her left and saw the Berkeley Marina, fronted by a large expanse of lush green grass leading towards the water of the bay. It was full of all sorts of craft, with various sizes of both catamarans and single-hulled boats and a few larger pleasure cruisers dotted in amongst them. She also noticed a multitude of shops in the commercial section of the marina, including some interesting-looking cafes and restaurants.

"This is so exciting," thought Gabrielle to herself, as the marina faded into the distance and Giovani pushed his taxi eastward towards their destination. Her mother had been chatting away amicably to their driver and looked happy and contented, although, deep down, Gabrielle knew that she was apprehensive about leaving her only child alone in a foreign country.

Within ten minutes the imposing buildings of the university loomed ahead. Bianca had booked her daughter into accommodation at the Resident Halls Unit Three of the UCB, for the almost twelve-month stay at this prestigious seat of learning. Using the local map she had picked up at the airport, Bianca directed the taxi driver to turn right into Oxford Street from University Avenue. Gabrielle looked admiringly at the elegant buildings and the huge array of trees that made up the precinct, as they passed the Berkeley Art Museum and the Pacific Film Archive, as well as the famous Cal Performance Center. After a few blocks they had arrived at the place that would be Gabrielle's home for the next twelve months. In the same street as her accommodation, Gabrielle noticed a cute little takeaway coffee joint called the 1951 Coffee Company, nestled in the front of the building that housed the First Presbyterian Church of Berkeley.

"Hope they make good coffee!" Gabrielle quipped to her mother as they alighted, took out her luggage, and said their goodbyes to Giovani after settling the bill. After Gabrielle had booked herself into her new home and rolled her three suitcases of luggage into her first-floor unit, she turned to her teary-eyed mother, who was contemplating a whole year of being away from her one and only child.

"Oh, Mum, come on now… it will be over in a flash, I promise you. It is less than a year until I am back home at Nova. No need to blubber," said Gabrielle, as she gave her mother a loving cuddle and wiped a few tears from her eyes.

"I know, darling, but we will all miss you, you know," responded Bianca, with a soft kiss onto her daughter's head. "When you were at São Paulo Uni, you were only a couple of hours away by plane and I could always drop in to visit you, if I needed to. Over here, you are so far away and all on your own. Will you be okay?"

"Well, I won't exactly be alone, Mum. There are thousands of students here with me, plus the whole of Berkeley city centre and that little old place called San Francisco!" replied Gabrielle, rather cheekily. "I think I will be fine, Mother. I am almost twenty-three, I'll need to learn how to look after myself sometime, so why not now?"

Her mother smiled back at her brave girl, obviously proud of Gabrielle's positive attitude.

"Well, how about a celebratory dinner, my darling? Giovani, our lovely taxi driver, recommended me a place just around the corner from here. I think it was called Angeline's Louisiana Kitchen, on Shattuck Avenue… yes, here it is, I wrote it down in the taxi." Bianca, plucked a piece of paper from her black Gucci handbag. "He says that all the students rave about the wonderful, home-cooked New Orleans style food. Fried catfish and hushpuppies, shrimp Creole, baby back ribs… will be something different for you to get your teeth stuck into, hey, young lady?"

"Sounds wonderful, Mum, and I am starving! Let's go," shouted Gabrielle enthusiastically. "I will have a shower later tonight."

The new arrivals enjoyed a great night and dinner together, although Bianca had a little too much white wine. She had planned to go on a tour of the university with Gabrielle at 10am the next morning before heading back to Brazil on a late flight out of San Francisco, again via Dallas. However, she woke up in her hotel next morning with a start to the sound of Gabrielle frantically knocking at her door. It was 9am; she had slept in. With a little help from her daughter, Bianca was ready and presentable enough to meet any professor or Dean at UCB. Leaving her luggage with the hotel receptionist and thanking her for a wonderful night's sleep, Bianca finally slid into the waiting taxi that Gabrielle had organised whilst her mother was applying some final touches to her make up. By 9.45am they were on their way.

"Don't let me drink so much, next time... please!" pleaded Bianca to her daughter, who was teetering between amusement and exasperation at her mother's antics.

The tour of UCB was breathtaking. It took them through the amazing botanical gardens, the beguiling mixture of traditional and more modern buildings, the many social and sporting facilities, and the most up-to-date science facilities that Gabrielle had ever seen – especially the Genetics and Plant Biology Building, the Lawrence Berkeley National Laboratory, the Valley Life Sciences Building and the Lawrence Hall of Science. Bianca could certainly appreciate why the tuition fees and other additional costs were so expensive, but she calmed herself with the thought that Gabrielle would make it all worthwhile.

A short, quiet lunch together at Bianca's hotel ended her brief stay in the city. A long goodbye as Bianca got into her taxi to the airport left even Gabrielle a little teary. Bianca smiled weakly and waved as she disappeared up Shattuck Avenue in the taxi, heading back to Oakland International Airport.

"Okay, it's all up to me now," thought Gabrielle. "And I am going to do it my way!"

A Real Education

The first month of Gabrielle's compressed Master's studies was hectic, eye-opening and character-building. She had fitted in well at her accommodation with all the other students, including first-year hopefuls, postgraduate know-it-alls and aspirants furthering their education with Honours degrees and Master's like her. There was a vast array of subjects being studied by this year's young men and women, who were from various ethnic backgrounds, and this made for cosmopolitan and eclectic conversation. Gabbie's favourite hangout was the 1951 Coffee Company she had spotted across the road from her digs on the very first day – it was the place to be for a lot of her fellow boarders at Residents Halls Unit Three.

Gabrielle's particular study was based at the Genetics and Plant Biology Building, erected on the Berkeley campus in 1990 with the aim of revitalising the biological sciences at the university. The GPB was a three-storey, concrete building that housed four classrooms of various capacity, as well as laboratories that made her own Nova Coffee establishment at home seem limited in both size and equipment. There were only four other students completing their biology Master's degrees this particular year, although she found out that she was the only one hoping to get her specialist degree within a twelve-month period. The others had chosen the standard eighteen-month programme, with the regular fall, winter, Easter, and summer vacation breaks in between semesters. The four students comprised two young men, one Hispanic and the other of Asian descent, and a couple of women. One of the latter was a local San Franciscan, of similar age to Gabrielle, and the second was a mature student in her thirties from New York. This cohort of students certainly echoed the variety of gender and ethnic diversity that Berkeley was so famous for.

Their key lecturer was Dr. Robert Peyton, a tall man in his forties with a hint of debonair elegance about him. The first time that Gabrielle was introduced to her new teacher, their eyes met over a polite handshake, and Gabrielle smiled nervously as he introduced himself to the group.

The first semester of the young Brazilian girl's studies gave her hope that she had the ability to achieve a notable pass mark in her chosen specialist subject. She hoped that the information and knowledge that she took on board from this experience would set her up for a professional career in the field that she loved. She felt the weight of expectancy on her, especially from her grandfather, but she was confident that she had what it took to be successful. Certainly, that view was shared by her eloquent teacher as the first few months, between August and November, came and went. He had proved to be a hard taskmaster in the eyes of the two young men and the young local girl, Suzy. But Gabrielle and her older associate, Kate Needham, had taken to Robert Peyton's persuasive and energetic ways of imparting knowledge to his students. Whilst the other three aspirants seemed to be breaking under the pressure, Gabbie, as she had become known by her fellow students, and the more mature Kate had excelled in their studies. Off campus, they had also become quite close, as two out-of-town girls, with similar ambitions and no real knowledge of the local scene, sharing a friendly, empathetic bond.

They regularly kept each other company at Pat Reid's Coffee Shop, located adjacent to the main GPB building. Underneath the royal-blue table umbrellas at the front of the usually full coffee shop, Gabbie and Kate would often sit on the wooden bench seats to drink an excellent brew of coffee and discuss their studies or other issues that were concerning them. Most of all they discussed their learned lecturer, Dr. Robert Peyton.

In the months leading up to the end of the first semester, all five of the Master's students got to know their teacher a lot better. Through the general gossip that is generated within an establishment as big as UCB, or the "Cal" as it was colloquially known, it became apparent that

Dr. Peyton was now a single man again, although not yet officially divorced from his wife. He was the father to two boys who were twelve and ten years old. His boyish looks had seen many a female student's heart flutter throughout his career and there were constant rumours of his extramarital infidelities circulating the classrooms, staff-rooms and dormitories.

Both Gabrielle and Kate had been beguiled by Peyton's good looks, charm and charisma from the first few weeks of their time at UCB. Their willingness to work hard and both learn from and appreciate his knowledge heightened his interest in them, not only as capable students, but as individuals. Although Kate was closer to his age and by no means unattractive, the lecturer seemed to be more drawn to Gabrielle, because of her intelligence, her beauty, and her down-to-earth attitude.

Gabrielle often visited Kate at her rented bedsit in downtown Berkeley for nights out. The rents outside the university-owned housing were noticeably cheaper than those within the immediate vicinity of UCB's campus. Kate's budget, as a single woman from the other side of America, meant that she had to look for the best value she could to afford the eighteen-month stay at this prestigious university. Kate had put her career, working in the New York Health Department, on hold for two years in order to grasp this opportunity. She had progressed as far as she could have within the huge State Government department and was aiming to break into the executive level by gaining her Master's degree from Berkeley. Her area of expertise was medical research, and the knowledge she already possessed was like a magnet to young Gabrielle, who wasted no opportunity to learn as much as she could from her new classmate. This was not just confined to university matters.

Their social outings became a regular occurrence and Gabbie's many overnight absences from her own accommodation block had started tongues wagging amongst some of her newly acquired friends at Residents Hall Unit Three. Although Kate had visited Gabbie at her place and enjoyed a couple of nights with her and her roommates at the 1951 Coffee Company across the road, the young Brazilian preferred the downtown area.

Towards the end of November, many end of semester and pre-Christmas parties were happening in and around Berkeley. Gabbie and Kate had been invited to one such event at the Berkeley Marina complex. They had met and dressed at Kate's place and had gulped down a bottle of the finest sparkling wine that they could afford, before ordering a taxi to take them west to the marina.

Within twenty minutes they had arrived at the glamorous entry to the venue. Their pre-drinks had ensured that they were both in a jolly mood and ready to enjoy their night out. The festive party had been organised by the powerful Student's Union of UCB at the ballroom of the swanky DoubleTree by Hilton Hotel. Traditionally, as well as students, the Union often invited favoured lecturers and administration staff to their fundraising events to bolster the coffers. On entering the luxurious ballroom, the girls were glad that they had decided to buy new dresses for the occasion, as all the guests already there were beautifully attired. Kate looked ravishing in her halter-neck red sequinned gown, which showed off her curvaceous body, and she had worn her curly blonde hair up high. Her matching red stilettos added a couple of inches to her height as she stepped inside to the event. Gabbie had chosen a tight-fitting short black dress that drew attention to her long, shapely, tanned legs. Her silver shoes were not as high-heeled as those of her partner in crime, but featured strapping that wound enticingly around her ankles and lower calves. Their entry into the room certainly had the desired effect of gaining attention from the well-dressed invitees, both male and female.

As they headed towards a waiter brandishing a silver tray full of champagne glasses, Gabbie felt a delicate tap on her bare shoulder.

"Why, if it isn't the Dynamic Duo!" declared the handsome man behind her, smiling radiantly.

"Oh, Dr. Peyton, so lovely to see you... I didn't know you would be here tonight," said Gabbie, rather flustered.

"Kate, look who's here!"

Her friend was grabbing two glasses of very bubbly champagne from the waiter.

"Good evening, Dr. Peyton. Wow, a three-piece suit. Looks like you are out to play tonight!" gushed Kate.

"You ladies look so wonderful this evening, I just love your dresses," drawled Peyton, in his cute Southern accent, clutching a glass full of bourbon and ice. "Please, call me Robert. After all, this is a social occasion. We can forget about work tonight, surely?"

Gabbie raised her glass and said softly, "Well, here's to the end of our first semester under your very able tutelage, Robert."

"And we both look forward to being under you for many more months to come!" piped up Kate with a cheeky grin, as she chinked the glass of her lecturer with her own, almost empty champagne glass.

The doctor smiled at them both, his blue sparkling eyes looking deep into each of his students' adoring gazes.

"Maybe we'll catch up a bit later on this evening?" he said, excusing himself and waltzing off to the other side of the room, where the Student Union boss, Sarah Houseman, greeted him with an intimate kiss to the cheek.

"That was a bit forward, Kate!" chided Gabbie, with a giggle. "We look forward to being under you, Robert!" she imitated in a comically bad New York accent. "Let's get a few more drinks and see who else is around that we know."

Both women enjoyed a wonderful night, linking up with a few of the students they already knew from campus and making friends with even more fun seekers. They had hit the dancefloor hard as the night went on. Gabbie surprised herself with her dancing skills, helped by her avid consumption of champagne, and attracted many admirers. Kate could also move well, and they had a fun time together. By close to midnight the place was emptying after what seemed like a successful and enjoyable night for all concerned. Kate and Gabbie were sitting with a rather drunk group of postgraduate students in the comfortable lounge next to the main bar area. A couple of the young men in the cohort clearly had designs on Gabbie and Kate.

"He's rather cute, the blond one," whispered Kate into Gabbie's ear. "But too young for me, Gab."

"Wow, I am feeling quite woozy. Maybe it's time to get a taxi home?" Gabbie said. "And yes, too young for me as well. Shall we make a move?"

As they finished their short, drunken conversation Robert Peyton appeared at the table and slid in to sit next to them both.

"Do you fancy a nightcap, girls?" he asked. He now looked a little dishevelled, with his tie loosened around his neck, but now even sexier in the eyes of both of his favourite students. "I've got a tab at the bar, as I'm actually staying here the night. Seemed the most sensible thing to do. Do you both wanna join me... at the bar?" he drawled.

"Great idea!" said Kate.

"I'm in," added Gabbie, with a smile in Robert's direction.

The trio stood up, rather gingerly, said their goodbyes to the other group at the table – including the now disappointed two postgrads opposite – and made their way to the elegant bar area. Their gentlemanly host pulled out two leather stools from under the lip of the marble-topped bar and offered them to his guests.

"Ladies, please be seated. What can I get you to drink?"

"Two Cosmopolitans would be simply fine, Robert. Is that okay for you, Gab?" Kate replied, looking at her younger friend.

"Sounds great to me. My legs are killing me after all that dancing. I'd love a good icy-cold drink."

Quite a few guests had mustered around the bar area, as the official part of the evening celebrations had ended. A loud shriek of laughter came from a big group of revellers, including Sarah Houseman, the Student Union boss, at the other end of the bar. Robert turned to look at the group and raised his freshly poured glass of iced Wild Turkey in their direction, a broad grin across his face. Sarah Houseman turned in his direction, threw her arms in the air and waved back at him excitedly.

"You seem to know Ms. Houseman quite well, is she staying here tonight as well, Robert?" enquired Kate.

"You've really got to show the Union some respect around here. You'll learn, wait and see," smiled Peyton, as he passed the two women their drinks. He purposely looked deep into their eyes as they thanked him for the oversized cocktail glasses full to the brim with the icy red liquid. He then stood between the women as they sat on their barstools and placed an arm around both of their shoulders.

"How about we finish off these drinks down here, then retire upstairs to my suite? I have a fridge full of cold champagne and bourbon up there. What do you say?" whispered their lecturer.

Kate took a sizeable swig from her cocktail glass, looked at Gabbie and raised her eyebrows. She looked into Gabbie's confused eyes and said softly.

"Let's go to the powder room for a little chat, "

She smiled at Peyton and excused herself, telling him that both the women needed to use the toilet before they moved on. He nodded in approval.

Once inside the powder room, Kate headed for the mirror and started adding a fresh layer of lipstick and touching up her smudged mascara. Gabbie followed her inside and also looked at herself in the mirror.

"I don't know, Kate. Do you think it is okay to do this? I am only a poor, young Brazilian student, after all. You are the worldly one!" replied Gabbie, giggling as she looked at her image in the mirror.

"What do you have to lose, partner?" replied Kate, "let's go girl!" as she headed out of the powder room, with Gabbie following her.

They returned to the bar area, where Robert Peyton was still chatting to the barman.

"Okay, Robert. We're on!" confirmed Kate with a nod of her head.

"I really do appreciate that, ladies. I really do. I'll ordered some food for the room," he added.

"Don't move, I'll be back soon. Finish off those lovely cold Cosmos."

As he walked towards the far end of the bar to organise some midnight snacks, Gabbie placed her hands on Kate's knees, looked at her straight in the eyes and said, "Are you sure this will be alright, Kate? This is all a bit new for me!"

"Relax, honey. You came to university to learn a thing or two, didn't you? Chill out, this'll be fun!" she replied with an assured grin. Gabbie smiled back.

Robert Peyton arrived back at their end of the bar and surreptitiously pressed a key card into Kate's palm. She grabbed it with a knowing wink, giggled and said in a low voice,

"What number, Robert?"

"507," he responded in a faint whisper. "See you up there in ten minutes. Feel free to use the amenities…"

"Oh, we will, Robert, we will!" quipped the brash blonde, eliciting a quizzical look from her teacher.

Within two minutes the girls had finished their drinks and Kate had whisked Gabbie off to the foyer area of the hotel where the elevators were. Once inside the confines of the lift she swiped Robert's key card against the fob-detector and pressed the number five. The number lit up as the lift ascended.

Gabbie stared at her reflection in the mirrored wall of the lift to her left.

"We're going to have some fun with Dr. Peyton tonight… aren't we, Kate?" she muttered.

"We certainly are, my dear!" exclaimed her smiling partner. "He won't know what hit him, Gabbie."

The lift doors slid open as they reached their destination and they stepped out onto to the soft carpet, arm in arm, giggling profusely. They found room number 507, Kate placed the key card against the lock, it flashed green and buzzed, she pushed down the handle and they were in. Kate went straight to the fridge and pulled open the door. A delighted smile came to her face as she spied a cold bottle of Moet & Chandon nestled in the bottom of the cold interior. Kate dragged the bottle out and looked around for some flutes, finding them in the cupboards above the cabinet. As she expertly unwrapped the silver foil top from the cork and twisted the metal wire to release the stopper, Kate saw that Gabbie had gone into the elegantly decorated bathroom and started to disrobe.

"Champagne coming right up, my little coffee girl!" she shouted, at the same time dislodging the cork out of the neck of the bottle, which resulted in a tremendous popping sound. As the sound of the cascading water from Gabbie showering hit her ears, the New Yorker quickly filled up the three champagne flutes and placed them down on the low tables either side of the huge kingsize bed.

"I think our handsome lecturer will be here any minute, Gabbie. You better get that beautiful Brazilian backside of yours out here soon!"

"Coming, Kate. Just drying off," called Gabbie.

Kate kicked off her heels, unzipped her red dress and stood unsteadily on the plush carpet that adorned the floor of the room. The sequinned dress fell to the floor, followed by her lacy brassiere and panties. She pulled back the bed cover and slipped excitedly under the crisp cotton sheets. A second later, the bathroom door opened and Gabbie appeared, totally naked, followed by a mist of warm steam escaping from the shower. She walked slowly towards the bed, her eyes transfixed on Kate, as her friend smiled gently. The young Brazilian slipped into the bed, leaned across, put her arm around her neck and pulled Kate towards her, kissing her forehead.

"Thank you for helping me to grow up, Kate, I wouldn't have done this without you," she whispered.

"My absolute pleasure, Gabbie. I suppose we should leave some room for our teacher."

At that moment, there was a light knock on the room door, then an electronic buzzing sound. The door slowly opened inward to reveal a smiling Dr. Robert Peyton creeping into the room with a silver tray loaded with strawberries, waffles, and cream in one hand, and a half-consumed glass of bourbon in the other. As he closed the door quietly behind him, he saw the vision that lay before him, cracked one of his sexy smiles and proclaimed, "Well, isn't that a beautiful sight?"

Final Months at Berkeley

Within a week of their little *ménage à trois*, Kate was heading back home to New York to celebrate Thanksgiving, Christmas and the New Year with her friends and family. This left Gabbie alone on campus, as the other three Master's students were also taking the break away from Berkeley. Robert Peyton was still occasionally seeing Gabbie for individual tutorials and for multiple social occasions until around mid-December. With most students taking the break, the Cal, and Berkeley itself, became a bit of a ghost town.

Gabbie had been flattered by her teacher's attention and perceived affection. She found their sexual encounters thrilling and exciting, even though Robert had intimated that he was being constantly harassed by his wife, who was pressing for a quick divorce settlement. Robert had shown her around the city of San Francisco, and they had spent a few evenings at his city apartment. Her studies were going well, considering their personal relationship, so she was surprised when he told her that he was considering a reconciliation with his estranged wife before Christmas. He said that he missed his two sons and he felt that he had an obligation to be with them during their later teenage years.

Gabbie was taken aback by this news, but not as devastated as she thought she might have been. Maybe the fact that she had seen Dr Peyton, only one week earlier, at one of the local restaurants accompanying Sarah Houseman at a very intimate dinner, had something to do with that. Gabbie had kept her appearance discreet that evening and managed to slip out of the eatery unseen by the couple. She recognised a car parked outside the establishment, a bright blue Renault adorned with Student Rights stickers, which she had seen many times before on campus. It belonged to the UCB Student Union boss. Without a thought she moved towards the vehicle, checked there were no potential witnesses around – it was an extremely quiet night in Berkeley – then proceeded to let air out of two of the tyres, unscrewing the valve caps from adjacent wheels and firmly pressing down on the pins to release the air, with a hairpin she extracted from her head, until they were flat. A satisfied smile lit up her face as she finished her task and smartly headed off on foot towards her digs.

"At least the son of a bitch won't get a free ride home tonight to his bachelor pad in the city!" Gabbie thought to herself as she made her way home. She had no quarrel with Sarah Houseman – Gabbie saw her only as another "love fool" who had fallen under the devilish charms of her teacher. Gabbie was angry with herself for all that she given during her relationship with Peyton, but even so she did not regret a single minute of it. Wait until she told Kate when she got back from her Christmas break!

The yuletide period passed quickly for an increasingly confident Gabbie. There were many phone calls to her family back home in Brazil and frequent interstate conversations with Kate in New York. She spent many days on her own, conducting visits to San Francisco and enjoying the freedom of doing whatever she wanted, whenever she wanted. The young Brazilian took many photographs of various places of interest around the exciting city, including the Golden Gate Bridge, of course. She sent multiple WhatsApp messages, along with some photos, to her mother, grandfather, uncles, aunty and cousins, and even to Esmeralda, the former nanny, who was still employed by her poppy at the Nova homestead. During all this time she had earnestly stuck to her concentrated work plan, pushing herself mercilessly to complete her studies in line with the strict timeline she had set herself. Gabbie needed to get a great result from this year of heavy study to legitimise the time and money that she and her family had invested in this project.

Dr Peyton finished up for his Christmas break on December 18th and was not due back until the last week in January, to prepare for the new semester which began officially in the first few days of February. Gabbie was happy that her preparation had been solid, and she had adequately thought through the torrid affair with her teacher and had compartmentalised it as the important life lesson that she felt it had been. Her strength of character shone through and she started the new year in a relaxed fashion as her fellow students in the biology Master's programme returned to Berkeley from their respective breaks. From then on, she saw Peyton as her teacher only. He had certainly moved on from their brief encounter, having succeeded in reintegrating with his wife and family over the Christmas period. Her friend Kate had met a new man during her vacation in New York and was in a positive and jovial mood on her return to the Cal. However, the women's bond with each other was still as strong as it had ever been, and they were overjoyed to be reunited.

The next six months passed quickly as the intrepid young Brazilian blossomed like a brightly coloured flower in the enthralling and sustaining atmosphere of university life. Her study was hard, yet exceedingly rewarding. Gabbie's capacity to take in the knowledge she was ingesting was seemingly never-ending and her work was gaining praise from her cohort students and teachers alike. The more practical, laboratory-based experiments she was taking part in were admired as groundbreaking efforts within the Agricultural Scientific fraternity of the campus. Her documentation abilities were also being exulted by her fellow scientists and the representatives of corporate sponsors which, importantly, pleased the administration officials of UCB. She had certainly grown as a human being during this short stay away from the comforts and confines of her Brazilian home. So, when the northern hemisphere summer season was approaching and her Master's degree was within her grasp, Gabbie felt that her time at this prestigious institution had been a special and productive time in more ways than one.

In late June 2014, Bianca and Luiz Almeida travelled up to Berkeley to attend Gabrielle's degree ceremony, and also to accompany her back home to Brazil. It had been an extremely successful twelve months of intense learning for young Gabbie. Her grandfather was ultimately pleased with her official success and certainly recognised that she had, indeed, grown into a capable young lady.

Felipe, Mateus and Bianca

Bianca Almeida was back to her maiden name after two failed marriages. The only real positive from her attempts at marital bliss was her daughter, Gabrielle. Bianca was now back in the family business looking after the administration and the financial management of the successful Nova Coffee Company, a job at which she was excelling. Her father, Luiz, was still the head of the company, but in recent years he had handed over most of the management responsibility to his three offspring, Felipe, Mateus and Bianca.

The three siblings were now quite a cohesive team, backed by a strong and loyal staff – between them they had the Nova Coffee Company sitting in an extremely healthy financial position. All their little quibbles of the past seemed to have disappeared and the future was looking good for all of them. Young Gabrielle had developed into an amazing asset for the family in terms of her abilities within the area of crop maximisation, using the scientific knowhow gained from her recently completed Master's degree in America. Since her return from Berkeley in late June, all her family had noticed that she had changed, in many ways, for the better. Young Gabbie had matured in an immeasurable fashion. The young girl that had left them the previous August had been quite an inexperienced young soul, who, although confident in her abilities, lacked the strong belief in her own worth within the family business. She had returned as a more complete individual who understood her true worth. She worked hand in hand with her uncle Mateus, the overall manager of the production area of the plantation processing and packing sections. Her key skill was to supply all the required scientific information to her uncle, gained from her work in the lab, which helped in maximising yields for Nova Coffee and ensured that the quality of their beans was always kept at the highest level. Certainly, her grandfather Luiz was pleased with Gabbie's growth as a person. It was a development that would only help the family business.

Bianca had received an email, quite out of the blue, from a coffee company in Vietnam. They wanted a representative to visit the Nova complex to discuss the possibility of a joint project, based on a new strain of crop herbicide that had been developed in their smallish coffee plantation and production factory in Southern Vietnam. After initial discussions with Felipe and Mateus, Bianca had consulted Gabrielle on the technical aspects of the proposal and then took a full report to Luiz to get his approval. The old man saw no reason to deny Nova Coffee a potential boon to their production practices, so sanctioned the visit on the proviso that Gabrielle should take the lead in the scientific side of the offer. The brothers agreed, so Bianca replied positively to the email, inviting Mr Dai Ca Phung to visit them at Nova Coffee to discuss his proposal at length.

The Plan Unfolds

Dai Ca Phung summoned his personal secretary, Tina Lei, into his spacious office at the Lam Dong Coffee corporate centre. Balancing carefully on the high-heeled shoes that accentuated her shapely legs, Tina entered his room from her desk area outside his door and gave a courteous smile to her boss.

"Please sit down and take a few notes, Tina," Dai started, as he motioned towards the leather-bound chair opposite. "I need to take a trip to Brazil, quite urgently, and would like to organise some accommodation, as close as possible to the coffee company known as Nova Coffee – it's situated close to a town called Nova Serrana in the Southern Highlands area of the country. I will travel alone, on a business-class ticket, and would like to leave Vietnam within one week, if possible.

Can you please organise that for me, Tina?"

"Certainly, Mr Phung. I'll book it with our usual travel company – will that be okay?"

"Actually, no… not this time, please. I would prefer that you organise this particular trip through this alternative travel company," Dai told her, handing over a business card. He needed the trip to go "under the radar", as he preferred that as few people as possible knew of his travel plans.

"Oh, I am sure that this can be arranged. How long would you like to stay at this place, sir?" replied his very loyal and long-serving secretary.

"Five days should be enough to complete what I need to achieve, so maybe four nights' accommodation would be best. Please try to get me into the best possible hotel available, although I doubt that there would be anything in the five-star range in such a place... I'll leave it up to you, Tina, you know how I like things," said Dai.

Dai then asked her to convene a meeting of all the Lam Dong Coffee scientific and research managers.

"Can you call the meeting for 9am tomorrow morning, here in my office? I expect all the managers to attend. We have an especially important project to discuss, so please ensure that they understand that their presence is to be prioritised. Thank you, Tina."

With that Tina got up from her seat and left the room at her boss' direction, her perfect derriere being admired by her superior. She sat behind her tidy desk and began to arrange all that needed to be done. Dai stretched back on his expensively crafted leather chair, closed his eyes, and said to himself in an inaudible whisper, "It has begun!"

Dr Chien

The next day, prior to the meeting, Dai was in his office early, the strong morning sun sending shards of bright yellow light through his open windows. Unusually, a crisp breeze freshened the normally stuffy atmosphere of the room and Dai felt greatly confident.

He was eager to meet with his four most senior scientific and research managers, along with the Director of that division, Dr Phan Chien. The doctor had worked with Lam Dong Coffee for nearly thirty years and was a trusted advisor to Dai's stepfather, Dung Lam, as well as a gifted biologist. If his plans were to succeed, he knew that Phan Chien's blessing had to be given, otherwise they would go no further. Therefore, the plan that Dai had devised had to have a dual purpose – firstly it needed to be seen as necessary for the good of Lam Dong, but secondly its intimate details and true purpose would only be known by one man – Dai Ca Phung.

As the four men and one woman congregated in the boardroom next to Dai's office, each of them poured coffee and made small talk. When he assessed that the time was right, Dung Lam's extremely ambitious stepson strode into the room, closed the ornately decorated door behind him and greeted the group confidently and boldly.

"Good morning, ladies and gentlemen, thank you for attending this important meeting. I am sure you are wondering what this is all about."

For a young man only just approaching the age of thirty, Dai had a presence and personality that enthralled most listeners, and today was no exception. The four managers knew their position and rarely questioned any senior company directors when being informed of changes or new systems that were to be implemented. Dai knew this situation and was well-versed in getting loyalty and the best possible results from his underlings, even though they were experienced managers. His charming manner and undeniable charisma served him well in moments like this and he used it to his advantage every time. Dr Phan Chien, on the other hand, was an entirely different matter. Being so close to Lam Dong's "Big Boss" was a mighty advantage each time the good doctor had battles to endure. Dung Lam trusted his old friend implicitly and would always call on his input to solve problems in the past. Dai had been taught by his mother, Mai Thi, and later by her husband, to respect his elders and to always seek wise counsel from those more experienced and knowledgeable adults who surrounded him at work. To this end, Dai had followed those teachings and was seen to be respectful by all who worked with him. In fact, Phan Chien was very gracious when talking of Dai Ca Phung and, outwardly at least, believed him to be worthy of his exulted position at Lam Dong. However, the truth was far from this, as he really saw Dai as a threat to his own position in the company.

Dai realised that he had to be seen to be respectful of his Head of Scientific and Research Division and at the same time not reveal the true purpose of his plans. It would be a challenge, but one that this young man had been made for.

As the congregated management group listened intently to their young leader, Dai related the reason for the meeting. He told them of how proud he was to have to have overseen all the wonderful work that his team, led by Dr Chien, had done to eradicate the scourge of parasites in the coffee plantations of Lam Dong. They had produced an effective chemical herbicide that numerous tests had verified, beyond doubt, could stop the disease-spreading parasites in their tracks and wipe out their breeding cycle. A result that was a first in the industry – achieved ahead of the powerful multinational chemical giants of Europe and North America – meaning that Lam Dong was in a very powerful position to commercialise this chemical breakthrough and produce a mighty windfall for the Vietnamese coffee industry.

Dai laid out his very well-thought-out and sensible plan of how the company could benefit from this situation and his vision of selecting certain markets to either sell to or arrange manufacture under license. Initially, however, they would need to apply for the necessary patents to ensure that their work would not be compromised by the greedy international chemical giants and, of course, legal advice of the highest measure to protect their intellectual property.

The gathered throng of scientists listened patiently to Dai's passionate speech, some in total awe of his persuasive and entrepreneurial skills, but more noticeably, they all felt a deep sense of pride for the part that they had played in getting their beloved little coffee company into such a strong position. Phan Chien, however, was inwardly concerned that his part in this success had been undervalued and his tight grip on power within the company's hierarchy was being threatened by this young upstart.

Dai finished his talk by thanking everyone present for their contribution to this great breakthrough. He then asked them all to keep this information to themselves until all the relevant patents and legal agreements were in place. As he was about to dismiss them all, Phan Chien stood up and asked his team to remain seated. For a Vietnamese, Chien was very tall, well over six feet, and his powerful presence ensured complete obedience from his scientific team. They all looked to him intently as he started to speak.

"Ladies and gentlemen... I am sure you are all as proud of our Managing Director as I am and heartily agree with him, and are excited about the potential of this fine result that we have, as a close-knit team, achieved for the company. It is of the utmost importance that we all go away from here and are careful not to pass on any of the details discussed at this morning's meeting. I would add that any breach of this condition, from any of you, will most certainly result in instant dismissal from Lam Dong and strong litigation against the person involved. As your leader, I have the greatest respect for all my group, but I must stress to you the delicacy of this situation and ask you all respectfully to recognise this. We are at the beginning of a journey that will bring immense prosperity to this great company and I assure you all that you will be well rewarded for your part in this effort."

Chien looked around at all his team as a silent pause ensued, suddenly broken by a spontaneous round of respectful hand-clapping in reaction to his words. Chien smiled; he knew that his power was still evident even at this late stage in his life. His gaze was distracted by a glimpse at Dai Ca Phung standing at the head of the table looking at him with great reverence and, with a nod of the head, Dai mouthed a silent "Thank you" to his tall and powerful senior.

As the meeting closed and the scientists strolled out of the office, Dai shook the hand of Chien, looked up to the slightly taller man and said, "I appreciate your support, sir, it means lot to me."

"Have you discussed this with your stepfather, Dai?" Chien responded.

"That would be my next step. How would you advise me to do so, Dr Chien?"

"Leave that to me, Dai. Then you and I must have a personal meeting to lay out the details and form a concrete plan to implement your ideas. Well done, young man, we are all proud of you," Chien replied, with a knowing smile.

"Let's meet for dinner this evening. Is that okay?"

"Certainly, sir, that would be excellent. I will get Tina to reserve a table for two at your favourite restaurant, I am sure that she will know your preference. Let us say... 7pm?" Dai offered.

"Ask Tina to email the details to me, I look forward to having a chat," replied Chien, as he nodded his head in Dai's direction and strode out of the office, smiling at Tina as he walked through.

Dai put his head around the doorway that separated his office from Tina's and called cheerfully, "I would love a fresh coffee, Tina!"

"Of course, sir. Coming right up," was the instant reply. She instinctively knew that today would be a happy one.

Dai sank into his office chair with a look of relief on his face and a smile radiating across it as he pondered the reaction to his meeting and what the future would bring. All being well, next stop Brazil!

"Thank you, Tina," said the happy young man, as Tina placed a steaming pot of Lam Dong's finest coffee and his favourite cup next to him on the desk, subtly bending forward to offer a pleasing view of her ample bosom to her admiring, and decidedly single, boss.

"Today, will be a good day, Tina," started Dai. "Could I ask you to reserve a table for two, tonight, at Dr Chien's favourite eating house? I am sure you can find out which one he likes best. 7pm would be good."

A seductive smile accompanied the answer. "Of course, sir. I already know his special place. I will organise it straight away... and, by the way, your flights and accommodation are organised for Brazil. I have emailed them to your personal address... to keep details discreet, as you asked."

"You are worth your weight in gold, Tina," said Dai, as he beamed back at her.

"Always a pleasure, sir," pouted back his stunning secretary, as she left the room. Dai savoured the delicate and arousing whiff of perfumed aroma that was left, momentarily, in his office after her exit.

Dai Ca Phung allowed himself a secret smile as he sipped his freshly brewed coffee, opened his personal laptop, and got on with his day's work.

Dinner with the Doctor

A little after 7pm that evening, Dr Chien appeared at the front reception desk of the Dragon's Tail restaurant, positioned less than fifteen minutes away, by taxi, from the Lam Dong Plantation and offices. He was a regular patron of the elegant, family-run restaurant, the owner personally greeting him with great pleasure and showing him to the best table, where Dai Ca Phung awaited his guest. After the usual pleasantries were dispensed with and the appropriate wines were matched and ordered for the required food, Dai felt that the right time was approaching to raise the issues that this dinner meeting was all about.

"What was my stepfather's reaction when you mentioned my plans, Dr Chien?" asked Dai.

"Very cautious at first, but I managed to bring him around to our way of thinking eventually. He seemed quite positive about the idea by the end of our talk – barring one consideration," replied the doctor, taking a sip of his Pinot Noir before continuing.

"Your stepfather – and I should say that I hold the same misgivings – wondered which markets you would target and also how you would convince our competitors on the world stage to work with us. We don't want them to try to undermine our virus control chemical by buying our product and replicating it for themselves," explained Chien.

Dai shuffled nervously in his comfortably padded chair, but came straight back at the doctor.

"But Dr Chien, we would need to get our intellectual property details fully safeguarded a long time before we offered the virus control to anybody. Our patents and legal paperwork must be tighter than tight, to ensure that an immediate response in the form of illegal copies of the chemical makeup can be repulsed. That is why I have arranged a short trip to Brazil. I will be leaving early next week to seek out the relevant coffee growers and exporters who may be willing to do business with us. That country is the biggest exporter in the world of the arabica and robusta beans and its main market, the USA, is the major consumer of coffee in the world. We may as well start at the top, don't you agree?"

"I see your reasoning, Dai, but how can you convince such big Brazilian enterprises that our herbicide is a guaranteed fix for their parasite problems?" asked Dr Chien.

"I plan to talk to the scientists involved in that side of their business and, with my knowledge of the chemical processes, run some controlled experimental tests in their labs. I will take some of the 'Bad Gene' virus with me, introduce it in their lab and then apply the remedial chemical compound that we have developed to eradicate the virus. It sounds simple, and it is simple. Under controlled conditions and talking to the right people I am confident that I can arouse enough interest in the possibilities from a specially chosen coffee plantation that has a huge export market to America."

"Which company have you chosen, Dai?" interrupted Chien.

"I have picked out a family-run business in the Southern Highlands region, called Nova Coffee. I have emailed their head office to establish contact – they seemed quite positive in their response."

"Well, you have been busy, haven't you? It is a good job that I am happy with your plans, otherwise your airfare and accommodation, which I assume you have already booked, might well have been a waste of money. Your stepfather lets you run your own game as head of the scientific branch, but in the end he trusts me to keep an eye on the section for him... and that, of course, includes the new Managing Director. Dai, I agree with your plans... but please let me know as many details as possible about the trip to Brazil so that I can reassure Dung Lam that this expedition is well thought out and productive. We need to work as a team if this is to succeed... Do you understand?" explained the doctor.

Although Dai, in his own mind, took this personal rebuke badly, he realised that it was important to retain the support of this pompous old man, so he answered accordingly.

"Of course, sir, I totally understand your thinking and agree that we need to work together. I had already planned a trip to Brazil to study how the coffee industry copes with crop pests in that country – my stepfather had already sanctioned the costs of that travel, by the way – so I thought that I would bring it forward to fit in with my prospective plans for the virus control project. I am grateful for your support over this matter, Dr Chien, and I mean to show that I have what it takes to help guide this company to the highest peaks of success in the coffee industry. I would like to think that I have your support in this matter, Dr Chien?" questioned young Dai.

"It seems we understand each other, young man… Let us keep it that way, shall we? I assume that you will take care of the bill. Thank you for your time and company, Dai, I'll see you at the office." With that, Dr Chien raised his large frame from the dining chair, shook Dai's hand and made his way to the front counter to organise a taxi home.

Dai Ca Phung was more than pleased with the events of the evening. As he sipped on an aged whisky, he pondered the conversation, raising his glass to the front of the restaurant where Dr Chien was just exiting the main entrance.

"Good night and good riddance, Doctor… things will change soon at Lam Dong Coffee and I will be the one that you will answer to!" he thought to himself.

Dai beckoned the waiter, paid the bill and left for home, looking forward to his impending overseas trip.

Destination Brazil

Dai Ca Phung had spent three days preparing for his Brazilian trip. He had organised enough clothes to last him a week, even though the excursion to Nova Coffee was planned to last only four days. Tina had ensured that his long trip was at least a comfortable one, by adding on all the "extras" that were needed into his travel and accommodation package. Most importantly, Dai had used his position and rank within the Lam Dong Company to ensure all the necessary visas and documents were in place, meaning no political or commercial barriers would be in his way whilst travelling abroad. He had also sent an Air Express parcel addressed to himself at the hotel he had been booked in by Tina – the Hilton in São Paulo. The contents of this parcel were marked as "commercial samples – no value". He had sent this parcel four days prior to his departure from Ho Chi Minh City International Airport, known to the Americans as Saigon Airport before the communist victory.

Today he sat in the executive lounge of that very airport, booked on an Etihad Airlines flight, looking forward to the long journey via Bangkok in Thailand, Abu Dhabi in the UAE and finally onto the Guarulhos International Airport in São Paulo, Brazil. It would be a total of over 34 hours flying time, including stopovers – a long way and a lot of time to fill in, but the services available on a business class ticket and the amount of work he had taken with him ensured that the trip was both comfortable and productively spent. Tina had booked a night's accommodation for him as the flight arrived after 7pm, and she had wanted to ensure that Dai was fresh and ready to face the Nova Coffee welcoming committee the next day. The hotel was situated in the Berrini Avenue region of central São Paulo and his luxury room overlooked the impressive Rio Pinheiros. As Dai showered in the luxury surroundings of the five-star hotel, he thought about Tina and smiled. One day, he might have to thank her properly.

The next morning, he arose early, well rested after the long trip. He had ordered, and already received, room service for breakfast. He had also packed his bags before calling reception to see if his parcel had arrived. To his joy the parcel of "commercial samples" had arrived on time and awaited him downstairs. After checking out and picking up his parcel, within an hour he was jumping onto a long-haul coach service that would get him to the small town of Nova Serrana by lunchtime. Tina had booked his accommodation there in the best quality hotel she could find over the internet. The seats on the surprisingly modern coach were comfortable, and the air conditioning worked well. As the trip would take more than six hours, Dai went over his notes again to ensure that his sales story was as viable as possible. His understanding of the Almeida family story was now complete, or as close as it could be. He had studied websites, testimonials, and LinkedIn listings to give him a working knowledge of how Luiz's business had grown to its present position and who the main people were in the organisation. In fact, his studies had given Dai a deep admiration for the family that had worked hard to get to where they were today and he was looking forward to meeting them all, even though his real intentions were less than beneficial to the Brazilians. The painful history of his family, and the perceived harm that the Americans had done to Vietnam, still spurred him on to inflict as much misery he could on the USA, even though the Almeida family all seemed like good people.

By twelve midday Dai had been dropped at the Liber Hotel in Nova Serrana, booked into his room and was preparing himself for the meeting with the Almeida family that was set for 2.30pm that afternoon. The room was a rather steep fall in quality from his previous night's accommodation, but it was clean and comfortable, as well as being situated only a short taxi ride from the Nova Coffee company offices.

Dai had showered and freshened up in the quaint hotel and dressed in a lightweight suit and open-necked business shirt to face the rather muggy, hot afternoon that awaited him as he stepped out of the hotel lobby into his taxi. The hotel itself was situated in a semi-industrial area of the town with many empty, yet-to-be-developed blocks of land surrounding it. The journey, although only a brief fifteen-minute drive, took him through much greener areas of bush, and gradually more trees became evident until he reached a set of imposing ranch-style entry gates, bedecked with the Nova Coffee Company name and logo. The plantation, which reminded him of his native Buon Ma Thuot, was situated at the base of a range of undulating hills populated by rows of mature-looking coffee trees. These were surrounded by larger indigenous trees, offering much-needed shade to the smaller berry-laden trees below. After the taxi had passed along a winding gravel entrance road lined with palm trees, Dai arrived at the front of the Almeida compound via the horseshoe driveway. There were three or four different sized buildings scattered around the lush, green area and a welcoming breeze cooled Dai as he alighted the taxi. Clutching his leather briefcase, Dai followed the sign which indicated the direction of the company office. As he walked across the loose gravel underfoot, he glanced to the left where the Nova Coffee factory stood. Faint aromas of roasting coffee permeated the air and plumes of smoke flew into the bright blue skies from the metal chimney protruding through the factory roof. The distant sound of horses caught Dai's attention as he approached the large homestead and, looking to his right, he could see a set of neat and tidy stables located in the distance. The Nova Coffee office was a freestanding structure next to the main house, painted in the same white stucco style as the Almeida family residence. The cobalt blue, wooden window shutters of the main homestead were also echoed in the smaller office building.

Immediately behind the impressive-looking house, he could see a full-size tennis court surrounded by a high fence. It seemed to have all the latest equipment installed within the court, the bright blue colour of the playing surface acting as a marked contrast to the mainly green surrounds of the homestead. As Dai walked closer to the entrance of the office area, an in-ground swimming pool came into view to the right-hand side of the buildings. Its deep still waters sent shards of light reflecting from the strong sunshine onto the walls of the outhouses built next to the pool enclosure.

This was certainly an impressive home, with all the extras that made life a little sweeter.

Just as he reached the office, the front door of the main homestead burst open and he was greeted by an attractive lady, who he thought was maybe in her forties.

"Good afternoon, Mr Phung, I assume? My name is Bianca Almeida, welcome. Can you please join us in the house? It is a lot cooler in here." She beckoned to the visitor. "Thank you so much for coming to see us," she added.

Dai smiled and made his way up the entrance stairs of the house.

"My position is head of Finance and Administration for my father's company. So pleased to meet you." she said, offering her hand in a friendly gesture.

Dai took her hand in a very businesslike manner, smiled, and shook it quickly. "I am Dai Ca Phung from the Lam Dong coffee company in Vietnam. Thank you so much for agreeing to meet with me. I am so pleased to make your acquaintance, Ms. Almeida," proclaimed Dai.

"Oh, please, call me Bianca... we are not really that formal in these parts. Come this way; we are ready for our meeting with you. Can I get you a cold drink to cool you down a bit? It is very warm today."

"That would be very agreeable Ms. Almeida... um, I mean, Bianca," replied Dai as he followed her inside.

As they entered, Bianca issued some instructions in the native Portuguese dialect to a young woman situated inside, whom Dai assumed was the office junior or maybe a housemaid.

The entry hall to the family home was cooled by a huge wooden fan, hanging from a beautifully ornate plaster ceiling. The floors were polished maple wood that shone immaculately, the furniture was of an era long past, yet it perfectly matched the rest of the décor and it was clear to see that the Almeida household exuded a welcoming warmth that, no doubt, came from the loving family that owned it. It fitted in with the image he had built up in his mind from all the hours he had spent researching this family on his long journey from Vietnam.

He followed Bianca through a set of double doors that opened into a meeting room, perhaps the company boardroom, which was a lot cooler than the outside hallway. Seated around the huge, wooden table that took up a good deal of the space in this room were three men. Two of them stood up as he entered with Bianca and made their way towards the entrance to greet him.

"Mr Phung, these are my two brothers, Felipe and Mateus," said Bianca as they both stepped forward to introduce themselves personally to the visiting Vietnamese businessman.

"Good to meet with you both, gentlemen," replied Dai, as he shook each of their hands, maintaining a solid grip with both the brothers. They proffered him a businesslike welcome and smiled broadly in return.

"And this is our father, and head of the Nova Coffee Company... Mr Luiz Almeida," continued Bianca, waving in the direction of the elderly man, still seated at the head of the boardroom table.

As Dai Ca Phung strode towards Luiz Almeida, the elder statesman of the family rose from his seat, quite deliberately and slowly, extended his hand to his overseas guest and a smile spread across his still-handsome face.

"So good of you to travel so far to see us, Mr Phung. We look forward to listening to what you have to say, and hopefully we can make your trip worthwhile. Please take a seat."

"I am very honoured to be in the presence of the great Luiz Almeida, sir. I have read much about you and your coffee company and know of how you have helped promote the Brazilian coffee industry around the world, especially in the great US market to the north," said Dai, as he shook Luiz's hand and took his place at the table.

The housemaid, earlier summoned by Bianca, entered the room at that moment with a tray of coffee, cool water and sweet biscuits, laid them on a beautifully carved side table and silently left their presence with a sweet smile to the visitor. Dai nodded his head in appreciation and returned the smile.

The discussions started at around 2.45pm, and the ideas offered by the man from Vietnam proved very intriguing to the gathered Almeida clan. Mateus, as head of production, was more than interested in what Dai had to say. He had seen many a fine crop of coffee devastated by any number of diseases over the years. He understood, even though Nova had an excellent scientific section, that it seemed the pesticides that they produced themselves, or were bought in from the international chemical companies, were always running one step behind the multiple parasites that spread havoc amongst their crops. Anything that would help in this crucial area of coffee production was always welcome.

Luiz, although knowledgeable in the scourge of parasites and their inevitable consequences, was not so excited about the groundbreaking antidote that Phung's company offered, but instead pondered on the reason why this Vietnamese competitor would want to offer Nova Coffee a chance to boost its production capabilities and help it win the war against pests. He had done his own homework on the Lam Dong Company and was mightily impressed by the abilities of its Scientific Managing Director, Dai Ca Phung. Especially since he was only at the tender age of twenty-nine. In his mind, Luiz drew comparisons to his own career and the relatively young age that he himself had taken over control of Nova Coffee, and he saw Dai as someone who should not be taken lightly.

Luiz's eldest son, Felipe, was also aware of the commercial advantages that a disease-free run of crops could bring to the company. His extensive marketing expertise told him that the greater the turnover in dollar value, the more effective he could be in promoting the Nova Coffee brand on a worldwide basis. He had argued for years with his father about the dangers that marketing to the US almost exclusively held for Nova. Felipe had wanted to extend his marketing prowess into the emerging markets of China and South-East Asia, but his father reasoned that it could never be cost-effective. Luiz put forward that with Vietnam, the second-biggest producer of coffee in the world, being in that region, Nova Coffee would prove too expensive in comparison to the local opposition. Maybe the increased productivity that this Vietnamese "bug killer" could almost guarantee would open the door to a more expansive marketing push into Asia. Felipe made a mental note to discuss it further with his father.

Dai mentioned to Mateus that he would like to work with one of their leading scientists to run tests, under very tightly monitored conditions, to verify the abilities of the new pesticide. His plan was to introduce some of the "super-bad" genes into a small amount of coffee trees, within the confines of the Nova Coffee laboratory. Then he would apply the antidote pesticide to the affected trees and gauge the results scientifically. The whole process should take less than three full days to complete and then they could compare the results and analyse whether the process could be successful in Brazil. The confident Vietnamese offered results of similar tests recently carried out in his homeland, which had been very promising. Although they were each very able in their own fields, the Almeida clan were confident that their "ace in the pack" – Gabrielle – would be able to understand the nuances of the scientific reports and confirm their authenticity.

"Later we will introduce you to my daughter, Gabrielle Souza, who is Nova's technical expert in all matters chemical and biological, Mr Phung," mentioned Bianca, at an appropriate stage of the talks. "She is only in her early twenties but has studied at the absolute best university in America for her chosen subjects and has worked with all of our top laboratory staff since she was 12 years old. I am sure it would allow you to talk and work with someone on a more technical level, more suitable than any of us around this table. We trust in her informed input for all matters involving this especially important segment of our business and expect great things from her in the future."

"That sounds most agreeable, Bianca. How soon could I meet with her?" asked Dai.

"As you are staying so close to our home, would you be open to having dinner with us this evening, Mr Phung? We would be happy to have you as our guest... wouldn't we, boys?" said Bianca, turning to her elder brothers.

"Well, both Mateus and I are expected at the Coffee Exporting Association of São Paulo this evening, for the monthly meeting, but I am sure Father will be available to host our guest. Okay, Papa?" answered Felipe, with a glance to Luiz.

"Yes, yes, of course, Felipe. It will give me more time to acquaint myself with Mr Phung, I very much look forward to spending some more time with you," announced Luiz with a wide grin and a quick look at Dai.

"You are all so gracious to invite me into your home. I would be honoured to attend and look forward to meeting Miss Souza. Thank you," replied Dai, with a courteous bow of his head.

Mateus offered to drive Dai back to his hotel in the centre of town and the meeting ended with cordial handshakes all round. Dai collected his briefcase and followed Bianca's brother to his truck, parked in the large garage next to the main homestead. They both jumped in and headed out past the coffee plantation, through the main gates of the complex and onto the main road heading into Nova Serrana.

"Are you married, Dai?" asked Mateus as they roared out of the main gates.

"No, sir, that opportunity has not yet come my way," replied Dai. "What about you? Do you have any family?" enquired Dai.

"Yes, for many years... My wife is Clara and I have two sons: Luiz Junior, who's thirty-one, and married to Livia. The other boy is Vitor, who is maybe a little bit younger than you, twenty-eight. Not married yet, but has a beautiful girlfriend named Ingrid; I think they may get together very soon. No grandkids yet, Dai, but it's something that Clara and I are looking forward to. We all dote on Bianca's kid, Gabrielle. She is such a lovely girl and has the brains to go with it... I am sure that you will like her when you meet her tonight. My boys think she's great."

"Sounds like a beautiful family, Mateus. I shall certainly look forward to meeting your niece this evening," replied Dai.

Within fifteen minutes they had reached their destination. Mateus instantly recognised the hotel.

"They have a great restaurant at the Liber, Dai. They are one of our best clients in town, relatives of ours as well. You will not be disappointed if you eat there, always first class and you'll love the coffee... it's Nova, of course!" quipped the driver.

As he dropped Dai off at the front door of the hotel lobby, Mateus turned to Dai and gave some advice to the young man.

"Don't underestimate Gabrielle, Dai, she's a very smart cookie. Enjoy your night," said Mateus, with a chuckle.

He released the handbrake with a slight screech, pushed down his foot on the accelerator and sped away back to the Nova compound.

Hatching the Plan

As Dai entered the foyer area of the Liber Hotel, he recognised one of the hotel staff members who was just arriving to start his shift behind the bar of the hotel restaurant. The young man, Marcel, whose name Dai remembered from his arrival earlier in the day, was just placing his bicycle in the bike stand, positioned down the side walkway next to the foyer entrance door.

"Busy night tonight, Marcel?" asked Dai as the flustered youth skipped quickly by him, surprised that the overseas guest had remembered his name.

"Yes, Mr Phung... I have been called in to cover for one of the barmen who has called in sick, and we have a full restaurant tonight. Will you be eating here tonight, sir?" asked Marcel.

"Not tonight, but I shall require a reservation tomorrow night probably, but not until maybe 9pm, as I'll have a lot of paperwork to do and a report to write up. Could you ask the maître d' to book a table for that time tomorrow night for me? Will you be working?" enquired Dai.

"No problem, sir... consider it done. I will also be there tomorrow night, but now I must rush," Marcel responded with a youthful grin, as he quickly made his way past the young Vietnamese businessman and inside to the restaurant area.

As Marcel raced past, Dai followed him inside and made his way up to his room on the first floor. He had just solved a problem which had been worrying him ever since he had arrived in Nova Serrana, a solution which would make things a lot easier for him the following night.

Back in his room, Dai dropped his baggage on the floor, tore off his suit jacket and poured himself a cold beer from the small in-room fridge. As he sat on the foot of the bed he looked across to the bedside table. The old-school alarm clock ticked over to 5.15pm and his head was full of excitement, yet at the same time tinged with a modicum of regret. He was determined to carry out his plan to the letter, but even in the very short space of time that he had spent with the Almeida family, he had grown to admire them and was very impressed with their solidarity, something that he had missed out on as a young child growing up in Buon Ma Thuot. Thank God for his Ba, he mused, as he finished off his cold beer. He then stripped off his clothes before jumping into the shower to refresh himself before his dinner appointment later that evening.

Gabrielle and Dai

Dai had taken the time afforded him to reread the notes on the virus, which he planned to discuss with young Gabrielle, before booking the taxi to transport him back to the Almeida household. By 7.30pm the hot sun had slipped beyond the canopy of the vast coffee plantation and darkness was imposing its fading colours onto the landscape. Through the open taxi window, Dai felt the heaviness of the air, and the threat of a stormy night was apparent as he neared his destination. The dark clouds overhead seemed even blacker than they really were against the fading embers of the day's sunlight. He got out of the taxi at the Nova Coffee front entrance, paid his dues to the driver and walked slowly towards the tall man awaiting him at the opened door. A bright light flooded out from the inside of the house, silhouetting the figure ahead of him, but as he approached he recognised the features of Luiz Almeida, as the older man put forward his hand to greet his guest.

"I like a man who is punctual, Mr Phung. It's good to see you again… please come inside," said Luiz, as the men met on the threshold.

"The weather looks like it may storm a little later on," commented Dai, as they entered the homestead.

"Yes, hopefully it will. The plantation could do with a good downpour, it's been a little dry of late… the coffee needs its fair share of moisture, as I am sure you no doubt know, Mr Phung," answered the sage old gentleman.

"We Vietnamese coffee growers love the rain, too, Mr Almeida," agreed Dai, as the two men were shown through to a beautifully decorated sitting room by another older man, dressed in the manner of a butler.

Awaiting Dai was Bianca and another young lady, whose olive complexion, long dark hair and alluring jade green eyes echoed the beauty of her mother.

"Hello again, Mr Phung. May I introduce you to my daughter, Gabrielle? We have told her of our earlier conversation, and she is very keen to meet with you and discuss your ideas on disease control and scientific matters in general," offered Bianca.

Gabrielle, as confident as ever, offered a hand in welcome to Dai. The young Vietnamese took it swiftly and said in well-practiced English... "So wonderful to meet you at last, Gabrielle, I have heard so much about you from your family, even though I have only been here for a short time." His dark eyes glinted as he responded.

"I too, Mr Phung, have been well informed about you and the reason for your visit to our company. I am very intrigued to find out as much as I can about your terrific research and look forward to working with you in the Nova lab. Can we offer you a glass of wine to start off the evening? I am afraid that Mum and I have already started our first glass and I think that Poppy has been partaking of his usual sherry a little longer than us. Is a light Pinot Noir okay for you?"

"Certainly, Gabrielle, that would be most agreeable," responded Dai, as Luiz chuckled to himself at his granddaughter's forward approach to their dinner guest. The butler came forward to fill a glass for the guest and Dai accepted it quite eagerly.

"Shall we all be seated for dinner? I am famished," put forward Gabrielle. They all moved towards the elegantly laid table, tastefully lit by candles perched in an elaborate, well-polished silver candleholder in the centre.

Luiz took his accustomed position at the head of the table, with his daughter and granddaughter to his right. The visitor was seated immediately across from Gabrielle, to Luiz's left. He took a first sip of a very well-matured Pinot Noir and offered a quick toast to his hosts. "To the Almeida family!" said Dai. "I am so pleased to have made your acquaintance." He raised his glass to the two ladies opposite him, then at the patriarch. Gabrielle's eyes dipped as Dai smiled at her and she was aware of a warmth enveloping her face, which changed the hue of her complexion from its original healthy olive hue to a pinkish glow. The effect did not go unnoticed by her grandfather.

The dinner was a very amiable affair and the two younger members of the quartet seemed to hit it off wonderfully well. Their conversation was certainly not stilted or reserved, and their obvious advanced intellects made for some stimulating exchanges.

Luiz was impressed with Dai's maturity, for one so young, especially regarding his business knowledge in general, and seemed to be warming to his would-be adversary as the evening progressed. It was also clear to the patriarch, as well as to his daughter, that Gabrielle was somewhat enamoured with the confident young man, evidenced by the fact that she could not keep a smile off her face all night.

A sumptuous meal of premium-cut Picanha barbequed steak and a fresh salad was prepared and served by Luiz's in-house cook, Pedro, and his staff and it was heartily eaten by a hungry Dai. As the dinner progressed to a grand crescendo of a homemade Brazilian dessert called *brigadeiro*, a popular local dish made from condensed milk, chocolate powder, sugar and fresh butter, Dai was feeling very much at home. All the excellent food was washed down with generous amounts of wine. It was clear that both youngsters would be looking forward to spending the next few days together in the Nova laboratory. This fact was pleasing to Luiz, but it also worried him for some reason he could not quite pinpoint. Bianca was excited to see her offspring being so natural and so attentive with a member of the opposite sex, a sight she had rarely seen in the past.

The evening ended with a couple of nightcaps for the men in Luiz's study before Dai was whisked off by Bianca to the waiting taxi at around 11pm. They had arranged to meet again the next morning at the Nova lab, situated only 100 metres from the Almeida homestead. It was agreed by Luiz that Gabrielle was to look after Dai over the coming three days and to resolve whether the confident young man's biological breakthrough was all that it had been made out to be. Luiz went to bed wondering what the next three days would bring and if it any of it would be beneficial to the Nova Coffee Company's future. Gabrielle was enthralled by this courteous young man from faraway, who had been catapulted into her life and aroused feelings that had been all but alien to her since her return from the States. She sighed as she kissed her mother and poppy goodnight, raced to her upstairs bedroom, and peeked out of her curtained window to see Dai's taxi disappear into the darkness. Its red brake lights flashed as it approached the main gates of the complex, then disappeared from view. Dark storm clouds gathered above, and the crescent of the new moon sent a crisp shard of light hurtling towards the foliage of the plantation below. It had been an enlightening evening for all concerned.

The phone rang noisily in Dai's hotel room the next morning, waking him from a deep sleep, and the pain he felt in his thumping head was a stark reminder of how much alcohol he had consumed the previous evening.

"Hello, this is Dai Ca Phung," he muttered blearily, as he sat hunched on the side of his bed.

"Good morning, Mr Ca Phung, this is Tina back home in Vietnam. How are you?" came the response.

"Oh, hello, I am sorry, I have just woken up from a heavy sleep and am feeling slightly groggy... Why are you calling, Tina?"

"Sir, I have Dr Chien on the line for you, he asked me to ring you. I am sorry for the early hour," apologised his secretary.

"Okay, put him through please, Tina," replied Dai, summoning his faculties to negotiate the difficult conversation ahead.

"Hello, Dai. How is it going over in Brazil... have you been successful?" demanded the surly confidant of his stepfather. "You did not give me all of your travel details before you left, young man. I had to get them from Tina. I sincerely hope that all is going to plan and that this 'adventure' of yours will provide some positive results."

"Sir, of course I am on track to succeed with the plan. You should not feel that I cannot achieve the results that have been very meticulously planned for. All is going well and today I will be working in the Scientific Laboratory of the Nova Coffee plant. Please have faith in my abilities, Dr Chien, as does my stepfather, Dung Lam. Can you please give my love to him and my mother and I will look forward to being back in less than a week from now? Must go now, I have a long day to plan for..." And with that, an indignant Dai slammed the phone down onto its cradle.

At the other end of the phone a rather startled Dr Chien roared into his mouthpiece, "Dai, are you still there? Dai, where are you? Disrespectful young pig!" he shouted, slamming down the receiver when he realised he had been hung up on.

"I will teach that young upstart the meaning of respect when he returns," thought Chien to himself.

Dai immediately rethought the conversation after his rash outburst and knew that he would have some explaining to do when he got back to Vietnam, but he was confident that his return would see him regarded as a hero to the company. He put that thought to the back of his head, strode towards the welcoming shower, and washed away his headache.

Gabrielle was eagerly awaiting Dai, as he pulled up in his taxi at 8am as arranged. She was standing at the door of the Nova Coffee Laboratory, situated within the main processing plant of the plantation. Next to her was her well-built Uncle Mateus, in protective mode after his sister had relayed the events of the previous evening to her youngest brother over breakfast. "I hope you have come to work hard with Gabrielle, young man. There is a lot to do and we need to see that your concoction will give us the advantages that you have promised. The last thing we need is to waste time and resources... do you hear me?" demanded a rather curt Mateus.

Dai was taken aback by this greeting. Where was the lovely, friendly and amiable Uncle Mateus who had given him a lift back to his hotel yesterday?

"Gabrielle will show you around. Let's hope it will be a successful time spent together, for all our sakes. See you later, Mr Phung!" boomed Mateus, turning and striding off.

"I am sorry, Mr Phung," said an apologetic Gabrielle. "Uncle Mat is very... protective of me and we've just had some rather negative feedback from one of our bigger customers in the States about the quality of our arabica bean shipment sent a few weeks back... he takes it very personally. Come this way and we'll begin our experiment."

"Please, Gabrielle, call me Dai. After all, we will be working at close quarters for the next couple of days and, hopefully, we will get on well enough to become friends, or at least to respect each other's abilities. What do you say?" chirped Dai with a smile.

"Okay... Dai. Let's go, I'm looking forward to this!" replied Gabrielle, returning his smile.

The main laboratory area was quite small compared to the same space at his own Lam Dong lab, but a lot of the scientific equipment was newer and more advanced than the equivalent apparatus used in Dai's lab. He was happy that he understood, and could use properly, the updated gear that Gabrielle had obviously learnt her craft on.

The pair set up the experiments well as a team. Each understood what the other was talking about in relation to the science. The elder Dai was very impressed with the knowledge and ability that young Gabrielle had gleaned from her mix of hands-on practice at the coffee plant and the theory she had committed to memory from her time spent at university. He was further impressed by the skills that she had recently acquired at the prestigious University of California, Berkeley, where she had completed her Master's degree. As her uncle had warned him, she was indeed a very smart cookie – a statement that he quickly came to agree with wholeheartedly.

By the end of day one, their bond had grown even stronger. They seemed to enjoy each other's company, as well as relishing in their shared quest for knowledge regarding the best way to eradicate the dreaded parasites from their beloved coffee plantations. The other, elder scientists who were working in the same space often came across to see what their young prodigy and the mysterious man from the East were conjuring up. Dai treated the men with the respect that he always afforded those more senior than himself and soon endeared himself to the other lab workers, much to the delight of Gabrielle. She was most impressed that the theory, so painstakingly described by Dai, of how the pesticide had been developed in Vietnam, seemed to be working in practice under strict laboratory conditions here in Brazil.

By the time they decided to call it a day at 5.30pm, Gabrielle could not wait to get back into the lab the next day. She was keen to see if the artificially infected young coffee tree, which they had used in the experiment, would be showing signs of deterioration by the morning. Dai had kept the chemical makeup of his compound very secret throughout the first day. He packed up his briefcase containing the mysterious mix very deliberately before they left the coolness of the air-conditioned laboratory and sauntered into the relative heat of the outside courtyard.

"Wow, I really enjoyed our first day, Dai," said Gabrielle as they left the building. "Can't wait until tomorrow…"

"Yes, it was very agreeable working with you, Gabrielle," added Dai, in his very conservative manner. "Within a day or so we should have the data to prove that my idea works and hopefully your family will be willing to invest in the project, or at least work with Lam Dong to our mutual benefit," said Dai, a beaming smile spreading across his face. He had indeed enjoyed his day with Gabrielle in the Nova lab, for more reasons than one, and at many different levels.

"I'll get the office to call you a cab, it shouldn't be long... I have to rush off to play tennis this evening with Uncle Mat's sons. Would you like to join us, Dai? I am sure they wouldn't mind," offered Gabrielle, with a hopeful look.

"I am sorry, Gabrielle, I must ring back home this evening to speak with my stepfather, Dung Lam, the boss of our coffee company. Otherwise, I would have been honoured to spend some social time with you and your cousins. Perhaps another time," replied Dai.

They smiled at each other and the young girl, who had only just met this charming man yet felt that she had known him forever, sighed internally as she headed to the office to organise Dai Ca Phung's taxi ride back to the Liber Hotel.

Dai strode across to the stairs outside the office area. Placing his briefcase down and sitting on the top step of the elegant entrance in the comforting shade of the imposing Almeida house, he felt a soft breeze cool his warm face and was well satisfied with his day's work. He had plans for the coming evening, but it did not include any phone calls back to his homeland. He would be coming back here, to the Almeidas' coffee plantation, to execute a particularly important part of his overall plans. One that Luiz Almeida and his family would soon regret.

Within fifteen minutes the local taxi, driven by the same driver who had dropped him at the plantation earlier in the day, was pulling up outside the big house. Dai saw no-one inside the office to say goodbye to, so jumped into the front passenger seat, put his briefcase between his legs and instructed the driver to take him to the Liber Hotel. Once again, as the taxi sped out of the Almeida compound, Gabrielle's jade eyes were sadly watching him leave from her bedroom window.

"Wow", she thought to herself. "I'd really like to get to know him a lot better."

The Evil Deed

By 6.30pm, Dai was back in his hotel room. On his way through the downstairs lobby area of the establishment, he had purposely taken a detour to the bar of the in-house restaurant to see young Marcel, resplendent in his navy blue Liber Hotel uniform. Dai walked up to the bar and caught his attention.

"Is the booking okay for just after nine tonight, Marcel?" queried Dai. "Just need to get all this annoying paperwork out of the way first, so I can start afresh in the morning."

"Oh, yes, sir, Mr Phung… it's all booked. I look forward to seeing you later this evening," was the reply.

With this, Dai beckoned Marcel closer and placed a sizeable tip of folded Real notes into his hand, more than a whole day's wages to the young barman.

"Thank you very much, Marcel. Much appreciated. I'll see you later this evening," replied Dai, with a radiant smile.

Marcel looked down at the generous tip, smiled and thought how much he loved dealing with overseas customers, not that too many came to his small hometown.

With that, Dai turned and made his way swiftly to his upstairs room. Now contemplating his moves for the night, he quickly took off his daytime clothes and changed into a pair of black jeans and a long-sleeved black tee shirt. He found the black balaclava, leather gloves, torch, backpack and black running shoes and socks that he had packed. He then slipped on the comfortable socks and shoes and placed the remaining items into the backpack, along with some bottles of a chemical liquid and a syringe that had been part of the parcel he had sent himself from Vietnam. He pulled off the cardboard backing from a Liber Hotel notepad that was lying next to the telephone and placed it in his jeans pocket. Finally, he turned on the in-room radio, tuned onto a station playing a middle-of-the-road range of tunes, making sure that the volume was audible from outside, but not too loud. Throwing the zipped-up backpack over his shoulder, he opened his hotel room door slowly and deliberately. The radio warbled out an old Elvis classic, as he prepared to leave.

By now it was after 7pm and the staff of the Liber Hotel were busy downstairs preparing for a full night of hospitality or serving pre-dinner drinks to the guests in the restaurant. He gently closed the door behind him and then descended from the first floor via the stairs through the emergency fire door without being seen by any hotel guest or staff. At ground level, after checking that it wasn't alarmed, he opened and then peeked around the door that led into the side alley. No-one was around. He slipped out and half-closed the door quietly behind him, ensuring that he left a small wedge of the cardboard at the bottom of the door that would enable him to re-enter the stairwell from the outside on his return. He quickly commandeered Marcel's unlocked bicycle from the rusting bike stand, smiled wryly and thought to himself, "Well worth the tip, Marcel!"

Without looking backwards, he cycled out of town via a couple of back streets and then on to the main road towards the Nova Coffee plantation, his backpack securely in place on his shoulders and a confident grin on his face. He had estimated that the trip, along mostly flat terrain, would take him around 35-40 minutes. By the time Dai arrived just outside the main gates of the Nova Coffee compound, it was 7.50pm exactly on the Fossil watch that Dung Lam and his mother had bought him for his 21st birthday.

He had noticed on his previous two visits to the Almeida property that the amount of security at the estate was minimal. Only the factory, office and production areas had internal security systems in place and there were no external systems installed on the perimeters or plantation areas. "I suppose no-one would want to steal a coffee tree!" he thought to himself.

Dai dismounted the bicycle and leant it against the inside of the low-level fence that surrounded the plantation, making sure that it was out of sight from any passing traffic on the main road. Not that there would much traffic at this time of night in such a remote area, but he wanted to make sure that he was not seen by anyone.

The new moon was a very slim crescent way above his head, leaving the whole area that surrounded him draped in a blanket of darkness. The cloudy night also aided his illicit act and, as he took the backpack from his shoulders, he unzipped the top compartment and carefully put on his balaclava and black leather gloves. He had become almost invisible.

He walked into the dense foliage of the coffee plantation, torch in hand to light his progress and seek out trees full of plump ripe berries. For twenty minutes he infused dozens of mature trees with the deadly "Evil Gene" mixture, using the syringe. He emptied each bottle one by one, until he had run out of the rogue chemical. Carefully placing each used bottle into his backpack, by 8.20pm he had finished his evil deed. With a full backpack of empty bottles and syringe, along with the torch, he returned to where the bicycle was resting. Before getting back on board, still wearing the secretive black balaclava and gloves, he sat down on an old fallen tree and sighed. He suddenly felt a tide of remorse flow across him as he finally realised what he had done and how the result would affect the lives of the friendly Almeida family, especially Gabrielle. Had he done the right thing? Could he justify his actions, could he live with the guilt? Was his hatred of all things American worth this dastardly act? He convinced himself that it was, by thinking of all the harm that the Americans had inflicted on his nation during the war, his family and especially his beautiful Ba, Mi Ling. Dai looked at the face of his watch and saw that it was nearly 8.25pm. With at least a thirty-minute ride back to town, he had to hurry. He mounted Marcel's bike and started pedaling as fast as he could.

Within twenty-five minutes he could see the approaching lights of Nova Serrana. No-one had been on the road all night. He had been lucky. On entering the back road that would lead him to the alley next to his hotel, he stopped momentarily to dispose of his backpack's contents and the backpack itself. The commercial dump bin, which he knew was emptied and taken away to the local dump on a daily basis – it had woken him abruptly at 5am for the last two mornings as he lay in his hotel bed – stood fifty metres away from the Liber Hotel's back roller door. It also serviced the adjacent supermarket. As he approached the bin, he could see it was quite full, so he placed the backpack and its sordid contents deep into the bottom of the smelly waste. Finally, he discarded his balaclava and gloves, as well as the torch, in the same manner.

Without wasting a moment, he speedily made his way to the fire exit door in the alley next to the Liber. He placed Marcel's trusty bicycle back onto the bike rack in the same position that he had found it and made his way to the stairwell door. The wedge of cardboard was still in place, untouched, and had done its job to perfection. He removed it and slipped silently inside, carefully closing the door behind him and making his way up the stairs. As he reached the top, he put his hand on the internal doorknob and started to turn it. As he did this, he heard voices echoing from the hallway on the other side. He pulled back and placed his ear to the door to try to understand where the voices were coming from.

"Darling, I knew you'd come to see me," came a rather drunk-sounding female voice.

"How could I resist, Alexi? Are you going to let me into your room?" demanded her amorous male visitor.

With that the door squeaked on its hinges, the woman obviously having opened it to let in her lover. Dai then heard loud shuffling and giggling as the door banged shut. Dai smirked, opened the door slightly, and checked that the coast was clear. All was now silent, so he pushed open the door, slipped through the opening then quietly closed it behind him, swiftly walking along the hallway to his room. Retrieving the door entry card from his dirty black jeans, he swiped himself in, closed the door behind him and headed straight to the fridge. He quickly found a mini bottle of Jack Daniels and took a swig to calm his nerves. Looking across to the bedroom side table, he noticed that the alarm clock was already showing 9.06pm. He needed to get a move on to complete his evening's work and get to the downstairs restaurant before the kitchen closed. Throwing off his sweat covered tee shirt and filthy jeans, socks and running shoes, he went into the bathroom and toweled himself down, washed his hands and applied some aftershave. Slipping into a pair of fresh chinos and a polo shirt, he sat on the bed to put on a pair of natural coloured leather boat shoes, stood up, slicked his black hair into place with his comb and looked at himself in the full-length mirror.

"Are you proud of yourself, Dai Ca Phung?" he barked at his reflection.

Within thirty seconds he was downstairs at the entrance to the restaurant, which by now was at full throttle. The hotel manager, acting as maître d' on this busy evening, greeted his guest formally and showed Dai to his single table.

Dai sat wearily in his chair and viewed the menu.

"Can I interest you in a drink, Mr Phung?" came a voice from behind a startled Dai. It was Marcel.

"I could kill a big, cold beer, Marcel, thank you. Whatever you think is good on tap will be fine," replied the relieved Dai.

"Certainly, it won't be long. Did you finish your paperwork, sir?"

"Yes, Marcel, everything went like clockwork and I am now back on schedule, thank you."

"Enjoy your evening, Mr Phung, the bar is open until twelve midnight," finished the young barman.

Dai Ca Phung looked around the crowded restaurant at all the smiling faces and the happy guests, his mind wandering to imagine the pretty face of the girl whose world he might have just ruined... Gabrielle.

How could he face her in the morning? "Maybe a few beers and a couple more Jack Daniels will help me find the answer," he thought to himself.

Beginnings of Love

The next morning, Dai awoke early to the mechanical sound of the local garbage truck picking up the metal bin and dumping its rotting and smelly contents into the covered back container. It then dropped the emptied bin back to its original position between the hotel and the supermarket. He smiled to himself, knowing that his tools of trade from the previous night would soon be covered, out of sight, by tonnes of garbage from all the other local villages at the communal rubbish tip.

His next thought was about how he would manage the next couple of days at the Nova Coffee compound, especially when he saw Gabrielle again. The effects of his actions would not be apparent to the staff of the coffee plantation for at least a week. By this time, the protective shield of the leaves on the coffee trees he had tampered with would start to perish, and the leaves would fall off. This would leave the precious coffee beans open to the damaging rays of the hot Brazilian sun and lead to an eventual failure of the crop.

By 8am he had enjoyed a hearty breakfast in his room, showered, dressed and was about to get into the taxi that he had ordered for his planned visit to the plantation laboratory. He was eager to see Gabrielle, which again caused him to question his motives, but resolved within his head that he was doing the right thing for Vietnam.

As the taxi neared the end of its journey, Dai looked out of the window to see Gabrielle waving at the approaching car with a huge smile on her beautiful face. He thought how lovely she looked, and he smiled back at her as the taxi came to a halt outside the laboratory doors.

"Good morning, Gabrielle... did you win at tennis last night?" he enquired.

"Hi, Dai. I played well, but my cousins are extremely competitive boys and, as always, they would not let me win, but I really enjoyed it," she told him, with a sparkle in her eyes. "How is your stepfather? I bet your mum and him are missing you back home."

"Oh, they are both well and I've only been gone for less than a week, so far. So, I think they will be able to cope without me for a short while. I am really looking forward to working with you and your team again, today," said Dai.

"Me too!" exclaimed Gabrielle. "Let's get started."

The couple walked towards the doors, and as they approached Dai skipped quickly to the entrance ahead of his hostess and opened the door to let her in, displaying the gentlemanly manners he had been so diligently taught by his mother and his Ba. Gabrielle smiled appreciatively as she walked through the door and looked deeply into his eyes as she passed him. Dai responded with a shy smile and a typically Asian bow of the head.

Their working day was again a successful one. There was a telling difference in the condition of the poisoned coffee tree that they had administered the detrimental drug to the previous day, which they both had expected. Dai explained to Gabrielle that they would apply the antidote later that day and check the progress of the plant tomorrow. By then, he promised that the tree would have begun its recovery and the leaves would soon flourish to protect the coffee beans. If this were to be the case then Gabrielle, as she told Dai, would be in a position to recommend to the rest of the Almeida family that there would be a strong case to develop the antidote drug under license in Brazil. Perhaps Nova Coffee could even look at becoming a distributor for Dai's coffee company to the South American market.

The shrewd Vietnamese had been careful not to tell Gabrielle, nor divulge to any of the scientists in the laboratory, what the working ingredients of the antidote consisted of, or, more importantly, the vital percentage makeup of the drug's contents. During the last couple of days, Gabbie had often proffered chemical theories to Dai of what made up the contents, but he had resolutely declined to confirm or deny any such ideas that she had put forward. In her eyes, this understandable caution made Dai Ca Phung even more beguiling and mysterious, and he became instantly more attractive to the enchanted young woman.

By day's end Dai had, as always, been careful to pack up all the contents of his secure briefcase and ensure it never left his sight. This had been noted by Gabrielle and reported back to the family. They were all sure, if the experiments were successful, that the mysterious contents of Dai's briefcase were worth their weight in gold. When Mateus walked into the laboratory at the end of the working day and asked Dai if he would like to stay for dinner that evening, the tired-looking Vietnamese offered his apologies, saying that he again had a lot of paperwork and phone calls to catch up on. Dai did not want to get into a compromising situation with the Almeida family and certainly did not want to give them, especially Mateus, the chance of discovering the contents of his lethal briefcase. He knew that Gabrielle had the brains and the ability to dissect the antidote's makeup and the skill to recreate the drug in a short time.

Gabrielle said goodbye to her new colleague, as Dai's taxi arrived to take him back to his hotel. He placed his briefcase inside the back seat of the car, then turned to bid her farewell. Once again, their eyes met, this time a lot closer together, and both were aware of an urge to mark their goodbye with a kiss. As Gabrielle closed her eyes in anticipation of a lingering and passionate embrace, Dai noticed Luiz Almeida walking towards the taxi and pulled back from his advance. Gabrielle appeared startled at the lack of contact and then noticed her grandfather appearing from the house and understood Dai's reluctance.

"Hey, Poppy, we had a great day in the laboratory today... how was your day?" blurted out the embarrassed young lady.

"Rather successful, Gabbie. We have just been informed that our tender for the US Government has been accepted. It is a massive opportunity for Nova Coffee and with our next crop looking like being a big one, we are in a great position to make the most of it. I must say, Felipe did a fabulous job on the marketing of the tender," replied Luiz.

"That is great news Mr Almeida, well done," enthused Dai, after regaining his composure.

"I believe, Mr Phung, that tonight will be your last night in Nova Serrana, and... seeing as you have built up such a great rapport with my granddaughter, why don't you ask Gabrielle out for dinner at the Liber Hotel? They do a great meal... probably the best in town. In fact, why don't I come along with you both. I could do with a good night out, and, hey, we can celebrate our good fortune. The bill is on Nova Coffee!" pronounced the elder statesman, looking expectantly at young Dai. "Do we have a deal, Mr Phung?"

Dai was slightly stunned, and looked at Gabrielle, who was nodding in an approving manner. "Well, I suppose I could get all my phone calls and paperwork done by 7.30pm," he began, before being interrupted by Gabrielle and her grandfather, who said simultaneously, "We'll see you there at eight o'clock then!"

As Dai's taxi left the compound, he turned around from his back-seat position to see Gabrielle and her grandfather, arm in arm, happily strolling back to the house. Tonight will be interesting, he thought, and allowed himself a smile.

Dinner with Poppy

It was 8.15pm. The Liber Hotel was all abuzz with throngs of businesspeople in town for the annual "New Ideas" convention, which took place at the Nova Serrana Community Centre. Most of the hotels in town were fully booked, as usual, and the Liber, as one of the better eating houses in the town, was bursting at the seams with customers.

Luiz Almeida's status in the area ensured that the best table in the house was always available to him and his family. It also helped that his cousin owned the establishment. So, as Dai entered the restaurant area after coming down from his upstairs room, it was not hard for him to find the Almeida table. Gabrielle sat next to Luiz, looking altogether fabulous. Gone were the boyish-looking laboratory clothes that Dai had become used to seeing, replaced by a strapless, three-quarter length dress in black silk, subtly adorned with jade and silver jewellery to match her stunning eyes. Her olive skin and flowing locks of chocolate brown hair added to her natural beauty, in stark contrast to the strict ponytail look that Dai had been used to on the previous two days. He reached the table and stood next to Luiz, in utter awe of his transformed dinner date.

"Wow, Gabrielle, you look amazing and here am I with chinos and boat shoes... I apologise for my lack of formal clothing," he uttered.

Gabrielle blushed, graciously smiled, and looked at her grandfather, who had a smirk on his face, amused by Dai's bewilderment.

"Sit down, Mr Phung. What can I get for you to drink? You look as if you could do with one!" offered Luiz, winking at his granddaughter.

The night went well for Dai. He seemed to have slipped his way into Luiz's good books, and the attention that he attracted from the suave Brazilian's granddaughter was intense. Her charm mesmerised the young Vietnamese and it was clear to them that their relationship was far beyond the professional working stage. Each glance became stronger, each eye-contact lasted longer, and it became abundantly clear to the patriarch of the Almeida family that this pair of young, intelligent twenty-somethings were falling for each other. Ever the diplomat, Luiz excused himself from the table after he had finished his main course, to apparently visit his cousin, Ramos, who owned the restaurant. He left the table with a sly glance at Dai, accompanied by a knowing smile, and moved quickly away toward the area where a Manager's Office sign was affixed to an ornately decorated wooden door.

"Alone at last, Dai," sighed Gabrielle to her table companion.

"It would seem so, Gabbie. Do you mind if I call you Gabbie?" asked Dai, taking her right hand into his and looking intensely into her stunning jade eyes. "Would you also mind if I suggested that we get some fresh air outside for a few moments? It is getting rather stuffy in here and my heart seems to be beating at an exaggerated rate each time I look into your eyes!" professed a rather coy Dai, as his grip intensified on Gabrielle's trembling right hand.

Her mouth dropped open in amazement as he uttered these words and then exploded into a smile as she answered his question. "Yes, you can call me Gabbie, if you like, and, yes, I would love to get some fresh air with you. Lead the way, " she responded.

Her gallant beau immediately stood up, offered her his elbow and glowed internally as his beautiful partner wrapped her arm into the bend of his as tightly as she could, and they walked slowly towards the front door together.

The ever-vigilant maître d' noticed the move and was instantly at the exit, opening the door to let the two lovers outside. "Shall I refill your glasses whilst you take a short break, sir?" he suggested to Dai.

"That would be wonderful!" replied Dai, as the couple moved through the door into the freshness of the cooler night air.

Dai escorted Gabrielle along the raised boardwalk that surrounded the outside of the hotel until she stopped suddenly, turned towards him, and looked deeply into his eyes. As Dai placed both his arms around her slender waist, he slowly bent his head in the direction of her waiting lips and kissed her passionately. Gabbie responded instantly – the moment that she been waiting for had arrived. Words were not needed as they unlocked their entangled lips, looked at each other and fell into an even more intense embrace, followed by a longer, more passionate kiss, as she pushed her body closer to Dai's.

"Did that really happen?" whispered Gabrielle, as their lips parted for the second time.

"Apparently," retorted Dai, as a huge smile burst onto his face. "Wow, I think I felt my knees buckle!" he joked, and Gabrielle responded with a longing look into those almond-shaped eyes that she already felt that she loved so much.

"We shouldn't keep Poppy waiting… Let's go back inside," said Gabrielle reluctantly, standing on her toes to peck Dai on the right cheek before heading towards the restaurant door, pulling him after her, her fingers clenched in his hand. Dai felt a moment of sheer joy, as he followed her back inside.

"Control yourself, Dai, we don't want Poppy to get upset!" teased Gabrielle, as they made their way back to their table in the lively eating house.

Luiz Almeida was again sitting at the table, watching them return, and he beamed as they sat next to him, noticing that the young pair seemed closer than earlier in the night.

"The night air certainly had a positive effect on you both, by the looks of things. It's good to see that you are both so happy," started Luiz.

"I have had a wonderful night, Poppy. Can we get some desserts now, please?" answered his smiling granddaughter.

"Of course, darling, whatever you want. Are you still hungry, Dai?" asked Luiz of his guest.

"No, thank you, Mr Almeida… but maybe a final nightcap would be appropriate. Would you care to join me?" asked an obviously happy Dai Ca Phung.

Luiz agreed that he would love a brandy, with a glint in his eye, as he looked lovingly at Gabrielle and noted, "I think you two may be seeing more of each other in the future. You certainly seem to have hit it off tonight!"

Dai and Gabrielle stared at each other. "I'd like that!" said Gabrielle very happily.

"Me, too," responded Dai fervently, and they both laughed as Luiz looked on with a very contented gaze.

The Long Goodbye

The next day, Dai woke at 5am, his mind racing. He was stuck in the middle of a confusing situation, which threatened to eat away at his senses. His plan to ruin the business of the Almeida family's coffee plantation was in process and set to succeed, but he had fallen head over heels in love with Luiz's granddaughter, so how could he go through with the plan? More importantly, how could he spend his last day in Brazil with Gabrielle, knowing full well that his actions would devastate her young life? How could he resolve the intense nationalism that he had always felt for his mother country, and his hatred of America, against his newly found feelings of deep affection for Gabrielle? What was the lesser of the evils? He could not be around when the devastation that he had instigated upon the Nova Coffee Plantation took hold, and hated the fact that Gabrielle would be so hurt by its consequences. He was in a definite no-win situation.

After a couple of strong coffees to wake himself up, he stood at the window of his hotel room, looked out at the empty streets of Nova Serrana, and pondered his future. Within minutes, all was clear in his mind. He knew what he had to do.

Dai packed his luggage in a very concise and organised manner; he always did. He waited at reception for his taxi to the airport, which would travel via the Nova Coffee compound so that he could say his goodbyes to the Almeida family. He felt a strong sense of remorse for what was about to happen; however, his Vietnamese nationalism had won the battle against his emerging love for Gabrielle and he had concluded that the way forward was to execute his plans as he had originally set out to do.

Dressed more formally in a smart, lightweight, navy-blue suit, plain white shirt and a conservative necktie, he got into the taxi, delivered his goodbyes and best wishes to the ever-attentive hotel staff and sat in the back seat, as the driver filled the boot with Dai's suitcases. Dai held tightly onto his leather briefcase, as he would do for the entire journey back to his homeland.

Deep in thought, he was suddenly jerked back into reality when his driver braked heavily as they entered the main gates of Luiz Almeida's coffee plantation.

"That was quick!" Dai thought to himself as the taxi made its way through the big gates and up the main entrance road before gently pulling to a stop outside the Almeida family homestead.

Standing at the front doorway was Gabrielle, her face glowing and emanating a beautiful smile as she caught her first glimpse of Dai getting out of the taxi. She ran towards him and shouted out, "Congratulations, Dai! I checked the small coffee trees this morning that we used in our experiment and guess what? They are looking healthy again, so the antidote worked. Isn't that wonderful?"

"That's great, Gabbie. I was always confident that it would be a great success!" replied Dai.

Smiling sweetly, Gabrielle seemed even more smitten as she hugged him tightly. There was no restraint from either of them as Gabrielle met her new love, wrapped her arms around his neck and pulled Dai close to her. Their eyes and lips met instantaneously.

"Oh Dai, I have been dreaming of seeing you all night," she blurted out as their lips disentangled. "Do you really have to go back to Vietnam already?"

"I am sorry, Gabbie, but I have important work to do and a company to run back home. I would love nothing more than to stay a little longer with you, but I must get back to Vietnam... but I really would love for you to visit me soon in my homeland," offered Dai, before he had time to realise what he had said.

"Of course, Dai, I'd love to do that... let's go inside and tell the family – they're all here to say goodbye to you," replied Gabrielle.

She grabbed hold of his hand and dragged him towards the front door. Dai looked back towards the waiting taxi driver.

"I'll wait, shall I, sir?" asked the driver, with a huge grin on his face.

"Yes, please. Shouldn't be long…" he called over his shoulder as he was pulled towards the house by the enthusiastic young Gabbie.

"Well, is it goodbye or *au revoir*, Dai?" asked Luiz as his granddaughter and the young Vietnamese appeared inside the house.

"Well, Mr Almeida, I am afraid that I must get back to my home, but I have a feeling that I may well be seeing you again sooner, rather than later," replied Dai.

"Yes, Poppy, Dai has asked me to visit him in Vietnam. Are you okay with that?" Gabrielle interjected.

"Well, we have your work to think about – we will have to ask your mother, and there are still a lot of things to be finalised here at the plantation over the next few weeks… but, I suppose it could be a possibility," replied her grandfather with a wicked smile on his face.

A massive smile came over Gabrielle's face and she looked at Dai, who was slightly taken aback by the suddenness of events.

"I must thank you and your family, along with all of your lab techs, for being so obliging towards me and for all the help that you have given me. I look forward to finalising agreements with Nova Coffee, so that we can work closely and be successful together in the future. Of course, I am incredibly happy to have made the acquaintance of your beautiful and exceptionally talented granddaughter. I hope to renew the bond I feel with her… with your permission of course, sir," babbled Dai, as he put forward his hand to Luiz. The two men shook hands and exchanged smiles with each other.

Mateus had been standing behind Luiz for most of the conversation and now stepped forward to greet Dai and say goodbye to him.

"We still have a lot to talk about and negotiate regarding any future business we may, or may not do together, Mr Phung, but I look forward to continuing our talks via email over the ensuing weeks. Have a safe trip back," Mateus said quite sternly to the departing guest.

Gabrielle gave her uncle a concerned look as he made his way past his niece and out of the house, heading back to the production area. She glanced at Dai, who was looking a little less confident after Mateus' comments.

"Your taxi awaits, Dai," said Luiz, interrupting the uncomfortable silence that had struck them all.

"Oh, yes, sir, I must be off to ensure I don't miss my plane!" said Dai.

"Gabbie, please don't forget to pass on the full results to me via email."

"I will be in touch, Dai," said Gabrielle as she pecked him, rather less enthusiastically, on the cheek.

"I will miss you, Gabbie," replied Dai as he turned to go. "Thank you for... everything. Goodbye, Mr Almeida... it has been a pleasure and an honour to meet you. I will be in touch."

With one long, lingering look at Gabrielle and a quick embrace, he hurried off down the front stairs and jumped into the back seat of the waiting taxi.

Gabrielle stood with Luiz at the front door and waved goodbye as the taxi fired into action and manoeuvred towards the exit of the property. Dai held his arm out of the taxi window, glanced back at the girl who had changed his whole world, waved one last time, then slumped back into his seat, shook his head and thought of what lay ahead.

The return coach trip to São Paulo airport was a sombre affair for the troubled young man. In his mind he had weighed up his options and decided to continue with his original plans. The deep emotions that plagued him were a strong force to try to combat. They had been developed through all the painful baggage that he carried because of what his family and fellow countrymen had endured. But his feelings for Gabrielle had dragged him to the precipice and he was torn between the two. He was sure that the long-haul airline flight back to Vietnam would give him enough time to set his mind straight and to confirm the way forward. Gabrielle or retribution?

A week after Dai Ca Phung had left Brazil, Mateus had finished a hard day on the job. The weather had been hot and humid in the coffee plantation and the fact that Nova had landed the huge USA contract was heaping pressure on him to produce a bumper crop. A slight wind had finally developed, and it was slowly creeping over the compound, its cooling effect giving relief to the whole workforce.

He decided to inspect the condition of the growing crop to put his mind at rest, to reassure himself that he could finally deliver a great result for his father. As he made his way through the northern section of the coffee trees he came across a sight that sent a shiver down his backbone – and this was nothing to do with the cool wind, which by now had built up to a stronger level and moving the canopy above Mateus rapidly with its rhythm. However, with every gust of wind an unnerving amount of the precious leaves on his coffee trees were shedding from the branches. Leaves which provided vital cover and protection to the ripening coffee beans below from the hot and relentless sun. As the wind heightened, more and more leaves fell from the trees above Mateus, as he looked up from below.

"Why is this happening?" he thought to himself. "Why?"

Home to Vietnam

Dai Ca Phung had been home from his Brazilian trip for less than a week. He had not slept much since his return, partly due to the expected jet-lag, but mostly because of the internal battles going on within his head. He had never expected to meet a young lady who would so completely change his life. Gabrielle had undeniably shaken his world to the core. Lam Dong's Head of Science and Research, Dr Phan Chien, had been pushing Dai for an urgent meeting ever since he had returned to Vietnam from his Brazilian adventure. In fact, he had been insistent that the meeting be scheduled to take place by the end of the current week and that the only two attendees would be Dai and himself. On her boss' instructions, Dai's loyal secretary, Tina, had been putting off Dr Chien's demands during Dai's first week back. He wanted to carefully prepare himself for this meeting. It could have any number of outcomes, and he was still fighting himself about what his desired outcome would be. His stepfather, Dung Lam, the quietly spoken head of Lam Dong Coffee, had been kept in the dark by both Dai and Dr Chien about the importance and the relevance of Dai's trip to Brazil.

Both men had their own reasons for secrecy. It was quickly becoming apparent to Dai that the good doctor had seen that the course his young Managing Director was taking opened up a huge opportunity for him to exploit his lofty position within the company. Dr Chien's close personal relationship with Dung Lam enabled him to take that long-established bond for granted and it was true that familiarity breeds contempt. He had often felt aggrieved that Dung Lam's rise to power within the Vietnamese coffee industry, as well as within the Lam Dong Coffee Company, had come on the back of his own strong efforts. The Scientific and Research Director had never had the personable skills that Dung Lam possessed or the general knowledge of the coffee-making process that his boss excelled in. Therefore, his grievance had grown over the years, as he saw Dung Lam's meteoritic rise within the industry, and he felt that his own position as the boss' second-in-command had been dealt a blow by Dai Ca Phung's insertion into the position of Managing Director. Chien had seen this move as completely nepotistic and a resentment was sown toward his friend and boss, which was gradually festering into hatred. He felt he had been pushed out, but he now had plans to personally benefit from the current situation.

Dai Ca Phung had managed to avoid the doctor for most of the week, aided by the fact that his stepfather had been attending important coffee industry meetings in Ho Chi Minh City and Phan Chien had been battling through a heavy schedule himself, covering Dung Lam's absence. Dai's mother had insisted that her son should visit her whilst her husband was out of town.

Mai Thi was still a doting mum and looked forward to spending as much time as she could with her only son. Of course, she needed to know all the details about her son's trip to faraway Brazil and whether he had met any "nice Brazilian girls" over there. With Dai soon to celebrate his thirtieth birthday, she was anxious to get to the next stage in her life as mother-in-law to Dai's future wife and then hopefully a grandmother. Even though she had not yet reached her fiftieth birthday.

Mothers will be mothers, Dai thought to himself, as he tried to placate Mai Thi with a few titbits about meeting a highly intelligent and lovely Brazilian girl at the Nova Coffee plantation. He played down the seriousness of his current feelings, so as not to encourage his mother too much. However, she was so happy to see her "little angel" again and deep down was pleased by how he had developed into a fine young man whom she could be immensely proud of. She did, however, need to talk to Dai about the past again. Mai Thi, although she thought of him often, had never attempted to get in contact with Dai's father, David Maxwell. How could she? She did not know where he had gone after that fateful night in Ho Chi Minh

City and there had been no contact from David since that time. She now preferred to leave all the past where it belonged and to get on with her new life. But she worried herself about how Dai had been affected by her story and what his feelings might be.

On the other hand, Dai had no intention of revealing his sinister actions in Brazil to his mother or Dung Lam. He knew that they would be ashamed of him. Furthermore, he did not want to tell anyone, especially Dr Phan Chien, knowing that the old man would use the information against him.

Leaf Rust

Back in Brazil, the Almeida family were in state of panic. Mateus had reported the shedding of the coffee tree leaves to Luiz. They sat together on the wooden easy chairs set on the wide balcony that surrounded the back of the family home. Luiz had a worried look on his face; the news he had been given by his youngest son could have a devastating effect on the biggest coffee crop the Nova Coffee Company had ever produced.

"Is it the standard Leaf Rust, Mateus?" asked Luiz.

"Maybe not this time, Papa. It seems to be spreading at a faster rate than normal. We need to get our scientific team on to it as soon as possible and get a handle on what we are up against. Let's get Gabrielle on the case!" replied his equally distressed son.

"Okay, son, get them on to it straight away and initiate our usual spraying routine as soon as you can. I will contact Gabbie; she is out with your sister somewhere – Nova Serrano, I think. We need her input."

Mateus said, "Papa, do you think this is anything to do with the Vietnamese guy, Phung? I've felt uneasy about him and his intentions ever since he came here."

"What do you mean, Mateus? I know that, technically, he is our opposition in the coffee game – but after what happened between Phung and Gabbie, do you really think that he would do something so serious to our family? Surely not," replied Luiz.

"We don't know him well enough to judge him either way, I suppose," said Mateus. "But something irks me about him. It is a possibility. We will know when Gabbie and the team diagnose the reason for the rust, maybe? I'll get going and set things in motion, ring Gabrielle and ask her to get back as soon as she can." He looked at Luiz and sensed his unease. Mateus took two steps towards the father that he had adored all his life, opened his big arms, and gave him a giant hug. "It'll be okay, Papa. We will get through this... together."

With that, Mateus quickly went back into the house and left his father sitting alone, a determined look on his face and a tear in his eye. Luiz picked up the half-full whisky glass that he had left on the side table during his conversation with Mateus. The ice had melted inside the glass, leaving a refreshing, tempered amber liquid that eased the dryness in his throat. After emptying the glass, he sat in silence for a few moments, thoughts flowing through his mind. Was this something to do with Dai Ca Phung? Or was it a coincidence? Why had this problem hit him at a time when he thought that all was going so well? Lastly, as always, he thought about his beautiful Beatriz.

The Almeida Family Meeting

"Oh, Mum, do you think Dai would like me in this?" chirped a deliriously happy Gabrielle, as she bounced out of the changing rooms in the local Nova Serrano clothing store.

"I'm sure he wouldn't be able to resist you in that dress, Gabbie," replied Bianca. "But we haven't even discussed when – if ever – you will be meeting that young man again!"

"Mother, I will be seeing him again, I promise you," Gabrielle asserted, with a cheeky grin on her face.

In fact, Bianca was revelling in this moment in her young daughter's life. No other male had ever captured Gabrielle's attention in the way that Dai Ca Phung had managed to. (She was blissfully unaware of her daughter's romantic escapades in California.) Such a whirlwind relationship raised concerns with her mother, but at the same time Bianca had never seen her little girl so happy and that was something that had made her genuinely overjoyed as well.

Bianca's mobile phone rang out. It was Luiz. He asked if his two girls could come back to the family home as soon as possible, explaining to his daughter that the request was an urgent one. His ever-dutiful daughter responded in the positive. "Of course, Father, we'll be back within the hour."

By 2pm, the whole Almeida clan was sitting around the dining table, with Luiz at the head. Bianca, Gabrielle, Mateus and Felipe looked on expectantly as the patriarch started to talk.

"It seems we have a huge issue to resolve, one that will take every ounce of strength we can all muster to get to the bottom of. Our best-ever coffee crop is being threatened by an unusual strain of Leaf Rust. Our reputation could be devastated in the eyes of the huge US market. Also, the massive export orders that you have all contributed towards could be wiped out. So, financially and emotionally, this event could blow us out of the water!" started Luiz.

"Mateus has already mobilised the scientific team. Gabrielle, we need you to help the guys down there to isolate the cause of this disease and advise – as soon as you can – whatever you can do to eradicate this pest.

If we know what the culprit is, we have a chance to save as much of the crop as possible," added the Grand Old Man of the Nova Coffee Company.

Looking towards his eldest son, Luiz carried on, "Felipe, you have worked so hard to get this massive sales opportunity realised, and the technical knowhow of your brother Mateus has produced us a fine, fine crop of coffee beans, which is almost ready to harvest. We cannot lose it all now. It is important that no-one – I repeat, no-one! – knows about this issue outside of this family. Any hint of the Almeida family being unable to supply such a huge order to our northern neighbours could cause panic and ruin our chances of future orders. We need to keep this under wraps, get it fixed and then supply on time to the Americans as quickly as we can. Felipe, use all your PR and marketing skills to ensure that there is no doubt in the marketplace. Mateus, swear the scientific team to silence. Do not discuss this matter with any of the production staff, suppliers, drivers… none of them. Bianca, you must continue to operate under a 'business as usual' banner. No need to talk to our trading partners about any of this, unless of course we cannot fix this problem."

"Yes, Poppy," uttered Gabrielle solemnly.

"No problem, Papa," said Felipe and Mateus, almost simultaneously.

"We all understand. We won't let you down father," offered Bianca.

"I have great faith in all of you. Let's meet again at 7pm and see where we are heading by this evening," said Luiz, as they all rose from their seats and prepared to vacate the house, each with their tasks to pursue.

As Gabrielle slowly moved towards the front door of the grand old house, her grandfather called out to her. "Gabbie, can I please have a word with you alone, before you get to work with the team?"

"Of course, Poppy."

Gabrielle followed her grandfather into his office and stood just inside the door. "I am so sorry this has happened, Poppy, but I promise you we will get it fixed, I promise you!" blurted out a clearly upset Gabrielle.

"I need to ask you a question that you may not like, my darling," started Luiz, "Do you think that any of this has anything to do with Dai Ca Phung?"

"What? You mean... you think that Dai has damaged our crop on purpose! How can you think that?" shouted Gabrielle, now angry as well as upset. "He is too honourable to do something like that. What could he possibly gain from acting so horribly towards us? Towards me?"

"I only ask because, after all, he is in the same industry as we are. He could gain massively by taking Nova Coffee out of the market – even for a short time," said Luiz.

"But Dai wants to do business with us, doesn't he, Poppy? Did he not seek us out so we could work together? Didn't he?" queried Gabrielle.

"Maybe he did, maybe he didn't. But I think we need to find out the truth, don't you? I know how much you like him, darling, but sometimes, in business, you need to put those feelings aside. You are the only one who can find this out, by contacting him and asking him that question. I have great faith in you, Gabbie, to ask the correct question in a way that will get to the truth. Then, if you are right, maybe Dai will be able to help us eradicate this horrible thing. But I know that he can help you, more than any of us. You may be the youngest member of the Almeida team, Gabbie, but you are wise beyond your tender age, I know that. I need you to use your scientific intelligence to help isolate the problem here and then also use your loving heart to help us get a solution with Dai Ca Phung."

Gabrielle felt her eyes fill with tears as she listened intently to her grandfather's pleas. She loved her precious Poppy more than anyone else in the whole world. But she also had opened her heart up to a mysterious and wonderful young man from far away, who had captured her whole being. She was emotionally split. She was silent for a few moments as Luiz gazed at his granddaughter, her mind doing cartwheels.

"Well, my beautiful girl, do we have a deal?" he asked.

Gabrielle looked at him, a slight smile appearing on her face. "I think so, Poppy, I think so. I know what I have to do."

A few moments later, Gabrielle was in her mother's office. Bianca was busy working on some sort of paperwork, a determined look on her face.

"Hey, Mum, you will have to help me compose an email to Vietnam and then, all going well – in a few days' time – I'd like to buy that dress we tried on this morning."

Realisation

On a typically sunny Saturday morning in Buon Ma Thuot in the beautiful Western Highland region of Vietnam, Dai Ca Phung sat alone on the balcony of the Central Tea House. It was the place that this troubled young man often came when he needed solitude. He needed to think a problem through. He had to dissect all the confused thoughts that were running through his head and finalise a solution. The Central Tea House was his quiet place, his centre of zen. The old waiter walked over to the table, as he had done many times, to offer service to the young, confident Mr Phung. Dai smiled at the waiter as usual and ordered a pot of green tea. The table at which he sat, on the outside balcony, was the one that he had occupied on that terrible day his Ba had been killed in front of his eyes. Mi Ling's memory had always been indelibly etched on his heart; he had missed her terribly since the accident. However, he also had marvellous memories of the many happy times he had experienced, in his younger days, whilst taking afternoon tea with his beloved Ba at this incredibly special place. Would she agree with the actions he had taken?

The waiter took his order and immediately understood Dai's requirement for privacy that afternoon. Especially as the young Mr Phung had deposited an ample amount of the local currency into his grateful hand whilst being seated. After being supplied with his preferred tea, which offered him a welcome relief from the constant Lam Dong coffee he consumed at work, Dai sipped at his first cup, took a long breath, and went into deep thought.

For Dai, his dilemma had split into two opposing camps. After he had made his decision in Brazil, the long trip back to his homeland had furnished him the time to question his actions once again. Once he was back at work on Monday, he knew that he could not delay his meeting with Dr Phan Chien much longer. Therefore, he had to decide what story to tell him when they met.

At that moment, Dai was startled by the sight of a Golden-winged Laughingthrush perched on the balcony railing in front of him. His Ba had always fed the local birds in her immaculate back garden and she had said that this local species was a constant visitor to her place. She had often said to Dai that she believed that you had to be free to be happy, and if she were ever reincarnated after she had passed on, that she would like to come back as a bird. The words of his Ba echoed in his head as he stared at the beautiful little bird. The Laughingthrush stared right back.

"What do you think, little bird?" he said. The brightly coloured creature fluttered its wings as it quickly and effortlessly bounded onto Dai's table. The Laughingthrush pecked at a few little crumbs that had broken off from the sweet biscuits that the thoughtful waiter had included with Dai's tea order. With a little chirp the thrush stared at Dai again before flying off towards the bank of trees in the main street. Free, and seemingly so happy.

At that moment, Dai was startled by an electronic buzz on his mobile phone. It was an incoming email. When he looked to see where it came from, he understood. It was from the Nova Coffee Company in Brazil.

He stood up from the table, left another tip next to the empty tea set for the waiter and thought to himself, "I understand, my beautiful Mi Ling, my Ba, I understand."

Fifteen minutes later he was home, back at his apartment. Dai switched on his laptop, positioned it on his dining table, and sat down in front of the illuminated screen. Quickly accessing his email, he located the recently received message from Brazil, clicked on it and began to read.

The electronic message read: "Hello Dai, I hope you have returned home safely and have got back into the rhythm of work in your coffee business. Thank you for your help and input whilst you were over here at Nova. I have really missed you since you left. I think about you every day and I hope you feel the same. Having time to think about our brief time together, and being the rational, educated person that I am, I cannot explain my feelings for you at present. I only know that they are real and profoundly serious. I cannot wait to see you again, which sounds so weird. But my emotions are only reinforcing what my heart is telling me and I cannot ignore it. Hopefully, we can see each other sooner, rather than later... however, there is another reason that we need to get together.

"We have an enormous problem at Nova! Uncle Mateus has discovered that the coffee plantation has a huge coffee rust problem in the northern sector. It is threatening to devastate our crop – which was looking like being our biggest ever yield in the history of Poppy's business. We have recently sealed, thanks to Uncle Felipe, a massive export contract with the USA market and now that could all be put in jeopardy by our inability to supply, due to the leaf disease problem. As you know, we have developed an amazingly effective spraying regime to protect our trees from any sort of disease that nature can serve up. It has worked so well for Nova over the last couple of years – our crop-yields are getting better, year on year – and the mix of chemicals and the 'natural' anti-rust properties we have introduced are proving to be winners.

"However, the new rust that has just hit the trees is like nothing any of us have ever seen before here in Brazil. We need your help, Dai, if that is possible?

"Once you have read this email, can you please contact me via WhatsApp/ FaceTime/Skype (whatever you have)... Dai, I need to see your face – all our addresses/numbers are at the base of this email.

"Not sure what the time difference is between Vietnam and here, but please plan to call me anytime between 7am and 8pm Brazilian time, can't wait to see and speak to you – even if it is only on the computer. We need your help so badly. Love and best wishes, Gabrielle."

From his seated position, Dai wedged his elbows onto the table between himself and the glare of the laptop. He closed his eyes tightly and sank his head into his hands. "Shit, what am I to do!?" he shouted out in the loneliness of his bachelor pad. Only he was there, only he could answer. The troubled young man ripped off his clothes and immersed himself in a long, hot shower. The demons in his head buffered against one another for close to fifteen minutes before he turned off the taps. The bathroom was full of warm steam, as he looked at himself in the mirror. What he saw was a man who had made his decision, even though the thoughts in his head were as misty as his reflection. He wrapped himself in the thick bathrobe that was hanging on the hook on the back of the door and moved back into the living area.

As he walked across the apartment floor, a quick glance at the clock in his kitchen informed him that it was 2.40pm local time. He flicked on his mobile phone to convert local time into São Paulo time. The digital numbers indicated a time of 4.40am for the region where Nova Coffee was situated.

"Gabbie will still be asleep," he thought to himself. Another three hours, at least, until he could contact her. He went slowly across to the drinks cabinet and picked up a heavy crystal glass from the shelf above. Dai twisted the top off a fresh bottle of Glenfiddich Scotch and poured, very slowly, a double-plus measure into the ornate glass before gently emptying the contents between his lips. As the single malt's strength and flavour hit the back of his throat, he realised that he was ready to talk to and see Gabrielle again. He smiled. He had his answer for her. Immediately, he wrote a quick email response to Gabrielle in Brazil and firmly hit the "Send" icon on the screen.

As he walked back to his bedroom to dress, Dai's mobile phone indicated an incoming text with a monosyllabic ding. He quickly looked down and read the contents. "When are we meeting, Phung?" A curt question from Dr Phan Chien.

Time to Talk

In Nova Serrana, the sun was up early. Gabrielle Souza had risen, after a restless night, at around 6.45am and nervously checked her laptop for emails. There was a short, but encouraging response from Dai in Vietnam.

"Thank you for the email and so sorry for your current situation. But so wonderful to hear from you, Gabbie. I will Skype you at 08.45am today (your time), that will be 6.45pm our time in Vietnam. Please be ready for the call, please have Mateus there also. Looking forward to seeing your smiling face again. Best wishes, Dai Ca Phung."

Back in Vietnam, after Dai had written the email, he had set the alarm on his mobile for 6.30pm, giving him time to prepare himself for the call with Gabrielle and Mateus in Brazil at the agreed time.

He also rang the Dragon's Tail restaurant, Dr Chien's favourite place to eat, and booked a table for two for later that evening. Even though it was a Saturday night, there would always be a table available for Chien, even if the place were already booked out. He then sat on his sofa, spread his tired body across the length of the soft furniture and laid his head on a comfy cushion. Holding his mobile phone in two hands in front of his face, he simply replied to Dr Chien's text.

"Thanks for your text, doctor. I have booked a table at Dragon's Tail, see you there at 8.00pm tonight. We have a lot to discuss."

With an outstretched arm he gently laid the mobile on the coffee table next to the sofa, closed his eyes and fell into a deep sleep.

Honesty

Gabrielle, emboldened by the email from Dai, had rung her Uncle Mateus immediately after she had read it. She asked him to be at the company office by the expected time of the Skype from Vietnam. She had also spoken with Bianca, her Uncle Felipe and her Poppy. They had all agreed to be there before the 8.45am call from the other side of the world.

The night before, Mateus Almeida had had a deep and honest conversation with his father. He had raised the possibility that the cause of the virus currently infecting the precious leaves of their coffee trees may not have been natural. He put forward the theory that the visit of Dai Ca Phung may not have been the friendly and positive event it seemed to be. Mateus stressed to Luiz that the strain of virus was not one that had been experienced in South America – let alone Brazil – before. He had been, and still was, wary of the confident young Vietnamese businessman's real intentions. It all seemed too good to be true.

"But Mateus," replied Luiz, "young Phung seemed to be genuine to me and the relationship that developed between your niece and him, granted that it was a very brief time they were together, well, I certainly thought that he was an honest guy... in my opinion, that is. I know you have always been very protective of young Gabbie. Ever since Bianca finished with the father, Rodrigo, and even more so when your sister started that ridiculous marriage to the actor. You have always stood by Bianca and helped oversee Gabbie's upbringing. I will always be grateful to you – and your brother – for everything that you have contributed to your niece's amazing development."

"Papa, we all love Gabrielle and would do anything to ensure her happiness. But with this guy, I just do not know. Maybe we should just contact him in Vietnam and have a straight talk with him?" replied Mateus.

A wry smile came across the face of the elderly plantation owner. He looked Mateus straight in the eyes and said, "Your niece has already beaten you to the punch, my son. Her mother told me that her headstrong daughter has sent an email to Dai in Vietnam this afternoon, asking for his input into our problem. She has some courage, our Gabrielle. Something that you and Felipe have instilled in her. Let us see how it pans out, eh? Gabrielle was hoping for a response by tomorrow morning, with the time difference and all that."

"You're the boss, Papa. Let's see what tomorrow brings. After that we need to take some drastic action – and soon!" With that he placed a solid kiss on his father's cheek and started to leave the room.

"Goodnight, son, sleep well. I love you,"

"You too, Papa."

The Call

Dai Ca Phung's mobile phone emitted an ear-piercing alarm sound, which dragged him from a deep and much-needed sleep. He tapped the small icon on the bottom of the phone's face to snuff out the sound, raised himself to a sitting position and then jumped to his feet. He had 15 minutes to prepare for his call to Brazil. He took off his crumpled bathrobe, put on some underwear from his bedroom's walk-in wardrobe, threw a casual tee shirt over his head, and stepped into pair of casual linen shorts. He brushed his teeth, washed and dried his sleep-logged face and combed his thick black hair into a presentable fashion. A quick glance into the bedroom mirror confirmed that Dai looked acceptable enough to see the Almeida family – and of course Gabbie – over the miracle of the internet.

By 8.35am all the Almeida clan were huddled around the oversized screen of Bianca's computer in her well-appointed office. It was an extremely hot morning in the region: Felipe, Mateus and Luiz had each donned short Khaki pants, loose polo shirts and casual shoes. Bianca and Gabrielle were rather more formal in lightweight tops and three-quarter length pants. The men had noticed that Gabbie had spent more time than was usual on her hair and makeup for such an early hour... but they understood why. Gabrielle had her iPad at the ready, in preparation for the taking of notes from this conference call. She also required it to refer to her own technical notes on the leaf rust problem, to help with the discussion. Her Uncle Mateus had a notebook and pen at the ready. Bianca, Luiz and Felipe just clutched mugs of hot, fresh coffee, the distinctive Nova Coffee logo adorning each side of their coffee holders.

At 8.42am the screen indicated a Skype call coming in. Bianca pressed the appropriate buttons on the computer's keyboard to allow the digital conversation to take place. Within a few seconds Dai's face appeared on the huge screen. A warm glow ran through Gabrielle's body as his image hit the screen and her face exploded into a huge smile as their eyes met.

"Hello, everyone," began Dai when he recognised all five of the Brazilian family's faces staring at his lonely features through the computer screen. "Wow, I wasn't expecting the whole family to be in attendance today... but I guess I can understand why you all wanted to be involved. Good morning to you all; it is early evening over here in Buon Ma Thuot, my hometown in Vietnam."

Luiz Almeida indicated to his family that he wanted to take the lead in the initial discussion with the confident Vietnamese. As respectful children they all ceded to his request.

"Hello, Mr Phung, good to see you again. So far away, yet so close at this moment. The wonders of modern science, hey?" started Luiz.

"As you know, we are in the middle of a somewhat grave situation over here with our precious crop. Something which I am sure you would appreciate. I will be brief with my comments. Can you please speak and work with Mateus and Gabrielle to help us try to eradicate this terrible beast that has come to visit us? Bianca and Felipe will, of course, be kept informed of all developments by them, as will I. But the most technical and informed team of Mateus and Gabbie – along with their Scientific team – are the ones who will be personally responsible for eradicating this terrible virus. Please help them as much as you can, Mr Phung. We will leave you now with Gabbie and Mateus. Goodbye and good luck." Luiz motioned to Felipe and Bianca to vacate the office with him and urged the remaining two to continue the conversation. Felipe and Bianca looked at their father quizzically, as they both wished to stay. But, as always, they accepted their orders.

Dai saw the three family members leave the room on his laptop screen. "Thank you, Mr Almeida," he replied. "I will do as much as I can."

"Hello, Dai, so lovely to see you again. You cannot realise how happy I am feeling now, even in our most desperate moment. It's only me and

Uncle Mateus here with you now," said Gabrielle, her eyes fixated on Dai's face. "Do you want to speak with Uncle Mat first, Dai?"

"You look beautiful, Gabbie, so great to see you. Maybe I should talk to your uncle to get some technical data on what is happening over there. I feel so bad for you and your family," replied Dai, suffering a sense of genuine remorse as those words came out.

"Thank you, Dai. Here is Uncle Mat," blurted Gabrielle as her uncle took prime position on the screen in front of the apprehensive caller.

Mateus, putting aside his previous suspicions, spent the next ten minutes giving Dai the details of what had happened since he had discovered the shedding of leaves on his coffee crop. The timelines of the tests that they had carried out on the infected leaves. The findings that had revealed that this virus was one that had never been experienced in South America before.

Dai could hear the desperation in Mateus' voice. He took note of all the information. He asked Mateus to instruct Gabbie to email all the test results to him in Vietnam, with as much technical information as possible, along with any other material that could help. He promised to get the Scientific team under his management to immediately work on the data, to see if there was a possibility of a fast-working cure that could arrest the development of the virus attacking the trees at the Nova Coffee plantation. Dai kept the conversation at a very businesslike level and ensured that he maintained a level of respect with Mateus, something that Mateus seemed to appreciate.

Of course, the young Vietnamese knew exactly what had caused the devastation of the Almeidas' crop. He had initiated the virus, a fact that he now regretted. Mateus finished off his part of the conversation with a "Thank you" and told his opposite number in Vietnam that he was leaving the office straight away to get all the required information together.

"All yours, Gabbie!" said Mateus as he left the room. "Thought you would appreciate some individual time with Mr Phung..."

Gabrielle smiled sweetly at her uncle and waved him goodbye. As the office door closed behind Mateus, she spun back towards the computer and Dai smiled with joy as their eyes once again locked together.

"Gabrielle, I thought we would never be alone," said Dai.

"We can be, if you want to," replied Gabbie. "My family are in dire need of your help now, Dai. And I am in dire need of you too."

"I understand, my dearest Gabbie. It has taken me a while to get to the bottom of my thoughts, my wishes, my dreams. But, finally, I have realised that none of them will ever happen without you in my life. Do you feel the same?"

"I do. I really do!" exclaimed the young Brazilian. "Where do we go from here?"

"Well, we need to get you over here in Vietnam as soon as possible, for more than one reason. We need to get an antidote applied to your coffee crop urgently before its spread becomes unstoppable. I know it may take some technical knowhow and a little deceit to get samples of your virus over here undiscovered by the border authorities. But I am sure that, as we only need a small amount to recognise its vile properties, you can handle that with a bit of help from your Uncle Mateus. The 'greater good' far outweighs the small legal issues we may be transgressing in this particular situation, don't you think?"

"I guess so," Gabrielle answered.

"Then can you get to work on that and book an airline ticket over to our Lam Dong Coffee plant immediately? Make it a one-way ticket for now, as I am not sure how long you will be over here for. My company will pay for your return trip, whenever that may be."

"I am sure I can, but Poppy and Mother will need to sanction it. After talking to my uncles as well, of course. I would also need my mum to come with me on the trip. Poppy would never allow me to travel so far all alone, especially with such a precious and dangerous cargo in my luggage. And with such a handsome young man waiting in Vietnam to sweep me off my feet!" Gabrielle replied with a smile on her face.

"Okay, Gabbie. Whatever you need to do is alright by me. It is so great to think that I will be seeing you so soon... and, of course, your mother. Speed is needed in this situation, so let us get on with it!" said a happy Dai. "Please email me all the information that you already have on your testing of the leaves and the tree bark – chemical analysis and your theories as well, if you have developed any yet. Anything that will help us – together, as a team – to get this thing eradicated. I am sure that we can succeed.

"Assuming you get the plan past your family, let me know your flight details into Tan Son Nhat. That is the international airport in Ho Chi Minh City. I will track the flight and arrange to pick up you and your mother when you arrive. You can both stay at my mother's house. I am sure that my mum would just love to meet you and Bianca. You'll probably need a phrase book or two to help with the conversation!" joked Dai with a chuckle.

"Okay, my darling Dai, leave all that with me. I will be in touch as soon as I have all the information together," said Gabrielle as she took one last look at the young man on the screen, smiled enthusiastically, blew him a kiss and clicked off the monitor.

Back in Vietnam the emboldened Mr Phung watched the screen on his laptop turn to black. But the face of his heart's content stayed in his mind's eye for a few moments. A smile lit up his face. "Now for that old bastard, Dr Chien!" he said to himself. Finally, he knew what lay ahead.

The Showdown

After getting dressed more formally for his dinner date with Dr Chien, Dai called a cab and within fifteen minutes he was sitting at his booked table at the Dragon's Tail Restaurant awaiting his guest. He took a swig of the whisky he had been served with, poured over a mass of ice cubes, and rehearsed his lines in his head.

A few minutes after 8.00pm, Dai glanced across the crowded restaurant and saw the tall and bulky Dr Phan Chien enter the restaurant, silhouetted against the brightly lit bar behind him. Dai raised his hand in recognition of his foe's entry into the establishment and jumped out of his chair to greet him.

"Good evening, Dai Ca Phung, better late than never young man," proffered the good doctor, as he shook Dai's hand with a very firm grip, before seating himself. He snapped his fingers at the looming, ever-gracious waiter, who had shown him to the table.

"Get me a large of my usual on ice," he barked at the waiter, who bowed his head and immediately hastened back to the bar to fulfil the order. "Now then, Mr Phung, what news do you have for me?" Chien directly asked of Dai.

Dai smiled weakly at Chien and commenced relating his story, including all that had happened. That is, all except for the poisoning of the trees. Dr Chien's face was getting visibly redder and angrier as young Mr Phung kept telling of his adventures in Brazil and of the wonderful rapport he had built up with the Almeida family. In between episodes, food was ordered by Chien and consumed by both men as the one-way conversation continued. Dai even told his dinner guest that there was a delegation of important members of the Brazilian company's team, Bianca and Gabrielle, now travelling to Vietnam in pursuit of an answer for their "virus" problems. The moment that Dai stopped talking to take a mouthful of the tasty food that lay in front of him, a very frustrated Dr Chien butted into the conversation.

"You seem to have taken charge of this 'Brazilian Expedition', young man, without a thought of including me in the decision-making. Why wasn't I consulted about any of this?" boomed out the angry doctor. "The discussions you have had and the consequent business you have offered this Almeida family is something that I should have been told about – to pass onto your stepfather – before any key offers were given to them. I should have been included! Don't you understand that, Phung? And now you have a couple of women travelling across the world to visit our company from Brazil, without consulting me!" continued a very heated Chien. "Do you realise what Dung Lam will have to say, once he hears about this?"

"But Dr Chien, my stepfather already has a full report on the trip and all of its results. I wrote it on the way back on the plane and emailed it to him on my return last week... I am sure that I had copied you in on that report, hadn't I? And I plan to tell Dung Lam and my mother about the visit of Gabrielle and her mother, Bianca, tomorrow," retorted Dai, with a smug smile on his young face.

"No, you didn't send me a copy of the email, young man. I will ensure that there will be consequences to your actions. I will speak with Dung Lam first thing in the morning!" shouted Chien, standing up violently at the table and upsetting food all over the delicate place-settings. "I will see you at your office, first thing tomorrow morning. You will pay for your disrespect!" With that comment he strode from the restaurant with a terrific scowl on his face, loudly telling the shuddering wait staff to order him a taxi home.

Dai took another large sip from his whisky, leant back in his chair and smiled to himself. "The war has begun," he thought.

Paying the bill with a hefty tip, he smirked at the stunned restaurant manager and apologised for the mess at his table. He slept very well that night.

From Rio to
Ho Chi Minh City

Back in Brazil, Gabrielle had done well with her list. She already had the notes from her laboratory tests on the virus affecting their coffee crop. She got more information from her Uncle Mateus and then bundled it all together in a concise email and sent it across to Vietnam to Dai's personal email address.

The next task was a slightly trickier issue: the planned trip to Vietnam. Cunningly she approached her mother first, using the romantic angle of the proposed visit. Then, having convinced her of the importance of her mother travelling with her – and also having the chance to meet Dai's family – the granddaughter and daughter of the ever-romantic Luiz went to see him together to sell the benefits of their trip to Vietnam. After a stiff half-hour's debate with him, they had won their case. It was then left up to Luiz to convince his two boys, Felipe and Mateus, that this was the best way forward. Women's logic, once again, won in the end, and the trip was planned.

After consulting the company's travel specialists in Rio, Gabrielle confirmed the agenda and dates. Now, all was set for Bianca and Gabrielle's long trip to Vietnam. A trip on which they would engage in numerous conversations with each other. Especially about Dai.

Mateus was to drive the women to the local Belo Horizonte Airport for an internal flight to Rio De Janeiro, from where they would connect with an overnight flight to Charles De Gaulle Airport in Paris. After an hour and a half stopover, they would board another Air France flight direct to Ho Chi Minh City, landing in the Tan Son Nhat International Airport just before 7am.

Because of the urgency, the trip would be tiring. But the increasing financial clout of the Almeida family ensured that Luiz could insist that Bianca and Gabrielle would fly first class all the way, especially as the Lam Dong Coffee Company would be financing their return trip. Gabrielle's ever-inventive Uncle Mateus had managed to secrete the required small quantities of laboratory test samples, including some of the affected leaf samples, into Bianca's makeup case in her hand luggage, with Gabrielle's help. There was next to no chance that these tiny samples would be discovered, even by the most diligent of border-control officials. The fact that Mateus had not told his sister that he had put them there would also increase the chances of them not being found. Gabrielle had been made aware of their hidey-hole, as she was renowned in her family as being the absolute best at keeping secrets.

Welcome to Vietnam

As the sun rose in Dai's hometown the next morning, he was quickly out of his bed, and by 7am he was at his desk in the company office. He had already been down to the factory floor and made himself a strong coffee, as Tina had not yet commenced her day's work. He always looked forward to Monday mornings at work, as it was often the case that his devoted secretary came in wearing a new dress or a blouse she had bought at the weekend. Tina made every effort to look good for her boss and Dai had appreciated this for many years. His newly acquired feelings for Gabrielle, however, had quelled his sometimes outrageous thoughts about Tina from earlier times. On reflection, he thought, as he sipped on his coffee, maybe he should have acted on these outrageous thoughts before now. But, then again, he was in enough trouble with his Director of the Scientific Department without complicating his relationship with Tina as well. Some things were just not meant to happen.

After opening his laptop and clicking his way to his incoming emails, he noticed that he had received the two emails he had hoped for. Firstly the technical information from Brazil, and secondly Gabrielle's flight details. He noted the early arrival time and date of the flight in his diary. He then picked up the phone to call his mother.

Mai Thi Phung, now Mrs Dung Lam, was overjoyed to get an early morning telephone call from her son. She had always been an early riser, ever since first arriving in Buon Ma Thuot, and she was still highly active for her age. Her strict morning regime was to get out of bed before 6am, no matter the weather, and partake of a leisurely stroll down the main street of the town. Over her many years of living in this little haven, Mai Thi had always remained so grateful for what this town had given her. During her time here she had grown as a woman and as a mother and had become a very respected member of Buon Ma Thuot's community. She still worked tirelessly in the Lam Dong Coffee plantation and factory complex, even though she was married to the boss. Her mind often strayed to thinking about her unfortunate start in life and the strains and struggles that she had endured to overcome the sadness of Ho Chi Minh City. She now had a respected and much-loved husband and a grown-up son who made them both immensely proud. On her walks she would always stop at the Tea House, where her dear friend, Mi Ling, had so tragically lost her life, and say a silent prayer.

"Good morning, Mother, how are you on this beautiful, sunny morning?" started Dai.

"Very well, my beautiful boy. Is everything okay with you? It is so early for you to be ringing, Dai," she replied.

"Well, I have some interesting news for you, if you have the time to talk," he said, intriguingly.

"Of course, Dai, I always have time to chat with my favourite son! What is so interesting?" she asked cheekily.

"I know that it may sound strange. But I would like to introduce you to an incredibly special lady, very soon in fact, who I met on my trip to Brazil. I did tell you about her last week, very briefly, you may remember? Her name is Gabrielle Souza," blurted Dai.

"Oh, this sounds as if it may be a serious thing between you and this... Gabrielle. But how can I be introduced to her if she is in Brazil, half a world away, and we are here in Vietnam?" asked his bemused mother.

"Well, because of certain events that are happening in Brazil, Gabbie and her mother, Bianca Almeida, will shortly be arriving in Vietnam as my guests," explained her son.

There were a few seconds of silence at the other end of the phone, as Mai Thi took in the meaning of her son's words.

"So, my son, this girl is a member of the Almeida family that you have been to see in Brazil, I take it? And after a week of being there with this

Gabbie, Gabrielle… whatever, she is coming here with her mother! My goodness, this sounds like such a whirlwind romance, Dai. What is the reason for their visit here, and why so soon? I do not understand. What will your stepfather say?"

"Don't worry, Mother. All will be revealed soon. It is all good news, I promise you. How about I drop round to Dung Lam's office later today and I will explain it all to you both over a cup of coffee?" he offered.

"I have got to go now, as I have a meeting with Dr Chien very soon. I love you, Mother. See you later today. Oh, I almost forgot – I said that Gabbie and her mother could stay at your house whilst they are here, it will only be a week or so. Is that alright with you, Mum?" he finished slightly sheepishly.

"Yes, that's fine, Dai, I will get it all arranged. Goodness knows the house is big enough to cope with two guests. They can even have a room each," said his mother.

"Great, thanks, Mum. I love you so much, see you later!" were Dai's parting words.

Mai Thi heard the phone go silent. She placed the handset back on its cradle, cupped the inside of her left hand over her mouth and thought to herself, "Oh my goodness, what is happening in Brazil that is so important? I must talk with Dung Lam. House guests, how exciting! I wonder what sort of food Brazilians eat?"

The Long Journey East

Bianca Almeida and her daughter sat very comfortably next to each other in the first-class section of the Air France flight from Paris to Ho Chi Minh City. They had been airborne for nearly an hour, after having endured the previous flight, unfortunately with some turbulence, between Rio De Janiero and the French capital. The extra dollars paid by Luiz for his daughter's and granddaughter's first-class seating and sleeping on both plane trips, was paying dividends for them. They were very happy with the excellent level of service afforded to them on the two legs of the journey. The food was superb, and the French champagne was constantly available. Bianca was also more than happy with the many admiring glances, and later conversations, that she was enjoying from more than one of the well-heeled male passengers on board. Flying first-class certainly had its advantages. Since her second marriage breakup from the bit-part actor Tiago Lima five years previously, she had thrown herself into the job at Nova Coffee. She was now a tremendous help to her father, especially as she was now regarded as the maternal head of the family, in steering the company forward. She also had a daughter to educate and raise. In both quests she been more than successful. But that success had come at the expense of her own personal life and she now was looking to, once again, be active in the game of love. Maybe "third time lucky" was still a possibility, especially as she was still only in her late forties and by no means unattractive.

Gabrielle, on the other hand, had only one man on her mind. She was quite happy for her glamorous mother to take centre stage on the social side of things. After all, Bianca had experience in these matters in her younger days, before she became a mother. Then, after her first marriage to Gabrielle's father, Rodrigo Souza, had run its course, Bianca had hit the singles merry-go-round again. It was not long before she had, prematurely in most people's eyes, remarried, a union that lasted less than two years before she was divorced again. Gabrielle thought that her mum deserved a bit of happiness in her life, so why shouldn't she flirt with all the eligible, young rich men and all the knowledgeable, older and even richer men who frequented the first-class facilities? Gabrielle, for her part, was certainly in no mood to contemplate looking any further than the young Vietnamese man who had stolen her heart.

Phung v Chien

It was 9.15am at the executive offices of the Lam Dong Coffee Company when the imposing figure of Dr Phan Chien appeared at the desk of Dai's secretary, Tina. The doctor loomed over the diminutive young lady with a scowl on his face.

"Is young Mr Phung in?" he enquired, very abruptly.

"Is Mr Phung expecting you, Doctor?" responded Tina, very politely.

"He most certainly is, young lady. Let him know I am here," boomed Chien, looking towards Dai's door.

After Tina had confirmed the appointment with her boss over the internal phone system, Dr Chien quickly made his way to Dai's door and entered, not bothering to announce his arrival with a courteous knock. As he entered the plushily decorated office, Dai stood up, with a determined look on his face, greeting Chien as he bustled his way in.

"Good morning, Doctor, please take a seat and let's finalise our discussions from last night, shall we?" said Dai very formally, indicating the seat opposite his own. Whilst still on his feet, Dai smiled at Tina through the open door and asked her to hold all calls while he met with Dr Chien. He then closed the door slowly and deliberately, before taking his place at the desk opposite his seated visitor.

Chien glared at his young nemesis, as Dai took his place in his own comfortable leather-upholstered seat. "Mr Phung, what do you think you will achieve from all that you have done in Brazil? You had no right to offer all the business and scientific opportunities which you did to this Nova Coffee establishment whilst you were over there. In addition, the invitation you have offered to the Brazilians to visit Lam Dong seems premature, in my mind!"

"Sir, if you had not stormed out of our dinner meeting so early last night, I could have explained the reasons for my actions," retorted Dai. "In fact, if you knew all the details, you would realise what an amazing opportunity we have to expand Lam Dong's influence in the South American coffee market. Locally, the deal helps us become a much more important part of the Highlands Coffee Corporation, as well as gaining an entry into the major US market. It is all good news, Dr Chien, I do not see what you are so upset about. Unless, of course, you are unhappy about my personal part in all of this and how my stepfather will react? Please, with all due respect, enlighten me with your thoughts!"

Chien sat upright in his chair, a quizzical look on his face, feeling that he had two choices. Firstly, to calm himself down, talk positively with his young colleague and then help the Managing Director take advantage of the possibilities ahead. Or secondly, fly off the handle in a rage and let this young upstart have a piece of his mind. He took in a deep breath and decided that the first option was the wisest. Dai had been staring impatiently back, awaiting his response.

"Okay, young man. Let us see how this plays out," said a surprisingly calm Dr Chien. "Tell me all the facts, and we shall go forward with your recommendations, on the proviso that Dung Lam agrees to them. I will need to analyse all of the data you have collected on the Brazilian virus and then my team will help you, if we can," he finished.

Dai, on hearing the unexpected answer to his demands, immediately stood up from his seated position. He then turned around and walked towards the huge window at the side of the office, deep in thought. After a few seconds of staring out of the window, he quickly swivelled around on the balls of his feet, smiled at the doctor, and said, "Okay, let us talk. Then we will go to see Dung Lam together."

For the next ninety minutes the two men discussed in detail the content of Dai's visit, the makeup of the Almeida family and Nova Coffee's position in the market. Dai was frank with the old man about the relationship he had developed with Gabrielle. He also detailed the scientific experiments and results that had been achieved in Brazil and the severity of the virus that threatened Nova's huge contract with the Americans. Rather annoyingly, in the eyes of an envious Chien, Dai had explained the wonderful technical abilities of the young Brazilian lady and what a great talent she was. Again, he refrained from mentioning his poisoning episode. He had put that into a sealed box in his memory, never to be admitted to. All he could see was a bright and prosperous future, both professionally and personally. Deep down he was happier than he had been for the whole of his life. Conversely, the eminent doctor – having now been made privy to all the relevant facts – was heading in his own direction. A direction that was imminently darker.

Dai had earlier asked Tina to ring ahead to his stepfather's office to set a time for a meeting, in the boardroom, with Dung Lam and Dai's mother. He indicated that both he and Dr Chien would be putting forward some bold proposals for their company and he also asked Tina to advise Dung Lam of the impending visitors from Brazil. He knew that his mother was already excited by this news and that Dung Lam would be highly inquisitive about the reasoning behind these actions. The time was set for a late afternoon get-together.

Dung Lam had taken the phone call from his stepson's secretary and immediately rang his wife. He was a little agitated about what all the fuss was about. Mai quickly calmed her husband down and told him that all would be explained when she got to his office, after she had finished her workday at 4.30pm. "Don't worry, my darling, our son knows what he is doing," she finished, as the Lam Dong Coffee chief replaced his phone on its cradle and stared out of the window that looked down onto the busy factory floor below.

"I hope so," he thought to himself.

Viva La France

On board the Air France flight that was winging its way to Ho Chi Minh City, Gabrielle was getting rather tired and thinking the time was right for a long sleep. The aeroplane was still 15 hours from its destination and her mother was engaged in an interesting conversation with a bright young man who seemed, to Gabrielle at least, to have more money than sense. Yet, he was devilishly handsome. Her mother had not planned to sleep for some time yet and had consumed her fair share of the premium champagne that flowed from the well-trained flight attendants in the first-class section. It had been quite a while since she had enjoyed the company of this type of crowd. But knowing that she needed to get at least six or seven hours' sleep before they arrived, she needed to pace herself to make the best of the time left.

Vincent Michel was an eligible and recently divorced Frenchman, currently living in Paris. In his late thirties, he had tried and failed at one marriage which, thankfully, had not produced any offspring. His former wife was a celebrated TV anchor on a Parisian news channel and had tired of his reckless ways less than three years into their marriage. His profession as a bank executive, successful only because of his rich father's influences, had led him to travel to many parts of the world. The handsome Monsieur Michel was on the same Air France Boeing 787 Dreamliner as Bianca and Gabrielle, heading to Vietnam for a two-week banking conference in Ho Chi Minh City. He had offered many glances in Bianca's direction during the earlier stages of the flight and had made his move after dinner service had been finalised an hour previously. Both Gabrielle and her mother had enjoyed an excellent meal on board and were relaxing together, discussing their plans for the visit to Dai's factory and the impending introduction to his family and their coffee company. Gabrielle, in her usual practical way, had invested in both an English/Vietnamese and a French/Vietnamese translation booklet in preparation for the visit ahead. Both Gabrielle and her mother had been taught to speak and understand the basics of the English language, along with their native Portuguese/Brazilian. Luiz Almeida had insisted on this for all his children and grandchildren. He understood that the English language was the basis of business, in a global sense. Therefore, he did not want his young family to grow up with the impediment of only speaking their native tongue, as he had as a boy. He was lucky that he had grasped the rudiments of new languages in his early teens and had managed to conquer this obstacle with the aid of his father's business contacts and especially José Costa. The man who was to become his father-in-law had mastered the "base" business languages of English, Spanish and Italian at an early age, and had taken great pride in teaching his great friend's son to do the same.

Earlier, after some deep and meaningful discussions with her mother, Gabrielle understood that her flight companion was probably in need of some company closer to her own age, and particularly of the male species. As a wise young lady, she understood that it was time to go when the handsome Frenchman appeared next to her mother, as he sauntered down the corridor between the seats. He had nobly introduced himself in his native tongue and then realised that Bianca was not comfortable speaking in French. He quickly reverted to the international language, English.

"Just going to the restroom, Mama. I need to freshen up before sleeping. Please excuse me," offered Gabrielle as she sidled out of her comfortable pod and headed to the front of the plane, giving the elegant Frenchman a warm smile as she left. Vincent Michel smiled back and then turned his attention to Bianca, who was more than willing to continue conversing with her handsome admirer.

Gabrielle spent a good half an hour preening and pampering herself in readiness for a long sleep. She emerged from the powder room and struck up a conversation with a tired, but still smiling, female flight attendant. Gabrielle had excelled in French during her high-school days and had been afforded a holiday in southern France at the age of 16 by her grandfather, as a reward for her excellent exam result in French. Her cousin Vitor, five years her senior, had qualified for a semi-professional tennis tournament in the region and his sports-mad father Mateus had jumped at the chance to join his youngest son for the two-week period. Vitor's mother, Clara, had asked Luiz if he would pay for Gabrielle's airfare and that she and Mateus would stump up the money for her accommodation and other expenses. Her lack of siblings had meant that Gabrielle had always gravitated towards her cousins, Vitor and Luiz Junior, and felt exceedingly close to the whole family. So, when the chance presented itself to take a trip of a lifetime with them, she begged her Poppy to say yes. Which, of course, he did. Having been such a good student of the French language, Gabrielle used the experience of that teenage trip to improve her French conversation.

All that earlier learning was now bearing fruit on this present trip. Not only did she have the ability to speak a quite decent quality of French – a language that many Vietnamese understood due to its history of colonisation by that country – but she quite easily understood what the Air France cabin crew and the lustful Monsieur Michel were saying as well.

After finishing her talk with Madeleine, the flight attendant, Gabrielle stood for a while at the front of the cabin and surveyed the whole first-class section. She instantly saw that Bianca was no longer in her appointed seat. She had obviously been wooed by the handsome Frenchman into moving her position. Gabrielle noticed that he had maneuvered her gullible mother into a seat next to his own and was ensuring that her champagne flute was constantly full. Being aware of where this might end up, as well as knowing of her mother's somewhat willing nature whilst sipping good-quality bubbly, Gabrielle decided that a little insurance was called for. She promptly returned to her recently acquired friend Madeleine, then had a short conversation in French with the ever-helpful staff member. They parted with a smile and a slight giggle, as well as a knowing nod of the head from Madeleine. Gabrielle made her way back to her allotted pod, which she quickly adjusted into the sleeping mode. Within ten minutes she was fast asleep, dreaming of meeting up again with Dai.

Across the aisles Bianca was, unfortunately, getting rather bored with her new admirer's forward advances. The ever-vigilant Madeleine, who had been viewing the episode unfold, as she had done many times during her long employment in the first-class cabins of Air France, made her move. Just after Bianca had excused herself to totter off to the restroom at the front of the cabin, Madeleine slowly made her way to the young Frenchman, who was glibly sipping his own champagne with a contented look on his face as she approached.

"Good evening, Monsieur Michel, how are you enjoying the flight so far?" she enquired.

"Wonderful," started Vincent. "Even better, now that you have decided to introduce yourself to me, err... Madeleine," he responded, with a quick glance at her name badge.

"To what do I owe the pleasure?" he asked.

"Well, Monsieur, I just wanted to give you some information which may be of help to you at a later date, especially when you disembark in Vietnam."

Vincent Michel stirred in his seat and became playfully attentive.

"Are you about to give me your mobile number, Madeleine?" he enquired, a lustful glint in his eye.

"Alas, not this time, Monsieur Michel. I was just going to advise you that the attractive lady who has been sharing your charming company with for the last hour or so is well-known to the flight crew. Her husband, who we understand will be meeting her on her arrival at the airport in Ho Chi Minh City, is also well known to us. He is a former middleweight Olympic boxing medalist from Brazil, who has a rather short temper, in our experience. As a valued guest of our airline, we would hate to see any harm come to you because of any misunderstanding of the relationship between the lady and your good self. I was alerted to this situation by the lady's daughter, who is accompanying her mother on this trip."

The Frenchman looked quite alarmed. "Oh, please do not think that I had any evil intent, young lady! But thank you so much for the information, I really do appreciate it," he finished. Vincent then polished off his flute of champagne with one nervous gulp. Offering the flight attendant the empty glass, he spluttered to her, "Maybe you could be a little darling and get me a large cognac to finish off my night, before I settle down for a sleep."

"Certainly, Monsieur. It would be my pleasure," replied Madeleine, as she turned around to return to the service area of the cabin. A satisfied grin spread across her face as she headed back.

At that same moment, Bianca appeared back at Vincent Michel's pod, her hair freshly brushed and with a new layer of lipstick elegantly applied to her smiling lips. Before she could sit down in the seat that she had previously occupied, the Frenchman turned to her and said, "My darling Bianca, I must sincerely apologise. I have the most dreadful of headaches and I feel that I should really partake of a lie-down before we arrive in Vietnam. I will need to go over rather a large amount of official paperwork before we disembark, as I have an early morning meeting in Ho Chi Minh City tomorrow. It has been an absolute pleasure making your acquaintance on this flight and maybe we could get together again in the future. You never know whether our paths may cross again. So, thank you, Bianca, and I hope you have a good sleep yourself," said a now strangely formal Michel.

"Oh, I see," replied Bianca, rather bemused by his change in attitude since she had visited the restroom. "Well, I will bid you *adieu*, Monsieur Michel. Thank you for your time," blurted an embarrassed Bianca, as she quickly turned on her heels and returned to her own seat.

Gabrielle was fast asleep as her mother took her place in the pod. "Maybe I am too old for this after all?" Bianca thought to herself, as she arranged her seat, rather tentatively, into the sleeping mode. With a final glance across the aisles to the seat from which she had just moved, the last thing she saw before falling into a deep sleep was Vincent Michel sipping a large cognac and chatting furtively to a very young and beautiful flight attendant.

Preparation for
the Brazilians

Dung Lam's office, which also served as an entry point to one of the company's elegantly furnished boardrooms, was comfortably cool as Dai Ca Phung and Dr Phan Chien arrived for their late-afternoon appointment. The eminent doctor greeted his old friend with a solid handshake and a huge smile. Dai was less formal, giving his mentor and stepfather a huge hug. After all, he had not seen Dung Lam in a while. He then turned his attention to his mother, who was already in the boardroom. Mai Thi had stood up from one of the expensive, leather-bound chairs to greet her son, with a massive smile on her face.

"Hello, Dai. Can't wait to hear all of your news and Dung Lam and myself are so looking forward to meeting the visitors from Brazil," she said in an excited tone.

"All will be revealed shortly," replied Dai, as his stepfather directed him and Dr Chien to be seated at the ornate boardroom table.

Over the next two hours Dai went through all the intricacies of his Brazilian trip, as he had done earlier in the day with Dr Chien. He again left out the details of his illicit night-time mission to poison the Nova Coffee Plantation. Instead, he concentrated on all the positive benefits that he thought would be available to Lam Dong Coffee Company and, by association, to their principal, HCC. He explained that if their Scientific and

Research department could analyse and eradicate the Brazilian virus – of which he was greatly confident – that there would be massive opportunities for their company. He explained how it would be possible to expand its markets for both their Vietnamese coffee bean sales and to get a foothold in the lucrative South American virus eradication market.

Also, because of the huge export contract to the USA that Nova were struggling to fulfil because of the leaf rust problem, another opportunity had presented itself. Lam Dong could now possibly supply coffee product to them to fill the void in both quality and quantity of the beans required for this order. At that stage, Dr Chien interjected into the conversation, which had been dominated by the younger Mr Phung and only occasionally interrupted by questions from an extremely interested Dung Lam on a few technical issues.

"Mr Phung, do you feel that we have the technical abilities within my department to eradicate this fiendish virus that the Brazilians have fallen foul of?" he queried.

"Yes, most certainly yes, Doctor. From the experiments that I initiated in Brazil alongside Gabrielle, the antidote that we applied to the 'Super-Bad' virus samples, which I had imported from our laboratories, showed positive results. It seemed to work perfectly on the Brazilian coffee trees we were working on within only a few days. Therefore, assuming the virus that Nova Coffee have acquired is not any stronger than our samples, I am more than confident that we can eradicate the problem from their crops. As soon as Gabrielle and her mother, Bianca, arrive with their sampling pieces, we should be able to do the required calculations and verify that our antidote will work. You have a great team of technicians who have been collaborating with me on this programme, Doctor. Therefore, they can work on the problem as soon the Brazilians get here, which, by the way, is tomorrow morning," answered Dai.

Dr Chien responded, "I will make sure that this will be completed as quickly as we can possibly do it. At the same time, I will personally ensure that, if the tests are all positive, we can ramp up production of the antidote serum in enough quantities to satisfy the needs of the Nova Coffee Company. Do you have details on the quantities required, Mr Phung?"

"We will have tomorrow when Gabrielle arrives; she has collated all the information required," answered Dai. "I will need to get all the costings from whatever we do over the next few days, so that we can work out our selling prices for the wonderful service that we will be offering to Nova Coffee, and in turn to the American coffee market," stated the young Managing Director.

"I agree, Dai," interrupted Dung Lam. "But please leave those details to me, as I will have to report to the Highlands Coffee board on all of this and extrapolate the figures to ensure adequate profitability. Especially as we will need to include the price of two, or maybe three, first-class airline tickets back to Brazil." As he said these words, a wide smile lit up his face as he looked directly at Dai Ca Phung and then across to his wife.

He felt enormously proud of what his stepson had achieved for one so young. Dung Lam then turned to his old friend, Dr Chien, with a more serious face. "My dear friend, I don't need to tell you how important your task will be to ensure that this project is a success. Dai has done a marvellous job in giving us this great opportunity. Please use your utmost efforts to get these tests performed quickly and correctly. Let me know if you need any more resources to make sure that we are successful. A huge amount rests on your big shoulders, Phan. Please do not let us down, I have great faith in you."

"After so many years together, sir, of course I will not let you down. Leave it to me," replied a subdued Dr Chien.

"Then let us get on with it, all of us!" finished Dung Lam. "Dai, maybe you would like to have dinner with your mother and me tonight? We are both most interested in hearing more about your friend Gabrielle and her mother," he added, then turned to the doctor, shook hands with his old colleague and bid him farewell. The elderly doctor nodded at both Mai Thi and Dai as he left the boardroom.

Mai Thi had been noticeably quiet during the meeting. After the doctor had left them, she gave her son a big hug and congratulated Dai on what he had achieved in the past two or three weeks. "I am so proud of my big boy, Dai. You have done so well with this project and I cannot wait to meet up with Gabrielle and her mother tomorrow. What time are they flying in? Are you picking them up personally?"

"They land just before 7am tomorrow morning, Mother. I aim to be there around 8am to greet them and drive them back to Buon Ma Thuot. Assuming they are on schedule, we should be back here by about 6pm tomorrow night. It is a seven or eight-hour drive, so I think we'll have a couple of breaks along the way," replied Dai. "So, I will be leaving in the Range Rover tonight at about 11pm to drive down there. I am looking forward to a leisurely trip, as it has been a long day today. I have already prepared the car and a small bag to freshen up at the airport. It is 6.30 now, so I will have a quick meal with you and Dung Lam, then I will have a couple of hours rest at home before preparing for my trip. Have you set up a couple of spare bedrooms at your place, Mum?" asked Dai.

"Don't worry, my son. All has been prepared at home. We shall not embarrass you, Dai," said his mother, as she took hold of his arm and walked him out of her husband's office. Dung Lam followed closely behind, a contented look on his face.

Papa Knows Best

"Hey, Papa, have you heard from Bianca or Gabbie yet?" asked Mateus, as he walked into the Almeida house and saw Luiz seated on the back veranda.

"Oh, hello, Mateus. No, not since they rang me from Paris Airport... that was earlier this morning. The flight from De Gaulle to Vietnam is quite a haul. Around 16 hours, I think Gabbie said. So, I doubt we will have any news from them until tomorrow, because they will have to get up north to the Lam Dong Coffee plantation after that. I believe that it is about seven or eight hours by road. Young Dai is supposed to be picking them up from Ho Chi Minh International when they arrive. It certainly is a long journey for the girls," Luiz continued.

"Well, the leaf cover is getting seriously scant out there. So, I am praying that Gabbie can get a positive result for us. It's a worrying situation, and it looks like the rust is resisting our own sprays, Papa," replied his youngest son. "I received an email from the US today, asking for an update on delivery times for the first shipment of coffee from us into New Jersey. I was going to wait on the call from Vietnam from Bianca or Gabbie before I replied to them. So, we will have to delay our response until that happens. Shit, I hate this waiting!" continued Mateus.

"Yes, it is hard, son, but just hold off until we get some indication. I reckon we will know if we can get through this awful time in two or three days. The tests should not take that long to carry out and, even if their

Scientific section is not that great, Gabrielle has the skills to sort it out. She reckons Dai has the necessary brains too, so let us leave it to the ones who know, hey?" offered Luiz to his despondent son.

Mateus, Luiz's strongest and most dependable child, gave a nod to his father, offered a forced smile, and muttered, "If you say so, Papa. If you say so."

Airport Pickup

Dai Ca Phung parked his Range Rover 4WD car in the short-stay section of the car park at the international airport on the south side of Ho Chi Minh City. After a pleasant early dinner with Dung Lam and his mother the previous night, Dai had sneaked in a couple of hours sleep at home before heading off in his car for the long trip down to the airport. At that time of night, the roads were not too busy and his recently bought Range Rover had navigated the journey well. After a couple of coffee breaks along the way, he had managed to reach his destination by 7.30am local time. Plenty of time, in his estimation, to freshen up in the airport lounge area and look suitably attired to greet Bianca and Gabrielle after they came through the Customs area.

He had brought along a casual, yet smart, extra set of clothing in his Ralph Lauren suit bag. The bag had been a thoughtful birthday present from his mother last August and it had accompanied him on many trips in the last twelve months. As he reached the entry to the busy airport concourse, he spied the familiar signage indicating the Vietnam Airways Business Lounge. Dung Lam had set his stepson up as a member of the exclusive VA Business Club after he had promoted him to the position of Managing Director at Lam Dong Coffee, well-earned in Dai's own opinion, eighteen months previously. He had had the opportunity to travel to a few local countries in Southeast Asia – Laos, Thailand, Cambodia and Taiwan so far – to promote and enhance the market penetration of Lam

Dong Coffee products and services. His efforts had certainly increased the profile of the company's brand in all these destinations. He hoped to conquer other, more populated countries like Malaysia, Indonesia and the Philippines in the years ahead. But for now, his firm concentration was on Brazil, South America, and its huge coffee-consuming northern neighbour of the USA. He entered through the doors of the swanky VA Business Club Lounge on the first floor. Within twenty minutes he had taken a refreshing shower and shaved. He changed into his fresh set of clothes and placed his old travelling clothes inside the suit bag. A final comb of his thick, jet-black hair and a peek into the mirror finalised his transformation from a ruffled traveller into the confident, youthful businessman that Dai perceived himself to be. He wanted to look good for his beautiful visitor and, of course, her mother. He even had time to purchase and quickly consume a welcome cup of strong coffee before heading down to the International Arrivals gate to meet Gabrielle. Looking up at the digital information screen, mounted above the food servery within the lounge, he checked Gabrielle's flight details. The Air France flight, originally due in at 6.40am, had been delayed and had landed an hour late. He calculated that, by the time they had passed through International Customs Control, they would not be coming out into the main entrance for a little while yet.

Down on the ground-floor level, he smartly nipped inside one of the many overpriced retail outlets that surrounded the main airport concourse area. He quickly chose a Hoa Lan, a multi coloured orchid indigenous to Vietnam, as a gift for Gabrielle. Dai then bought a beautiful silk scarf for Bianca. Without looking at the price, he quickly swiped his company Mastercard across the top of the machine at the service desk, asked for them both to be gift-wrapped and headed off to meet his guests with haste, one gift in each hand, the strapping of his suit bag draped over his right shoulder.

A mass of eager and excited people was already queuing four deep at the exit area, waiting for each of their loved ones to appear through the automatic doors. As every weary traveller came through the gates, pushing their over-burdened luggage trolleys, one or two of the waiting throng would uncontrollably burst into tears as their special people appeared. Dai was becoming quite emotional himself watching these interactions as he waited. He then saw, on the video screen above the doors, the image he had longed for. Gabrielle and Bianca came into camera view, making their way slowly along the white corridor leading up to the exit door. Gabrielle was wearing a huge smile and talking excitedly with her mother as they emerged through the door. They both started looking in all directions for their Vietnamese host. Gabrielle set eyes on Dai first and raced towards him, leaving her mother to push the well-stacked luggage trolley for the remainder of the way. Dai's face lit up with joy as he opened his arms wide to accept the embrace of his Brazilian beauty.

"Hello, Dai, so wonderful to see you again!" said an excited Gabrielle, as she melted into his arms and kissed him frantically.

"Wow, I didn't think that I had missed you so much until this moment," replied Dai, as he affectionately returned her kiss and held her tight. Looking over her shoulder he smiled at Bianca as she caught up with the loving couple. "Don't mind me, kids!" she stated drily, trying to suppress her own feeling of joy.

"Oh, Mum, isn't it so wonderful to see Dai again?" gushed Gabrielle, wiping a few tears from her jade eyes and smiling.

"Of course, it is, my dear. How are you, Dai? So lovely of you to meet us on our arrival," said Bianca, looking at him and holding out a hand to shake.

"Great to see you both looking so well, Bianca. Although we still have a long road trip back to my hometown, so I guess we'd better get going. Here, please accept these gifts from Vietnam to Brazil for you both."

Dai handed Gabrielle her Hoa Lan and Bianca her scarf, and they thanked him graciously. He gallantly took the heavy trolley from Bianca's grip in his right hand and deposited his own suit bag on top of the teetering luggage, before offering his free hand to Gabrielle and quickly sauntering off towards the airport exit. Bianca hastily followed behind them, only just managing to keep up with the exceedingly happy young couple.

Road Trip to
Buon Ma Thuot

Three hours later, the two women were in the comfortable back seat of the Range Rover and Dai sat alone in the front, driving in silence. At first, the Brazilians had marvelled at the lush, green landscapes of Southern Vietnam, as they were whisked past vistas of paddy fields and unusual tree varieties on their long journey northwards to Dak Lak Province. Both women had finally given in to their collective tiredness and had fallen asleep on each other in the back only an hour or so into the journey.

"I need to stop to fill up with petrol, Bianca," said Dai, as he saw her awake from her slumber, in his rear-view mirror. "Would you like something to eat or drink?"

"Oh, thank you, Dai, that would be great. Poor Gabbie is still asleep, though," she whispered back. "But I will try to wake her. She probably needs a toilet break as well, I know that I do. We must look rather ragged to you, Mr Phung, or should I say Dai?" As she spoke in whispers to Dai, she grimaced at her own image in the makeup mirror she had held up to her face.

"Yes, I could do with a break, too. There is a service station not too far ahead, I think. Maybe we will stop there for a rest and a freshen up, eh?" responded Dai.

At that moment, Gabrielle awoke from her sleep, very groggy and disorientated. "Hello, Mum, have we landed yet?" she enquired of her amused mother.

"Darling, we are in Dai's car, halfway to his hometown; you have been sleeping for almost two and a half hours. It's time for an R & R stop for the tired young man!" she replied with a smile.

"Oh dear, of course, so sorry," she said, leaning forward to place her delicate hand onto his tired shoulder and giving it a loving pinch. "Where are we? How far is it to your home, Dai?" she asked softly.

"You both must be so tired, after such a long journey. We'll stop here, at this service station," he replied, indicating right, before guiding the Range Rover onto the apron of the Petrolimex service station and stopping next to one of the multiple petrol bowsers. "Still another four or five hours to go yet, I'm afraid," said Dai, as he pulled on the handbrake, pressed the ignition button to kill the engine and flipped the petrol cap open from the internal catch. After the local attendant had filled the tank, Dai paid for the petrol and then drove the car into a vacant parking spot and all three travellers got out of the Range Rover and headed for the service centre.

The conversation at the service station and back in the car, on their way up north, was primarily about the problem currently affecting the Nova Coffee plantation. Gabrielle had now placed herself in the front seat of Dai's Range Rover, next to her "boyfriend". Her mother sat in the back section alone and spent most of the trip sending texts, via WhatsApp, back to her father and brothers, updating them on their progress so far. She realised that all three would be anxious about the results that would come from the Lam Dong Coffee testing facilities – so much was hanging on them getting some positives from this rushed visit to Vietnam. Despite this worry, she smiled to herself seeing the playful and loving interaction between her daughter and Dai in the front seats. They certainly seemed to be a good match for each other, intellectually and personally. Bianca was trying to keep up with some of the more technical issues that Gabrielle was discussing with Dai, but some of the scientific facts and figures that were being mentioned were beyond her comprehension. In her eyes, the main reason that Gabrielle had wanted her over here in Vietnam as a travelling companion was for her to perform a "babysitting" role, although her daughter was far from a shrinking violet, and she could hold her own in most social and work-related situations. The fact that she had fallen so hard for this eloquent and charming young man within such a short time meant that she believed there was a genuine chance of a future in the relationship. Gabrielle needed to have her mother's blessing on this matter, so the visit to Buon Ma Thuot was for two reasons. Firstly, of course, was to eliminate the virus problem in Brazil. But secondly, and maybe even more importantly, was the chance to meet and be introduced to Dai's family and their way of life. It was a task that Bianca had all the skills for, except for speaking the local language.

It was almost 6pm before the trio got close to Dai's hometown. The hot setting sun, low in the sky to the left of the Range Rover, was throwing long shadows across the green landscape, as Dai expertly drove his 4WD as quickly as the 100km-per-hour speed limit would allow him. Eventually, the signpost for Buon Ma Thuot appeared ahead. Dai smiled as he saw the familiar landmark sign. He directed the big 4WD off the major highway to get onto the smaller road that led towards his hometown. Within 15 minutes they were crossing the Dak Krong River over an elevated bridge. This river signified the border between the two provinces of Dak Lak to the east and Dak Nong to the west.

"This is the place where I was born, Gabbie. I have lived all of my life here," pronounced Dai very proudly. Twenty-five kilometres further down the highway they approached a large intersection that had a huge monument as its centrepiece. Dai explained to a very curious Gabrielle and Bianca that this was the Buon Ma Thuot Victory Monument, which was built in the late 1970s to commemorate the events of 10th March 1975, when VC and North Vietnamese troops liberated the city from the fleeing South Vietnamese soldiers during the last stages of the American War.

"You called it the Vietnam War, in the West. The Victory Monument is rather a modern sculpture, which consists of a column supporting a central group of figures holding a flag, with a modernist arch forming a rainbow over a concrete replica tank."

The women were mightily impressed with their driver's local knowledge and Gabrielle said, "Well, Dai, as well as being the Managing Director of a coffee company, you are also a local historian! Well done. What other skills do you have?"

"This town is a big tourism destination, so it helps to know about our history and all the places of interest. Vietnam is a quickly developing country, Gabbie – you'll grow to love it, I'm sure," advised Dai. "Wait until you see the Coffee Plantation area, not far away now!" he added with a huge grin on his face.

Gabrielle leant back, turned her head and made a funny face at her mother, who looked quite shocked at Dai's remarks. "He certainly is a patriot, Mother!" she said quietly.

Dai drove on as the outer suburbs of the city melted into a much greener and more heavily vegetated region of Buon Ma Thuot to the north-east of the city. After a short while he began indicating to turn right from the main highway, just after entering the district of Hoa Thuan. "Almost there!" shouted Dai, excitedly, as he pulled the steering wheel to the right onto a local road, signposted *Durong so 25B* – simply translated as Road Number 25B. It was a road of slender width, bordered on both sides by a mass of mature coffee bean trees. Gabrielle noticed a local café on the roadside, on her side of the car. "Oh, look, Dai. One of your local haunts, I bet... Cafe Pha May – do you know it?" she asked.

"Of course, I know all of the cafes in Buon Ma Thuot!" he responded. "They all sell Lam Dong Coffee." He added proudly, "That one is owned by Dung Lam's niece, Nhi. She is a lovely girl!"

Bianca was now taking notice of the very green surrounds from her view in the back seat. "I am so looking forward to meeting your stepfather and your mother, Dai. If they have done nothing else in their lives, they have certainly raised a fine young man as their son," she remarked.

Dai became strangely quiet after that compliment. After a moment's consideration, he glanced at Bianca in his rear-view mirror and quipped, "I couldn't agree with you more, Bianca. I am sure that they will love Gabbie just as much."

Within ten minutes the Range Rover had arrived at Dai's parents' house, a surprisingly modern-looking two-storey homestead, built close to the Lam Dong plantation. He had called his mother on his mobile, just as they arrived at Buon Ma Thuot, advising her that they would arrive within twenty minutes. Mai Thi and her husband Dung Lam were already outside their house, standing on their wooden balcony waving excitedly as Dai drove his car into the visitor's spot, in front of the garage door.

Both Gabrielle and Bianca were frantically adding last-minute makeup and lipstick to their faces using the internal mirrors, and seemed very keen to get out of Dai's car as soon as they could. Dai jumped out first to get the luggage out and waved at his parents as he spied them above him on the first floor of the building.

"Hi Mum. Hi stepfather!" he called out. "It's been a long trip, but it is so good to be home at last. Can you please open the garage door and we will come in that way to save you coming downstairs? I will roll the girls' luggage in there. Then I can introduce you all to each other."

Dung Lam had already had the same idea, and the roller door was on its way up before Dai could finish his sentence. Bianca and Gabrielle finally got out of the Range Rover and dutifully followed Dai inside the house through the garage door, which led through a door to the downstairs living area and then up a set of stairs, bordered by ornately carved wooden handrails. Although the exterior of the house had a modern appearance, the inside rooms were beautifully furnished and decorated in traditional Vietnamese fashion. When Dai and the women finally ascended the staircase, they were greeted by Mai Thi and Dung Lam, standing in the middle of their main living area, with broad, welcoming smiles on their happy faces. Dai took his cue and started the conversation.

"Bianca and Gabrielle, may I introduce you both to my mother, Mai Thi, and her husband, my stepfather, Dung Lam." Now he indicated the guests. "And, Mother and Father, can I please introduce Bianca Almeida and her daughter, Gabrielle, to you both. All the way from Brazil!" he added triumphantly.

Dung Lam could speak a little French and English, so managed to be courteous, charming and understood by his new guests. Mai Thi had a small amount of French to offer and both Gabrielle and her mother responded in whichever tongue they were addressed in. It was slightly embarrassing all around, but the Brazilians were certainly given a warm and friendly greeting.

Mai Thi, as chief hostess, ushered the two guests towards an array of food and drink that she had obviously been preparing all afternoon. Dung Lam, in his gentlemanly manner, indicated they should be seated in the comfortable chairs that surrounded the beautifully carved wooden table, which was covered with a feast of local Vietnamese food and cooling drinks. He immediately began, in slightly hesitant English, to slowly utter more kind words of welcome to their guests.

"So very lovely to meet you both, ladies. We hope that your visit here to our humble coffee plantation will prove a positive thing for your Nova Coffee business and that we can help you, in a good way, with the current virus problem you are experiencing in your homeland. We know how these things can affect you so drastically and we understand the hurt and the emotional upheavals that these issues can bring to a family business. We certainly feel your pain, as we have had our own struggles in this area in the past. We all look forward to helping you out. Our home is your home for the duration of your stay. So, please have some drinks and some food that Mai has prepared."

Bianca and Gabrielle looked at each other meekly, until the younger Brazilian took a slight intake of breath and responded to Lam Dung's heartfelt welcome. "Mr and Mrs Lam, my mother and I are so grateful for your amazing hospitality. We are so touched by your genuine warmth and understanding of our difficult situation at present, also by this beautiful welcome you have put on for us both. I was fortunate enough to meet your beautiful son, Dai, in Brazil and I am so happy to have had the opportunity to visit his homeland now and to also meet his parents. I can see now why he has such lovely manners and why he knows how to treat people so well. You certainly have done amazingly well to have raised such a lovely boy. A boy who has made me so incredibly happy in such a short time. Thank you both," said Gabrielle, all the time glancing at Dai's adoring face, in between smiling at his parents.

"And I would also like to add," added Bianca, "how grateful we are for your son's help in this matter and to you, dear Mai Thi, for letting us stay with you, here in your wonderful home. I hope that we can repay your generosity in the future with a visit to our home in Brazil, sometime soon, if you would like that."

Dai quickly translated both sets of words to his mother and her face lit up in joy; she bowed her head to both Bianca and Gabrielle as he told her what they had said. Dung Lam sat in his chair with a proud smile on his face as he heard the women speak, understanding and appreciating all the words uttered. It was then all smiles at the Lam household for the next hour or so, as everyone got to know each other better and the food and drink was devoured, especially by the tired travellers. Mai Thi introduced Gabrielle and Bianca to their respective guest bedrooms and Dai was looking forward to a well-deserved sleep in his own apartment as the night wore on.

"I think I will get off home to my place, Mum. I need a good sleep. Perhaps I can drop round in the morning and pick up Bianca and Gabrielle, how about 10.30? I can then take them to our office and factory and get started on what we need to achieve. The quicker the better, I think!" said Dai. "I know you will look after our guests."

"Of course, my boy, leave it to me. I have taken the day off from work tomorrow, so all is in hand. Do not forget to say goodnight to that beautiful Gabrielle, Dai. You are so lucky to have found such a lovely young lady!" teased his mum.

"Okay, Mum, I love you so much," he said, with a kiss to her cheek, before heading off to find Gabbie. He found her in deep conversation with Dung Lam on the outside balcony. His stepfather looked to be in awe of the young scientist he had been chatting to. "You have a good one here, young man!" he said as Dai approached.

Gabrielle's face lit up as Dai came into view. "Are you going home, Dai?" she asked. "I'll walk you to the car, if you like!" she added boldly. "I really need to get into my own bed too, I am so tired now."

"Yes, that would be great, Gabbie. I will come back at around 10.30am to pick up you and Bianca to take you to Lam Dong in the morning. Where is your mum?"

"She's just gone to bed; she is super tired after the long flights and road trip. You must be so tired, yourself, Dai," said Gabrielle. "Let's get you to the car, hey?"

With that the two lovers went off hand in hand down the staircase, through the open garage door and out towards Dai's Range Rover. Now out of sight of the parents upstairs, Dai stopped abruptly and turned to face Gabbie in the shadows of the coffee tree canopy. He drew the young Brazilian towards him, gently cupped his hands around her jawline and pulled her expectant lips towards his. They kissed long and passionately. He held her tight against his body and ran his fingers through her hair, looking deep into her jade-coloured eyes and kissing her again. Her eyes closed and a warm rush enveloped her body; she smiled wildly as she pulled

Dai closer and opened her eyes. He was smiling amorously.

"To be continued!" he whispered, as he prised himself from her loving grip. "Goodnight, my love. I will see you in the morning. Sleep well," he softly said as he slipped away towards the waiting car.

Gabrielle watched him go, turned around and walked through the garage door and up the stairs. She saw Dung Lam and Mai Thi sitting happily in their lounge area, waved them goodnight and found her bedroom. She quickly undressed, washed her face, brushed her teeth, and put on her nightdress. Within ten minutes she had slipped under the comfortable sheets of her bed and drifted into a deep, deep sleep. She was so excited to see Dai again, but even that would have to wait as sleep overcame her.

Lam Dong Coffee Company

The next morning, Dai had arrived punctually at his parents' home to pick up his two Brazilian guests. Both girls had slept soundly after their lengthy trip. His mother was on the upstairs balcony, waving to him as he pulled his Range Rover into the driveway. "Morning, son, hope you had a good sleep. Gabrielle and Bianca have had breakfast and are ready to go to Lam Dong with you. Dung Lam went into work earlier, around 7am. He said that Dr Chien wanted to talk to him about the testing procedures," called Mai Thi at Dai as he got out of his car. He entered through the open garage door and was quickly up the stairs.

Gabrielle was there waiting for him and embraced him as soon as he stepped inside the house. This time the kiss was more reserved, but still warm and loving.

"Hi, Gabbie, I hope you had a great sleep?" Dai asked, through smiling eyes and a cheeky grin. "Where is your mother? Is she ready to go?"

"Yes, Dai, we are both ready to go, thank you. Your mother has been an absolute angel, looking after both of us. She's just wonderful!" replied Gabrielle. "Mum is just applying a bit of makeup, you know that she likes to look good and make a positive impression."

At that moment, right on cue, Bianca appeared from her bedroom looking resplendent in a colourful lightweight blouse, three-quarter length pants and some sensible flat-heeled shoes. "Will this be okay to wear, Dai?" she asked.

"Looks fine to me, Bianca," responded Dai.

Mai Thi had silently entered the room behind Bianca and smiled sweetly at her guests and Dai. She gave her son a motherly hug and kissed him on the cheek. "Make sure you look after these lovely ladies well today, Dai. I am sure that all the staff will be excited to meet them both. I will have dinner ready for you all tonight when you return home."

"Thanks, Mum, for looking after our guests so well and for being a wonderful mum to me, as well," answered Dai, giving her a peck on the cheek. "Let's go, ladies." He pointed the way out with a courteous wave of his right hand. The excited women smiled, said their goodbyes to his mother, and headed off down the stairs.

As Gabrielle passed Dai, he asked her quietly if she had all the "things" that they needed for the testing. "All in my bag, Dai," she responded with a wink.

Within ten minutes they had arrived at the offices of Lam Dong Coffee. Dai parked his car in his allotted spot and quickly opened the back door to let Bianca out of the car, as Gabrielle collected her carry bag from the Range Rover's front passenger seat well.

"I am so looking forward to this, Dai!" she exclaimed, as they entered the front doors of the office building. Once inside, the air-conditioning system ensured some relief from the searing heat that had welcomed them after they had exited the car. Dai directed the visitors up a set of stairs towards the office level above. At the top of the stairs stood Dai's secretary, Tina, smiling sweetly at the trio.

"Welcome back, Mr Phung," started his pretty assistant. "And a big welcome to our two visitors, all the way from Brazil!" she continued, offering a courteous handshake to both Gabrielle and her mother.

"Thank you, Tina. This is Gabrielle Souza and her mother Bianca Almeida, from the Nova Coffee Company," said Dai.

"You have had such a long trip from your homeland, ladies. Welcome to Vietnam. I will prepare some of our local coffee for you all, while you get settled in. Shall I serve it in the boardroom, Mr Phung?" Tina enquired of her boss.

"That would be wonderful, Tina," he replied, as he ushered his guests towards his office and the boardroom.

Entering Dai's office, Gabrielle was extremely impressed with his choice of furniture and fixtures. "You certainly have great taste in office furnishing,

Dai. And Tina seems nice," she added, with a forced smile. "How long has she been working with you?"

"Since I have been in the position of Managing Director, nearly two years now, I think. She is great to work with, very loyal, and she looks after me," Dai responded.

Gabrielle took a seat at the boardroom table and proceeded to empty the contents of her bag neatly onto the ornate surface, sorting them into specific piles. Bianca sat down opposite her daughter and looked alarmed when she noticed a plastic bag containing coffee tree leaves and bark samples was amongst the group of things Gabrielle had laid on the table.

"You were lucky that the Customs Officials didn't find those in your luggage, Gabbie. You took a bit of a risk bringing those into Vietnam, darling!" she exclaimed.

"But, Mum, I didn't bring them in. You did!" replied her daughter, with a wicked smile on her face.

"What do you mean, I did?" queried her perplexed mother.

"You may need to talk to Uncle Mat about that when we get home. It was his idea. He asked me to hide them in your makeup bag and keep it quiet. Sorry, Mum!" laughed Gabrielle.

"I'll kill my brother one day! He has been doing things like this to me all my life. And you knew all along!" Bianca said angrily, although she was hiding a smile.

"We thought it best that you didn't know, you might have worried too much. At least we don't have to carry anything back with us. Except, perhaps, for some of the antidote if we find it," added Gabrielle.

At this stage Dai joined the conversation. "It is really my fault, Bianca. I was the one who asked for the samples to be brought across from Brazil, it would have taken weeks to get them sent over in the normal, official way. So sorry. We are up against it, timewise. You must understand that?"

"Oh, I know, I know!" said Bianca. "I do understand how important this all is, so I will talk to Mateus when I get back home. Let's keep going, eh?"

"We'd better get these samples down to Dr Chien right now, in fact," stated Dai, as he called in Tina, so that she could take the samples downstairs.

As timely as ever, Tina then arrived with a tray of coffee, milk, sugar and local biscuits. This broke the tension in the room and allowed Dai to set the agenda for the meeting in a businesslike manner. It also made

Gabrielle take notice of the fact that, as well as being an able and efficient assistant, Tina was incredibly beautiful. Might Tina's relationship with her boss have been more than a professional one, in previous times? "I'll have to ask Dai," she thought to herself.

"Thanks for the refreshments, Tina. Can you please drop this bag of samples down to Dr Chien in the lab? Also, let him know Gabrielle and I will be down there shortly to explain the contents," explained Dai.

Tina took the samples from Dai, nodded in response to his request and proceeded downstairs to pass them on to the laboratory, where Dai's existing antidote would be tested against the actual virus-laden pieces. All along Dai, of course, knew that the Vietnamese antidote would arrest the spread of the virus and they would be able to apply this to the Brazilian crop and avert the disaster. Only he knew this truth, so he needed to hide certain details of the testing from Dr Chien, as well as ensuring that neither Gabrielle nor Bianca found out that he had sabotaged the trees at Nova Coffee.

Dai then seemed to have an urgent thought, causing him to excuse himself from his two guests. "I am sorry, ladies. I just need to go down to the lab for a couple of minutes to talk to Dr Chien. Please, relax. Enjoy the drinks and biscuits. I will be back very quickly," he said in a serious tone. Then he was gone.

Bianca looked at Gabrielle with a smile. "I could do with a hot coffee!"

Dai returned within five minutes, poured himself a coffee and joined his two guests at the boardroom table.

The next two hours saw the trio discuss the whole problem of the leaf rust at the Nova Coffee plantation and how they proposed to fix it. Gabrielle and Dai took the lead, with Bianca following what she could understand, interspersed with strolls to the office window to stretch her legs when things got a bit too technical.

By meeting's end, Dai suggested that they all go down to the factory floor for a quick tour of the Lam Dong Coffee operation and then head over to the laboratory to oversee the testing of Gabrielle's samples. Bianca asked if, after the tour of the production area, she could be excused from the laboratory agenda to send some emails back to Nova Coffee and if Tina could help her in this task. Dai agreed and Tina, in her limited English, said that Bianca should just come upstairs when she was ready to begin her emails to Brazil.

Dai took great pride in introducing all the production staff to the esteemed visitors from Brazil and, in turn, Gabrielle and her mother were pleasantly surprised with the level of professionalism and quality of product that the Lam Dong Coffee Company produced in this Third-World factory. At the end of the tour, Bianca excused herself from the group and made her way back to the upstairs office area, ably escorted by one of the happy workers, to work on her messages home. Dai and Gabrielle thanked the production staff and then made their way on to the laboratory section of the factory. Tina had earlier informed Dr Chien that Dai and his visitor would be on their way after the quick tour of the factory was over. Chien had ensured that all his best staff were there to meet the important guest from overseas and had briefed his team on what was expected of them. As Gabrielle and Dai entered the main entrance doors to the scientific complex, Chien was standing there waiting to greet them.

"Hello again, Mr Phung, good to see you. I assume that this young lady is the budding scientist from Nova Coffee?" said Chien, offering a hand of greeting to Gabrielle.

"Gabrielle, this is Dr Phan Chien, Lam Dong's Head of Science and Research. Doctor, may I introduce Gabrielle Souza," said Dai.

Gabrielle looked up at the exceedingly tall scientist and began, "So wonderful to meet you, Dr Chien, Dai has told me all about you. I look forward to working with you and your team, so that we can find a cure for our problem in Brazil. Thank you for helping us out in our hour of need. Where shall we start, doctor?"

Chien then proudly took his guest on a short tour of the well-equipped laboratory and introduced Gabrielle to his team of scientists. They were most impressed with her knowledge of the scientific aspects of the coffee industry and she ingratiated herself even more by her attempt to converse with them in their local tongue, with Dai Ca Phung helping her out in the art of pronunciation. The translation books she had studied on the long plane trip over to Vietnam had given her a basic grasp of the language, which she readily admitted still needed a lot more practice.

Dai and Gabrielle were decked out in crisp, white lab coats before commencing on the testing processes required, alongside Dr Chien and his team. Dai had ensured, during his brief earlier meeting with Chien, that the use of the newly developed Lam Dong antidote serums were tested and analysed ahead of other options available. Dr Chien was watching his every move and Dai knew it. Gabrielle was, as ever, clinical and precise with all the tests she was overseeing. She might have been the only female in the laboratory that day, but she wanted to make sure that she left her own personal stamp on proceedings. Dai looked on with admiration, Dr Chien with a modicum of disdain and jealousy.

The Boys from Brazil

In the office of Nova Coffee, Felipe was looking at an email, recently received from his sister in Vietnam. It was rather a long correspondence, so he printed off two copies so that his brother and father could read it at their leisure. It seemed that Bianca was enjoying her visit to Southeast Asia and it appeared that Gabrielle was overjoyed to have been reunited with Dai Ca Phung. Although the final testing had not yet been completed, it seemed that, according to Dai and Gabrielle, there would be a very good chance that an antidote could be speedily produced that would eradicate the viral problem that Nova Coffee was experiencing. Bianca stressed that she would be able to verify this, hopefully within 24 hours, after getting confirmation from Gabbie. The email then went on for quite a while, describing the Lam Dong Coffee Company's attributes, including its people, machinery, and its size in relation to their own company. She was also very complimentary about Dai's family and how hospitable and welcoming they had been to Gabbie and herself.

Felipe read the whole email and a smile crept across his face. All the work he had done to make this deal with the USA become a reality now looked like ending in a positive manner. He understood the increased income and prestige from this huge venture could take his beloved Nova Coffee Company to the next level internationally and enable him to show his full worth to his father. He grabbed the two copies of Bianca's email from the office printer and quickly walked across to the Almeida homestead, where Mateus and his father were in a meeting. They would be overjoyed with the news.

"Positive news so far, boys!" said Luiz to his two sons, as he quickly scanned the contents of Bianca's email. "But before we get excited, let's wait for the okay from Gabbie first, then we can start planning how we get the antidote serum over to Brazil as quickly as possible, hey? What's your plan, Mat, to implement the spraying on the trees?" he asked of his younger son.

"Well, as you know, we have already bought and installed the temporary shade netting sheets that Felipe got up from São Paulo. So that should buy us a bit of time. Then, if we can get the serum from Vietnam in a strong enough concentration to allow mass spraying with our latest apparatus, we can have the whole northern area covered within two days. Then cross our fingers and pray, I suppose," replied Mateus.

"Shipping of the first consignment will take approximately seven days to the Port of New York and New Jersey out of São Paulo. We need to get that shipment there at the latest by the end of September to meet our contract terms," said Felipe. "How long will the harvesting and packaging take, Mat?" he asked, looking at his younger brother.

Mateus looked through his files, situated on his father's desk, to confirm his figures. "For the first drop, the quantity we need to ship should take us around three to four weeks to pick, sort and pack. Say, three days to containerise and haul down to the docks at Santos. Let's say five weeks in total once the berries are ready to harvest, assuming they are plump and healthy after we have applied the spray. Is that enough time, Felipe?"

"Maybe," answered his brother. "But it will be extremely touch and go!"

Luiz listened intently to his two sons and then asked his own questions. "If we fall short for the initial drop of beans into the US, do you think that any of our local suppliers could make up the shortfall, if we asked them? And if not, what are your thoughts on giving the Vietnamese a chance to help us out, boys? From what I have read on the internet and from the people I know in our industry, it seems that they have developed a great robusta-style bean, perhaps among the best in the world. They are also awfully close to growing an excellent quality arabica. The smaller portion of this contract for the USA includes robusta beans, doesn't it? They would have ample supply in Vietnam to get us over the line on the first consignment, wouldn't they?"

A worried-looking Mateus spoke first. "Good thinking, Papa, but the Quality Control section of the Tender document specifies that only South American produce can be used in the arabica portion of the order. However, the robusta portion can be sourced from wherever, as long as the quality is good enough."

Felipe added, "At the last Coffee Growers Association meeting Mateus and I attended, a few weeks back, it seemed that most of the growers in this part of Brazil, had their order books full, without a lot of room to move on their quota figures. But I can send out a general email to the ones that we have worked with in the past to see if they are holding any immediate overstock that we could utilise."

"I would rather not get local beans, if it can be helped," interrupted Luiz. "It has taken Nova decades to get to the position we are at now. Noted as clearly the best grower and supplier of the arabica bean in this country. We cannot risk putting any inferior product into the US market with our name on it. It could affect our future sales – we do not need that! So, I would say that we contact Gabrielle and Bianca in Vietnam. Mateus, you ring or Skype your sister in Vietnam. Work out with Felipe what exactly we need in robusta beans for the first delivery and ask Bianca to negotiate a price, including shipment direct to the US, for the smallest quantity, so we can buy off them to fulfil our obligations on this first order. Delivery must be by the specified date into Jersey, whatever we have to do," finished a now very fired-up Luiz.

He added, "Felipe and Mateus, even if we lose a bit of margin on this first shipment, we will make it up on future shipments. Ask your sister and your niece to get some assurances on the quality of Dai's robusta beans and ask her to insist that the packaging is branded 'Nova Coffee'. While you are at it, ask them if they also have any way of getting the beans to the US by the end of September, bearing in mind they may need to airfreight them. Get Bianca to check airfreight costs out of Vietnam. The girls will need to convince Dai and his company that, in the long run, they will benefit from all of this."

"Okay, Papa," said Mateus. "Let's give it a go, but we will need to keep the origin of the robusta content of the first order quiet within the association. We do not want to start any bickering among our fellow Brazilians, do we, Felipe?"

"Certainly not. The good news is that if you now only need to harvest the arabica beans, that may save us some precious time, hey?" chirped Felipe.

"Definitely!" replied his younger sibling. "And I am sure that we can supply the whole arabica content, as long as this new serum works on the foliage."

"Felipe, can you please make sure that we contact the relevant people in the States and advise we are on schedule with the first shipment as soon as we hear back from Vietnam? Thanks, son," requested Luiz.

"No problems," replied his eldest boy.

"I think I will have an early night. It has been a big day. Let me know how we are going in the morning, okay? Thanks, boys," finished Luiz, hugging both of his sons and heading off to his bedroom.

As he sat down on his bed, he held his hand to his head as a piercing, sharp pain made him grimace. He felt for the medication bottle that sat on the bedside table, turned the lid, and poured out a pill. Gingerly getting to his feet, he made his way to the bathroom to get a glass of water to help swill down his pill. Still not feeling that well, he undressed and settled into bed. Within ten minutes he was asleep.

A Testing Time

By the end of their first day in the Lam Dong Coffee laboratory, Gabrielle and Dai were excited by the results they were seeing. After analysing all the samples that Gabrielle had brought over from Brazil and feeding in the information that Mateus had sent over to Dai, it seemed that the local antidote from Vietnam had the ability to halt the virus successfully. They had conclusively determined what chemical combination had caused the Brazilian leaf rust to occur and which pests were spreading the disease. All they now needed to do was to "poison" a fresh coffee tree sapling with this concoction and then infuse the new antidote, once it was infected. If this experiment worked, then Dai and Gabrielle were agreed that Lam Dong Coffee could supply enough of the serum to send back to Brazil as soon as possible. Dr Chien had his misgivings about the speed in which the result had been achieved, but would wait on the physical results before he was sure. The results would be apparent within 24 to 36 hours.

Dai thanked all the scientists in the laboratory, who had worked so diligently to get the experiments finalised so quickly and successfully. He left with Gabrielle around 6.30pm, by which time Bianca had already decided to go back to Mai Thi's house to help prepare dinner for the evening. After sending her email back to Brazil with Tina's help, Bianca became quite weary. Tina offered to call a taxi to take her back to Dai's mother's house around 3pm. The attentive secretary realised that, after Bianca's long journey and all the excitement that she had experienced, maybe she needed a rest before dinnertime. Bianca was very appreciative of the offer, and also welcomed the chance to spend some time together with Mai Thi before her daughter and Dai returned home.

"Sorry, Gabbie, I just need to check my desk before we go to my mother's house. There might be some messages for me to attend to," said Dai, on their way out of the laboratory area of the factory.

"Okay, Dai. Do you think that Mum will still be here?" she enquired.

"We'll soon see," responded Dai, as he started up the stairs. Reaching his office, he saw a written note placed on his desk from Tina.

"Mr Phung, Ms. Almeida has decided to go home to your mother's place. I organised a taxi at around 3pm for her (she has sent her email). No other messages this afternoon, I have dealt with all the phone calls and have emailed some notes into your laptop diary for tomorrow... nothing urgent! Enjoy dinner with your guests and family. Regards, Tina."

"Hey, Gabbie, your mum went home at 3 o'clock. Tina got her a taxi. I wonder what our two mothers are talking about?" queried Dai, as Gabrielle walked into the office behind him.

"My mum will probably be sleeping by now. It has been a long couple of days for us both. I am feeling a bit jaded myself. I hope your mother has not gone to too much trouble with dinner tonight. I reckon that I will be in bed early. We'd better get back, eh?" replied Gabbie.

They quickly drove to the Lam household in the comfort of the Range Rover, both incredibly happy with their day's work, ready for a solid meal and an early night. Dai, of course, really wanted to take Gabrielle back to his apartment, but that moment would have to wait a little longer. Gabrielle would sleep well tonight after her previous few days of travel and Dai knew that.

Communication

The next day Gabrielle and Dai were at the coffee factory by 8.00am. Bianca had decided to have a quiet morning at home with Mai Thi before heading into the office. The two mothers had an entertaining evening the night before, mainly trying to communicate with each other. Mai really could not understand English and Bianca was struggling with Gabrielle's translation books, even though she tried. They found some middle ground by utilising their limited French skills, but all in all they got on surprisingly well and managed somehow to understand each other's meanings. Mai's husband had helped with some translations after he returned home from work and Dai had been immensely helpful over dinner that night. Bianca was slightly younger than her Vietnamese counterpart, but they were of the same generation and both of similar character. Their love of family was equally strong and both mothers were exceedingly happy with the budding relationship between Gabrielle and Dai.

Gabrielle's mother was invigorated after her long sleep and had taken a short stroll after breakfast with Mai Thi around the local area, enjoying the warm temperature and slight breeze. She was already feeling comfortable in this strange new land and Mai Thi's smiling company made it an even better experience. After a shower and changing into some more formal clothing, Bianca headed off to the Lam Dong offices in a taxi with her host, who had planned to return her much-loved and important work in the Coffee Roasting section at Lam Dong.

Gabrielle and Dai had entered the laboratory area with great anticipation that morning after Dai had picked her up in his range Rover from his mother's house. Gabrielle was eager to see how the experiment was unfolding and Dai was more than confident in the results being positive – with good reason. The looming presence of Dr Chien was immediately apparent as they walked into the Scientific area of the offices.

"Good morning," started the tall doctor. "I hope you both slept well. Today will be an interesting day, I feel."

"Good morning, doctor. Yes, we are both keen to see if the experiment will work. It's especially important for the Nova Coffee Company and hopefully for Lam Dong as well," replied a refreshed Gabrielle.

"Is the sapling ready to be checked, doctor?" said Dai abruptly. "There really is no time to waste."

"Yes, Phung, I have personally checked it this morning and the virus seems to have taken hold," responded the aggrieved scientist. "I will let it develop further then apply the antidote serum after we notice more deterioration of the leaves. We should see results later tonight if the serum is successful. Let us hope that we have done our research correctly this time," finished Chien, before tersely excusing himself with a false smile.

Dai seemed quite upset with the conversation. He turned to Gabrielle and asked her to find their lab coats and meet him at the sapling tree sample. "I just need to talk with Chien on my own, if you don't mind, Gabbie. I won't be long," he said calmly, pecking her lovingly on her cheek then storming off towards the doctor's office. Gabrielle moved away, smiled, and said her morning greetings to the scientists already working, in her best Vietnamese. They gracefully bowed their heads and responded in kind. As she moved around the laboratory, she noticed that Dai and Chien were in an animated and heated discussion behind the closed door of the Head Scientist's office. Deciding to stay clear of the argument, she put on her lab coat and laid down Dai's on top of the work bench close to the area where the poor coffee tree sapling was suffering the effects of the controlled poisoning.

When Bianca and Mai arrived at the factory complex, they said their farewells to each other, as Mai headed into the Coffee Production area and Bianca made her way upstairs to the office. She was greeted by Tina and asked her if any response had been forthcoming from Brazil. To her delight, Tina's reply was positive. An email from her brother Mateus had been received during the night and Tina had printed off a copy and placed it on the boardroom table for Bianca to read.

"Thank you, Tina. You have been so helpful, and I really do appreciate it," said a smiling Bianca.

"Thank you, Ms. Almeida. Would you like a coffee?" responded Tina, in her stilted English.

"That would be wonderful. Thank you again, and please call me Bianca, there's no need for formalities, really!"

Tina responded with a shy smile, not fully understanding Bianca's meaning, but understood the drift of her reply.

Bianca walked through towards Dai's office and sat down at the boardroom table. She turned over the sheet of printed paper that had been thoughtfully placed face-down on the highly polished wooden surface and began to read its contents. She searched for a pen from her quilted leather Chanel handbag and made some notes at the bottom of the printed page. Her eyes widened as she read the details of the tasks she had been asked to perform by her brothers and her father. Tasks which she and Gabrielle would be more than capable of doing, but she wondered how her requests would be received by Dai and his stepfather. By the time Tina had reappeared with a tray of coffee and sweet biscuits, Bianca had finalised her notes. She folded the piece of printed paper in half and placed it into her handbag, along with her pen. Taking a sip of her black coffee, she was pleasantly surprised by the depth and flavour of the steaming and aromatic drink.

"Excuse me, Tina," she called out. "What style of coffee is this?"

"It's our latest arabica style. We have been working on the blend for over twelve months now. How do you like, Bianca?" she probed.

"Very good flavour, Tina, very good," she replied with a wide smile, selecting an inviting baked biscuit from the tray. "We Brazilians will need to watch out for the Vietnamese!" she added with a slight laugh.

Headache

Luiz Almeida awoke from a fractured sleep, beads of sweat running down his forehead. The pain was back in his head; a heavy pressure had established itself inside the old man's skull and was causing a throbbing sensation. Flicking on the bedside table lamp, he reached for the bottle of prescribed pills from the table beside his bed, feeling dizzy and noticing that the numbers glowing from his alarm clock read 3.58am. Swallowing down a pill, he reached for his mobile phone and rang Felipe, who lived closest to the Almeida homestead with his partner Eduardo. His call was answered after only three rings by Felipe, who had been awakened suddenly by the shrill ring of his Apple iPhone. His little dog, Olive, ensured that both his parents heard the phone call by yapping incessantly and jumping on Felipe and Eduardo's bed to wake them up.

"Hey, Papa, what's up? It's 4am, are you okay?" spluttered Luiz's eldest son.

"No, son, I think I will need to get to hospital and see a doctor. Can you please call an ambulance? I have headaches... strong ones... Can't speak much longer, please do it as soon as you can!" pleaded a distressed Luiz.

"Stay on the line, Papa, and keep your phone on hands-free, please. I will get someone, and I will be there as soon as I can! Just rest, Papa, and keep this line open," replied a stunned Felipe.

Felipe placed his mobile phone on hands-free and placed it on his bedside cabinet. He quickly picked up the landline and called the closest local ambulance depot. He knew there was one located in the Nova Serrana suburb of São Marcos, fifteen minutes away, and the phone had the number preset. Thankfully, it was quiet at the UPA Call Ready Unit and the operator confirmed that an ambulance was on its way. He switched to his mobile phone and called out to his father, "Papa, can you hear me? The ambulance is on the way, fifteen minutes. I am on my way over to you now, hold on!" Next, he used the landline to call Mateus and finally his father's doctor and friend, David Alma. Mateus answered his call immediately and said he would be over straight away. The doctor took a while to be stirred from his sleep, but when he heard that it was his close friend Luiz Almeida in trouble, he promised he would come straight away and meet them at the hospital in São Marcos.

"Felipe, I am sorry to tell you like this, but you will need to advise the paramedics attending that your father has a tumour in his head and will need to be handled extremely carefully on the way back to the hospital. He did not want to worry you all about this, but now you need to know. I will see you at the hospital," explained Dr Alma, then he hung up.

Felipe replaced the handset, dressed quickly and then, picking up his mobile phone, ran from his house, on the way grabbing his car keys from the hook by the front door. Eduardo was left sitting up in bed, comforting little Olive in his lap, a bemused look on his face.

"Papa, can you hear me? Papa, Papa!" yelled Felipe at the mobile, as he hustled into his car and screeched out of his driveway. Felipe lived only 500 metres from his father's house, so he was there within two minutes. All was deathly quiet as he opened the front door with his spare key and bolted to his father's bedroom, his right leg dragging slightly as he ran. Felipe took in a deep breath and hesitated for a second, before pushing open Luiz's bedroom door. Once inside, he saw his father stretched out on top of the bedsheets, holding his head and obviously in pain – but alive and kicking!

"I am here, Papa, I am here!" he yelled, sitting down on the bed and gently cradling his father in his arms. He mopped the old man's wet brow with the corner of the sheet and kissed him tenderly. "You'll be okay, Papa, you'll be okay!" he whispered softly.

Within ten minutes, Felipe heard the wailing sound of the approaching ambulance and then he saw the flashing of the red lights outside his father's window, as the speeding vehicle braked quickly outside the front of the house. Then another vehicle arrived. The familiar heavy grunting sound of Mateus' 4WD truck was easy to recognise and the sound was so appreciated by his elder brother. At that moment, the paramedics were entering the bedroom after coming through the still-open front door, wielding a stretcher on wheels. Felipe got to his feet and advised them of his father's condition, then left them to tend to his sick father. Almost immediately Mateus' solid frame appeared at Luiz's bedroom door, looking incredulously at what was before him. He hugged his elder brother and Felipe fell into his embrace, weeping uncontrollably.

"The doctor said that Papa has a brain tumour, Mat. He never told us!" Felipe managed between sobs.

"He is in the best hands now," replied Mateus, staying calm. "You did really well, Felipe, really well. We will follow the ambulance in my truck back to the hospital and we can talk to Doc Alma after he has checked him out. Do not worry, Felipe, he is a strong old guy. If anyone can get through this, he will," asserted Mateus to his brother.

"I hope so, Mat, I hope so."

Almost two hours later, Mateus and Felipe were nervously waiting on Dr David Alma's assessment of their father's condition at the Emergency Ward of the local hospital. The waiting room, which had been quite empty on their arrival, was now slowly filling up with locals requiring various levels of medical attention. Finally, the door to the internal Emergency Ward opened and Dr Alma stepped through it, a worried look on his face. The Almeida brothers moved towards him and he beckoned them into a small office next to the waiting room.

"Okay, boys, your father is out of the initial danger. But he needs to have an immediate operation to remove the tumour growing in the frontal lobe of his brain". I know that Luiz had not told you of his problem, so this must come as quite a shock to you both, but it was his decision. As his doctor and as a dear friend, I agreed to stay silent and keep his secret from all you children. It was his wish and he was very keen that I did not tell any of his family about his medical condition. He knew the consequences of his situation, and now the only way of him surviving is to try to remove the tumour. I have put plans in motion with the staff here at the hospital to set up the operating theatre for tomorrow morning. I have contacted the best neuro surgeon I know, Dr Voss from São Paulo, to perform the operation and I will be in attendance with him. He is flying up later this morning. At this stage, your father is under a heavy sedation and is being monitored around the clock, so you will not be able to see him until later this evening at the earliest," explained Dr Alma to the concerned Mateus and Felipe.

"So, we can't see him at all today?" queried Mateus.

"No, I am sorry, he needs to rest totally. But tonight I will check on his situation and call you at Nova Coffee. The facilities here at the hospital are excellent, so he will be in the best of hands, I promise you," the doctor replied. "Please go home and look after your father's beloved Nova Coffee Company, I know that is what he would want you both to do. I have heard that Bianca and Gabrielle are away overseas. Maybe it would be better if they were not told of Luiz's situation until after the operation. Although I will leave that decision up to you both, of course."

"Thank you, Dr Alma, we appreciate all your help and advice. We will get back home now and see what happens from there. Here are both of our mobile phone numbers," said Mateus, handing him their business cards. "We look forward to seeing Papa tonight if we are able," he continued, as his distraught brother put his arm around his stronger sibling and nodded his head in agreement.

"Yes, thank you, Dr Alma," Felipe uttered, as he shook the doctor's hand before walking slowly out of the busy waiting room with his brother leading the way.

Business Lunch at the Café Fa May

Dai Ca Phung and Gabrielle had worked hard all morning verifying results from the ongoing testing of the sapling. As the day wore on, it seemed that the "Lam Dong Antidote", as Gabrielle had begun to call it, seemed to be ticking all the boxes and providing the positive results that she had prayed for. With a smile on her face and a playful pinch of his shoulder, as she looked on at Dai analysing the data, she blurted out, "Poppy will be so happy when we tell him the good news, Dai!"

"Well, it is looking good so far, Gabbie. By tonight we will know for certain," he joyfully replied.

"Let's get a bite of lunch with your mother, eh?"

The couple whisked off their lab coats, hung them on the nearby stand and headed off up to Dai's office. Dr Chien looked on from the inside of his laboratory office as they headed out of his Scientific area, then he opened his office door and walked towards the recovering sapling tree, an evil look on his face. Whatever Dai had said to him earlier in the morning had made him a truly angry person.

Bianca was in deep conversation with Tina as Dai and Gabrielle reached the top of the stairs. She smiled quickly at Tina then turned to Dai and said, "*Xin Chào, Dai. Ban cómuốn ăn tra không?*" Which roughly translated into English means, "Hello, Dai. Do you want lunch?"

A stunned Dai looked at Tina and then back at Bianca and replied, "*Vâng, điều đó thật tuyệt vời!*"

"What does that mean, Tina?" a puzzled-looking Bianca asked.

"Mr Phung says, yes, that would be very good!" responded Tina in her limited English. All four laughed out loud.

"Well done, Mum!" said Gabrielle in her native Brazilian and gave her a spontaneous hug and a kiss on the cheek.

"Well," said a more sedate Dai. "Shall we go out to get some lunch now? We have a lot to discuss."

Dai led the way down the stairs and asked Tina to take calls for him until they returned. Bianca and her daughter followed him, arm in arm. Dai chose to take them to Dung Lam's niece's Café Fa May, which was the closest eating house to the coffee factory and plantation. Dai introduced the Brazilian girls to Nhi, who ran the café, and then she, in turn, introduced them to some wonderfully fresh Vietnamese cuisine. The aromatic smells of coriander, fresh mint and lemongrass greeted the trio as they entered the seating area of the homely eating establishment, as did the more pungent aromas of garlic, ginger and *nước mắm* (fish sauce). Tables were set with decorated bowls, chopsticks and plastic drinking cups.

Dai asked Nhi to serve up a selection of the local dishes for his Brazilian visitors to try. She chose bowls of delicate beef soup (*Phở*) and chicken and winter melon soup, crab omelette, squid stuffed with pork, roasted chicken with lemongrass and beef with bamboo shoots. Each of these were accompanied by steamed rice, cellophane rice noodles and freshly sliced raw vegetables. Dried lily flowers and lotus roots added marvellous flavour and complimented some of the dishes. Dai loved his hot chilli and fish sauces, so Nhi made sure that there were plenty of options for him to choose from. Bianca found the chilli way too hot, but Gabbie loved the heat also. All these dishes were served up at the same time in a banquet style, with desserts and cakes served as between-course snacks, not as a separate, later part of the meal.

During the meal they discussed the successful laboratory tests that the two young scientists had performed during the morning and how happy Gabrielle was with the results. Bianca was comfortable enough to broach the questions that her brother had asked her to discuss with Dai regarding the supply of Vietnamese robusta coffee beans to the US market, direct from Lam Dong Coffee. Dai was ultra-positive about this suggestion and assured Bianca that Lam Dong had plenty of stock of high-grade robusta bean coffee, which could quickly be shipped or airfreighted to the USA. He would have to check costs with his stepfather first and how long it would take to brand the bags of beans with the Nova Coffee logo, as specified by Mateus.

"Bianca, please advise the exact amount your brothers require and where, exactly, we need to ship to in the States. We will also need the consignment details, so that we have no problem getting the beans in to the port. I really understand Nova's need to have excellent quality beans delivered," he said to an exceedingly satisfied Bianca.

He also offered to supply arabica beans, if Nova needed them, as Lam Dong had just perfected a high-quality blend that he was sure the Americans would be happy with. Bianca explained the details of the Tender, which precluded any other arabica styles apart from South American. Therefore, she gracefully declined Dai's offer.

"But maybe, in the future, Nova could incorporate some of the Vietnamese arabica styles in their offerings. Who knows? I was lucky enough to taste your new arabica style at your office this morning. Your lovely secretary offered me a cup. I must say it was rather tasty," enthused Bianca.

Gabrielle was listening in to this conversation and was buoyed by the fact that, if Nova and Lam Dong could work together to their mutual benefit, then the future for Dai and herself looked promising as well. "Oh, Mum, isn't it all so exciting?" she exclaimed.

Dai settled the bill for their lunch and guided Bianca and Gabrielle back into his 4WD for the short trip back to the Lam Dong complex. It had been a very profitable lunch for him and his company if the numbers could be sorted out and the short lead time fulfilled. It had also been a very eye-opening and mouthwatering taste experience for the Brazilians.

The Doctor's Decision

Dr Phan Chien was deeply upset, after his earlier argument with Dai Ca Phung. His younger nemesis had told him, in no uncertain terms, that his days would be numbered at Lam Dong, if he kept on insisting on his "old-fashioned" methods in the laboratory. He had also been berated by Dai Ca Phung in relation to the way in which he treated his staff. Earlier in the day, even his former close friend Dung Lam had belittled him at their morning meeting, when the Lam Dong boss had told Chien that Dai Ca Phung and his ilk were the future of this industry and that maybe it was time for the doctor to step gently into retirement, whilst he still retained some dignity.

He stood in his office, which he kept immaculately clean, and tidied up his desk with a sense of finality. The place was pristine. He opened the top drawer of his desk. Inside was a silver-framed photograph from the seventies, portraying a beautiful Vietnamese girl in her early twenties. Next to her in the pose was a tall, good-looking older man in military uniform. Phan Chien held the frame delicately in his huge hand with a sorrowful look on his wrinkled face, and tears began to flow down his cheeks. This was the final photograph in which the doctor and his beloved fiancée, Chau Lim, featured together. He turned the frame over and slid open the tiny black catches that held the photo inside the back of the frame. He delicately took away the piece of card that supported the photograph and flicked it into the rubbish bin under his tidy desk. He then read the faded, handwritten wording that had been etched onto the back of the picture. It read, "To my darling Phan. Cannot wait to see you in Saigon next week. Love as always, Chau Lim - July 1974", followed by six kisses. She had posted the photograph to her lover as his infantry division were fighting off a Viet Cong military advance, just north of the South Vietnamese capital. The doctor looked aimlessly into space after he had read those words. They cut into his heart, as he remembered how beautiful his fiancée had been and how devastated he was when he returned to Saigon to hear of her death in a North Vietnamese air raid. Their hopes and ambitions for the future had been tragically cut short by this savage act of war, leaving Phan Chien devastated and wishing that he too should have lost his life fighting for his country, rather than facing a life without the woman that he had loved and cherished.

The doctor stirred from his thoughts, ripped the picture from the silver frame and placed it in his jacket pocket. Discarding the elegant silver frame into the rubbish bin, and with an angry look of distain across his grief-stricken face, he strode out of his office for the last time. Walking across to the area where Dai and Gabrielle had been conducting their experiments, he went up to the sapling coffee tree that sat on the laboratory table and viewed it with scorn. The leaf rust appeared to have subsided and the young tree was recovering. He picked up the small tree and tucked under his arm.

"There is no place left for me at Lam Dong!" he thought to himself and stormed out of the Scientific and Research premises and headed out towards the coffee factory and storeroom area of the complex.

Figures, Figures, Figures

Once back at the Lam Dong complex after their delightful lunch, Dai left Gabrielle and Bianca in his office with Tina to organise an email response to Mateus' requests. He rang his stepfather to organise a meeting to discuss the planned business with the Brazilians and to settle on a mutually agreeable price per pound for the required American-bound robusta coffee beans. He had to persuade Dung Lam that the Nova Coffee label could be used for this specific shipment of their beans and needed to check whether the lead time of the end of September was a feasible target. Because of the urgency of this matter, Dung Lam agreed to cancel his planned afternoon agenda to work out a suitable pricing structure with his stepson and evaluate the most effective form of transport to get the goods to the east coast of America from Buon Ma Thuot. He asked Dai to come to his office immediately to ensure they could get the prices sorted out as soon as possible before emailing a written quote to Brazil. Dai indicated to Gabrielle that he was on his way to see Dung Lam and asked if he could get the exact quantity of robusta bags required to meet the poundage needed by America on this first shipment. He explained to Gabrielle that Lam Dong's standard jute coffee bags held approximately 60kg (around 130 pounds in American terms). He would be with Dung Lam until the numbers were crunched, so he needed the required figures back from Nova Coffee as soon as possible.

Gabrielle passed this information onto her mother, who was busy composing an email to Mateus back in Brazil, utilising Tina's reception area. The time was just before 3pm in Buon Ma Thuot, making it just shy of five in the morning in Nova Serrana. Therefore, Bianca was confident of getting an answer back from her brothers within three to four hours. If Dai and Dung Lam could get a price to her before 6pm today, then she could send a supplementary email at that time to confirm costings for Mateus. She first wrote that Lam Dong had the quality and the quantity required of the robusta beans to fulfil the smallish amount that Nova needed, but she needed firm quantities so that packaging, shipping or airfreight and product costs could be calculated. Then she gave Mateus the good news about Gabrielle's testing, and the fact that results would be available in a few hours' time. She would then need to know the approximate area of tree foliage that needed urgent spraying to preserve the valuable arabica beans currently hanging on the affected trees. Finally, she needed copies of the Tender papers for the USA consignment, so she could give Dai the information needed for shipment and port entry purposes and also artwork from Felipe for the Nova Coffee logo to be printed onto the shipping bags. Bianca had to explain that Vietnam still packed in the older style jute coffee bags, even though Nova had recently changed across to the newer polypropylene version. Signing off, she advised how well she was getting on with the team at Lam Dong and that Gabrielle and Dai were getting on better than ever. She finished with a message for her father. "Tell him we are both thinking of him, hope he is pleased with the good news about the virus control and we are looking forward to seeing him when we get back," was her final line.

At 4.30pm Bianca received an email from Mateus with the information needed to get Dai's quote finalised for the quantity of robusta bean bags that were necessary to fill the initial order to the USA. Thankfully, the quantity was the relatively low number of 200 bags with an estimated total weight of around 26,500 pounds. Mateus also added that he was overjoyed with the positive news about the virus testing and that he had his fingers and his toes crossed about the final results, asking his sister to send the information to him as soon as Gabrielle and Dai could verify the good news. He said that he had attached all the relevant paperwork concerning the first shipment to his email and if any more information was required, he asked Bianca to get straight back to him. Mateus confirmed that Felipe would be sending artwork for the Nova Coffee logo branding later, ensuring that the format would be relevant for printing onto jute bags. He also promised to work out how many litres of the virus antidote they would need to successfully spray the affected trees and that he would email that across a little later.

Just as Bianca had finished reading her brother's email, Dai came up the stairs and walked into his office area. On the way through he asked Tina to ring Dr Chien and then send the call through to his office. He approached Gabrielle and Bianca, seated at the boardroom table.

"Any word back from Brazil yet?" he asked.

"Just got the quantity figure back from Mateus, it is not a big figure, only 200 jute bags. But that gives us, or should I say you, the opportunity to airfreight them over to the States. Shipping by container is going take too long, I think. Is that quantity okay to supply, Dai?" replied a nervous Bianca.

"Yes, that figure is perfect. I agree, we do not have the time to ship over by container. But if we need to supply any larger amounts in the future, container shipping is a lot more cost-effective, assuming we have 30 to 40 days to deliver. That is good news, well done, ladies. Dung Lam has finalised costs for quantities by airfreight from 50 to 500 bags, so we should be able to give Mateus a firm cost on 200 bags straight away," responded a relieved Dai.

"Here are the papers for the Port Authority at New York and Jersey, Dai," said Bianca, handing him the copies she had made from her brother's email. "If you need any more information, let me know and I can contact Mateus again. But it looks like everything you will need is there."

"Thank you, Bianca. I will start drafting an official quote to Nova Coffee and get Tina to forward it directly to Mateus. Can you please give her the best email address to reach him? The sooner we get the price okayed by Mateus, the sooner we can start planning production. Oh, also, what about the Nova Coffee logo artwork, do we have that yet?" enquired Dai.

"It will be here by the morning. Felipe is sending it direct by email and it will be formatted for printing onto the standard jute bag. So it shouldn't need any extra work from your printer," chirped Bianca.

"Great. I'd better get on with the quote," said Dai.

At that moment, Tina interrupted their conversation. "I am sorry, Mr Phung, I can't seem to find Dr Chien anywhere in the building. He's not answering his phone or his mobile and no-one has seen him since lunchtime."

Dai asked Tina to ring Dung Lam and see if he knew where the doctor had disappeared to. He then turned to Gabrielle and asked her to go downstairs and check the scientific laboratory. "I will just brief Tina on this quote for Mateus, then I'll meet you down there in a few minutes. Thank you, Gabbie," he said with a forced smile. Gabrielle smiled back and headed out of the office and down the stairs towards the laboratory.

"Can we confirm the virus test results soon, Dai? Mateus will need to know before he confirms the quote, I assume," queried Bianca.

"Yes, of course, Gabbie and I should be able to check downstairs and verify the results very soon. As soon as we find Dr Chien," replied a concerned Dai. "Give me 30 minutes, please, Bianca."

"Yes, of course, I understand," finished Bianca.

Dai turned towards Tina and motioned for them both to go to her office area to get the quote written up and ready to send off to Brazil.

Where is the Doctor?

Downstairs in the laboratory area the last two scientists were leaving work for the day as Gabrielle walked in through the main entrance. She smiled at them and bade them "good evening" in their native tongue. Both smiled back and responded happily, as they clocked off for the night. The room had an eerie, quiet feeling to it as she progressed further into the laboratory, with most of the office lighting turned off as the day's work was over. There was no sign of Dr Chien as she passed by his office, noticing, as she surveyed his desk inside, that it was immaculately clean and tidy. She ventured over to the workbenches where she and Dai had worked on the sapling coffee tree, lit only by the neon flashes of the various testing equipment which glowed constantly, even after lights out. As she turned past the wall that divided the room into administration and scientific areas, she stopped in her tracks. The sapling coffee tree was nowhere to be seen. It had been in the same position all week since they had started the experimentation. Thankfully, Gabrielle discovered that the results pertaining to the finalisation of the virus testing, had been updated in the manual workbook. They had already been signed off as being transferred into the analysing laptop by Dai's diligent team of scientists prior to them finishing work for the day. Taking a deep breath, she signed in and then opened the computer screen, finally clicking on to the page that would show the ultimate result of the testing. As her eyes scanned the screen Gabrielle finally saw the figures that she and Dai had hoped for. There was a "zero" reading recorded for traces of the virus within the sapling, logged in at 4.45pm that day. The Lam Dong Antidote had worked! "Yes!" she whispered softly to herself, and a broad smile lit up the young Brazilian's face.

Her moment of self-congratulation was sharply interrupted by the piercing sound of a fire alarm, echoing throughout the scientific laboratory. Alarm lights had also illuminated, and their strobes were sending wild streaks of blue ricocheting across the white walls and ceiling. Gabrielle was shocked into action and instinctively closed the lid of the laptop, unplugged it from the wall and placed it under her arm. She then picked up the manual workbook containing a log of all the work carried out for the virus testing and headed for the exit door leading into the office area. As she got close to the door, it burst open and she stopped suddenly as Dai appeared at the door from outside.

"Thank God you are safe, Gabbie!" he shouted, above the noise of the alarm system. "Come quickly, there is a fire spreading in the production section of the coffee factory," he barked, hugging her closely and leading her out of the laboratory.

"I've got the laptop that has all the results on, Dai, and the workbook," shouted Gabrielle. "We did it, Dai. We did it! The results were good, no virus readings. It worked!"

"That is great, Gabbie, but let's get you out of here," said Dai.

Dung Lam met them as they ran towards the office entrance doors. Dai's mother, Bianca and Tina were all bunched outside in the car park, along with some of the workers from the evening shift.

Dung Lam shouted at Dai, "The fire service are on their way, Dai. Leave Gabrielle with the ladies and come with me to the factory. Maybe we can do something to stop the fire; we have extinguishers inside, next to all the machines. Come!" he ordered, as Dai urged Gabrielle towards her mother and his. Together Dai and his stepfather headed back towards the coffee factory. They reached the main entrance to the roasting area and pushed open the door. There they were met with a smoldering heap of loose jute coffee bags, which had been stacked up against piles of packed bags on pallets, containing freshly harvested green robusta coffee beans. The stack was three pallets high, ten pallets across and two pallets deep. The fire, which had started within the loose, empty bags, was heading directly towards the huge stack of palletised, bagged green coffee beans.

Dung Lam quickly assessed the situation and shouted at Dai to get two of the extinguishers, which were mounted on the end of the nearby roasting section machinery. Once secured, both men attacked the flames with the extinguishers as they quickly intensified. Amid the smoky and brightly lit atmosphere of the impending disaster, Dung Lam spied a silhouette amongst the higher levels of racked pallets. It was a solidly built, tall man. A man he instantly recognised. It was unmistakably the towering figure of Dr Phan Chien, carrying a flaming baton of wood. For a split second, Chien looked directly into the eyes of Dung Lam down below him. Misery, hopelessness and regret were all evident in his face. Then he was gone, lost in the heaving mass of flames and smoke.

The small fire-quenching devices being used by Dai and his stepfather were having little effect on the intensity of the raging fire, but both men bravely kept on trying to douse as much flame as they could. Dai soon heard the welcome sounds of the fire service trucks arriving from Buon Ma Thuot. He turned to see a group of four firemen entering the factory and unfurling long rolls of hoses. Within minutes there were eight firemen on site, using their professional skills with the fire-fighting equipment to attack the flames and bring the inferno under control. The Fire Chief herded both Dai and Dung Lam away from the dangerous area, advising that his team would finish the job and stop any more spread of the problem flames.

As Dai and his coughing stepfather emerged from the smoke-filled factory area through the huge doors, Gabrielle and Mai Thi came running towards their heroic loved ones. Both couples fell into embraces.

"You stupid man, Dung Lam!" started Mai Thi. "Why did you go into the fire, you could have been killed! You could have made me a widow; I don't want to be a widow!" she shouted out, whilst kissing and hugging her brave husband.

"Oh, Dai, are you okay? You should not have gone in there like that, you could have been injured or burnt. You stupid, brave idiot!" Gabrielle screamed, before bursting into tears and hugging her man. Bianca approached the embracing couple, sidled up close to her daughter and hugged them both.

Within an hour the Fire Chief had reported back to Dung Lam that the fire was under control and that the police would be contacting him shortly, along with fire-service inspectors. There would be an investigation into the cause of the fire, although he inferred that it had been deliberately lit. He then had the solemn duty of letting Dung Lam know that there had been one fatality of the fire, a male. He was an employee of the firm, as a Lam Dong name badge was attached to his charred clothing – Dr Phan Chien was his name. Dung Lam's heart sank as he heard the news. Thankfully, the remaining sections of the coffee complex – most of the warehousing, the offices, and the laboratory – were spared.

Mai Thi had gathered Dai, Gabrielle, Bianca and Tina in her husband's office whilst Dung Lam was being briefed by the Fire Chief downstairs. Once she been told of the discussion by her husband, she pulled Dai aside and whispered to him in their local tongue.

"Poor Dr Chien," she said. "Why would he do such a thing? Do you know, son?"

"I think he was very unhappy about his life, Mother. I feel he was upset about my successes and he thought that Dung Lam had treated him badly, in favour of me," replied her dejected son. Dai had certainly wanted Dr Chien out of the way, but not like this. Dung Lam approached his stepson and hugged him fondly.

"Do not blame yourself, Dai. Phan Chien was a good friend of mine for many years, but I needed to put the future of this company and its employees ahead of my personal feelings. Phan Chien was a man of his time, but his time had passed. It is my fault that this tragedy has occurred, Dai, I should have dealt with him more compassionately. You and your generation are the future of this industry. New blood, new energy and new ideas are what is required to take us forward. You and Gabrielle can do this," stated his proud stepfather, obviously overcome with the immensity of what had just happened.

He composed himself, hugged Mai Thi and started to speak to Dai again.

"Now, there is work ahead! We will need to check the factory in the morning, see what shape it is in, recount stock levels, see what stock has been damaged and start planning for a new, bright tomorrow. Firstly, advise Brazil of the positive test results and confirm our small order with them. Let us hope that they can salvage their crop over there, with a little bit of help from Lam Dong, and then we can start looking to build a positive relationship with Bianca and Gabrielle's company. But for now, let us all go to the safety of our own homes and wash off this terrible day. What do you say? I don't know about all of you, but I could do with a good, strong drink!" Dung Lam stated, looking at the whole group.

"A good idea," said Bianca. "Let's go. But first, can I request that Tina sends off that quote, now that the office area is safe, and give my father and brothers the great news about, as Gabrielle calls it, the LDA – the Lam Dong Antidote!"

Mai Thi insisted that they all, including Tina, came back to her place for dinner and drinks. They all agreed, except Dung Lam who said he would follow later. He needed some time alone with his thoughts, to grieve the loss of his old friend.

Pre-Op Blues

Dr David Alma rang the Almeida brothers later that day and asked them to come into the hospital to see their father. Luiz had regained consciousness in the late afternoon and was asking to see his sons. By the time they both arrived it was almost 6pm and Mateus and Felipe were overjoyed to see that Luiz was resting peacefully as they entered his room. Dr Alma had already briefed them about what was going to happen over the next 24 hours and had explained the risk factors involved. He also told them that Luiz had previously, a few weeks earlier, advised his lawyer to activate the power of attorney clause in his legal papers, in favour of Bianca, Mateus and Felipe jointly, regarding the Nova Coffee Company and his personal matters. Their father had every faith that his daughter and two sons could run the business and sort out his affairs, if the emergency operation proved unsuccessful. Luiz, as always, was still a very astute businessman at this very uncertain moment in his long life.

"Hey, Papa, we are here. Can you hear me?" asked Mateus of his father, whose eyes flickered slowly open at the sound of his youngest son's voice. A faint smile emerged as he saw Mateus and Felipe standing at his bedside.

"Thank you, boys," started Luiz. "I am so sorry to put you through all of this when you are so pre- occupied with the problems at Nova Coffee. Has David spoken to you about what I have organised with our lawyer?"

Felipe responded, "Yes, Papa, all is in order. Please do not worry about all of that. Just concentrate on getting through the operation and rest up.

Mateus, Bianca and I can look after business matters, we promise. In fact, Mat has some positive news to tell you."

"Yes, Bianca and Gabrielle have advised us that Dai's company is almost finished developing the antidote we need to clear up the leaf rust problem. Also, they can help us out with supply of a very high-quality robusta-style bean for the US order. We are just waiting on exact figures and costs, but Bianca is confident all will be good. We have not told the girls about your situation, Papa, just yet. Do you want us to tell them?" added Mateus, gazing lovingly at his fragile father.

"That is great news, boys. I will leave all of that for you to handle, I am sure you will come up with the best response. With the girls, I agree with you, please keep my illness quiet until they get back home. There is nothing that they can do, being on the other side of the world and all that. If worse comes to worst, I have left a letter for you all. But please do not read it unless I don't make it through tomorrow morning," Luiz replied. "Sam, our lawyer, has all these details."

"You'll be okay, Papa. You are big enough and ugly enough to get through this challenge," said Mateus, with a cheeky grin.

"Yes, you are strong enough, Papa," agreed Felipe. "You have always been the strength in our lives, and we need you to be there for us in the future, all of us," he added, tears appearing in his eyes. He leaned forward and tenderly kissed his father on the cheek. Mateus held Luiz's big hand and kissed him on his tanned forehead. Luiz closed his eyes and smiled, content in the fact that he had been blessed with such an amazing family. His only regret was that Beatriz was not here with him to see what marvellous children they had.

"Thank you for coming in to see me, boys. Get this US order sorted out and give my love to the girls overseas and your beautiful family, Mateus. And make sure that Eduardo looks after you, Felipe. I look forward to seeing you all after the operation. David tells me that the doctor doing the work is special. The best, he says!" quipped their father, as Dr Alma entered the room.

"I am sorry, boys; you will need to leave your father to rest now. He has a big day ahead of him tomorrow. I will call you when I think it is best for you to come in here again. Thank you so much for being here for my dear old friend," said Dr Alma to Mateus and Felipe.

"Bye, Papa, we love you," said the two sons in unison as they left his bedside. "See you tomorrow!"

As the two Almeida brothers left, Luiz looked at his lifetime friend. "I certainly hope I do," he said with a wry smile.

Doing the Deal

The next morning, both Mateus and Felipe were up early, starting work at the Nova Coffee compound at 7am. Mateus opened his computer and was happy to see a couple of emails from his sister had arrived. After reading them both, in order of receipt, he called Felipe on his mobile and asked him to meet him at his office. Then he picked up his calculator and started hitting the keys, referring to the figures on Bianca's correspondence. He did a rough calculation on the extra costs involved in getting the robusta bean component of the USA order sent directly from Vietnam. He screwed up his face, slightly disappointed that the extra costs of the airfreight, and of course buying green robusta beans from Vietnam, was leaving Nova Coffee short by about 20% on the projected gross profits of the whole operation. But, after careful consideration, he knew that he had no choice but to give the go ahead to Dai Ca Phung's company, through Bianca. He waited for his brother to get into the office, went through the numbers with Felipe and told him that Bianca was more than pleased with the quality of the robusta beans produced by the Vietnamese. They both agreed that the initial cut to gross profits on this first shipment to America could soon be recouped with future orders included in the Tender. Therefore, Felipe agreed with his brother that Bianca should go ahead with the deal and get the internal paperwork done between Nova and Lam Dong Coffee to make it happen as soon as possible. Mateus advised that he would immediately ask Lam Dong to supply an invoice by return email. Then he would arrange the required payment in US dollars through their bank, as requested in the quote from Dai Ca Phung. Mateus gave a copy of the emails from Bianca to his brother, after confirming with Felipe that he could supply the relevant artwork to Vietnam, as requested by their sister. Both brothers seemed happy with the result, especially Mateus. He was looking forward to getting the antidote airfreighted over by DHL, the fastest method in his experience, and getting his precious trees sprayed. It would take a few days after spraying to see any physical evidence that the chemical mix had done its job, but he had confidence in Gabrielle's knowledge and ability to have ensured the testing was foolproof. He had always believed in his niece's choices in life so far, and now maybe even her budding relationship with Dai Ca Phung.

"Okay, Felipe, I will send an email back to Bianca now and sign off on the quote. If you can get the artwork over to her directly from your department, we should be on our way. The sooner we get this sorted out, the sooner we can get back to Nova Serrana to see Papa. Let me know if you get a call from David, will you? I'll see you later," said Mateus to Felipe, as his older brother left the office with a wave and wearing a confident smile across his face.

How's Papa?

Later that day, Mateus was in the middle of the coffee plantation, surveying his crop and still worrying about the loss of the coffee tree leaves. His mobile phone rang out, stirring him from his thoughts. It was Felipe, telling him that someone had just rung him to ask them both to come into the hospital again.

"Is Papa okay?" asked Mateus.

"They didn't say, Mat. Just that we should come straight away," answered Felipe. "Can you pick me up at the main office in two minutes, please? Clara is here and she said that she'll look after the office whilst we are gone."

"Will do, see you soon," replied his worried brother.

Within twenty minutes they were both jumping out of Mateus' vehicle at the hospital car park, heading towards the reception area of the Surgical department. As they hurried through the automatic front doors, Dr Alma was waiting for them, leaning against the reception desk and talking to the ward sister. As soon as he saw Luiz's sons, he walked purposefully towards them. They stopped dead in their tracks, looking straight into David Alma's eyes, searching for answers.

"How is Papa?" blurted out Felipe.

"Can you both please come with me this way, boys?" stated the doctor firmly, ushering them both in the direction of a spare office at the side of the reception area.

They quickly and silently followed Dr Alma as he entered the room and slowly closed the door behind them. Both Almeida brothers had blank looks on their faces, as David Alma asked them to be seated.

"I think that we have some good news for you about your father," he started, slowly. "Luiz has come through the surgery and Dr Voss will be joining us shortly to report on how the procedure went. The operation was a long and delicate one. The recuperation period may be extensive, dependent on many factors, but initially, signs are looking more on the positive side, rather than the negative."

"Did you remove the tumour?" asked Mateus.

"I believe that we got all of it. But, until the internal swelling goes down, we cannot 100% confirm that. I am sure that Dr Voss can give you a more accurate assessment, I was just assisting with the operation. But this is excellent news so far, boys. These operations are always difficult."

There was an extended silence in the room, broken by a slight knock at the door. Mateus and Felipe turned their heads to see a small-statured man in a smart grey suit enter the room.

"May I introduce Dr Michel Voss?" said Dr Alma.

"These are Luiz's two boys, Felipe and Mateus," he added for the benefit of the new arrival.

"So good to meet you, gentlemen," started the surgeon. "You have an extraordinarily strong and determined father. Mr Almeida has endured a tremendously hard time these past five or six hours, but I do think that he has the strength and the determination to get over this. I am sure that, with the help of his family, he can enjoy a few more years yet on his coffee plantation," said Dr Voss, an assured look on his face. "He will need a long time to rest and recover from this experience, but I do believe he can get back to, hopefully, a less hectic existence when that period has successfully passed. From what Dr Alma has told me, he has a strong and loving family that will no doubt rally around him to ensure that this happens."

"Oh, thank you, doctor, I am not sure how we can ever repay you for saving our beautiful father. Thank you!" responded an exceedingly happy and emotional Felipe.

Even the usually unflappable Mateus was overcome, as he shook Dr Voss' hand and thanked him profusely for his efforts.

"Well, Dr Alma, I must get along. I need to get the plane back to São Paulo. My taxi should be arriving any moment now," Dr Voss said, then turning to address Luiz's two sons. "Please do not worry about your father; Dr Alma will take good care of him and the services here are excellent. I will keep in touch with all the results and can advise from São Paulo. So good to meet you both. Look after your father and each other."

With that, the eminent surgeon shook Dr Alma's hand and left the room.

"Can we see our father, Dr Alma?" asked Mateus.

The doctor shook his head. "So sorry, not yet, Mateus. Maybe tomorrow afternoon. I will monitor his progress and call you when I think the timing is right. Maybe you can contact your sister and Gabrielle now and break the news to them gently?" he advised. "I also suggest that you contact your lawyer, Sam Ramirez, and discuss how this all affects your business. I am sure that Luiz would have briefed him on what he wanted to happen, either way."

"Thank you, David, we'll get all the ends tied up now," chipped in Felipe. "And thank you for all your help and guidance over the past few days. You are a true friend to our father. Mateus and I appreciate all the help you have given us."

With that, the boys each shook David Alma's hand and proceeded towards Mateus' truck.

"Will you call Bianca and Gabrielle, please?" Mateus asked later, as they approached the Almeida compound.

"Of course, Mat. You have enough on your plate to get the US order organised. I will ring Bianca's mobile later this evening. I think that will be early morning in Vietnam," replied Felipe.

Aftermath of the Fire

The morning after the factory fire Dai was at Lam Dong Coffee early and so was Dung Lam. As they sipped on hot, sweet coffee amongst the blackened ruins of the factory, Dai turned to his stepfather and asked him, "Why would Chien do all this?"

Dung Lam took a mouthful of his steaming coffee, shook his head, and looked aimlessly into the charcoaled residue of the previous day's incident before finally answering.

"He was jealous of you. He was jealous of me also. Chien and I both started working at Lam Dong at the same time, when I was only 16 years old. He was my senior by nearly twenty years. He headed off on the scientific route and I preferred the production side of the coffee business, but we still got on well and worked productively together. As the company grew, Phan Chien excelled in his area of biology and chemical developments; technically he was brilliant. But he never dealt well with people, either his workers or those above him in management. In fact, he annoyed everyone he worked with. He never married after his fiancée was killed in the bombing of Saigon during the war, and has lived alone for all these years since. Later, as I climbed up the levels of management at Lam Dong, he stayed on the scientific side and virtually stagnated. When I was made General Manager of this factory, he became very surly with me and from then on he only talked with me about business matters, shunning me socially. When I promoted you two years ago, he barged into my office and demanded that he should have been elevated above you. Yesterday morning, after the two of you had words in his office, he told me of your conversation and that he had finally had enough. He rang me and said that it was all over for him, as he believed that his seniority was not respected. Then he went missing until I saw him high above us yesterday, right here, amongst the flames, just before the fire crews turned up. It is a tragedy, but it is one that could have been avoided if I had acted sooner. He should have retired from here years ago, but I let him stay on for old times' sake. So, there is only me to blame, Dai."

"No, you are not the only one to blame, sir. I also have been unfair to Chien over the last few years, especially since my promotion. I learnt a lot from the doctor in my younger years, but maybe I should have been more understanding of his personal problems," replied Dai.

"The Fire Investigator is coming in soon to check out the site and talk with me about his findings. I had better go back to my office and prepare for him; I will talk to our insurance agent as well. Can you please start working towards the Brazilian order, if we have the official order back from them, that is? We can meet again this afternoon to discuss it. I should be getting the stock figures from the factory warehouse in a few hours' time, so I will email details to Tina. Let's get moving, eh?" said Dung Lam, as he touched Dai gently on his shoulder and headed back to his office.

Dai silently walked around the black-stained stacks of ruined coffee beans and hoped that enough stock of robusta was still available to fill the order for Nova Coffee. He then walked off towards his own office to start his workday.

Phone Call from Brazil

Mai Thi had just served a breakfast of coffee, hot croissants, and fresh fruit to her house guests. Bianca and Gabrielle had slept soundly and were looking forward to getting into Dai's workplace to finalise all the paperwork to help the USA order become a reality, as soon as possible. Communication was becoming easier between the Brazilians and their Vietnamese hostess. All three had developed a tight bond and Gabrielle's grasp of the local language, although stilted, was enough to ensure that Mai Thi could understand her thoughts and wishes. Mai Thi was becoming increasingly impressed with her son's ability to capture such a beautiful and intelligent young lady as his girlfriend, and the feeling seemed mutual with Bianca as far as Dai was concerned. In the back of her mind, Gabrielle's mother knew that, because of the deep relationship she had forged with Mai Thi's son, her daughter would be faced with an important decision very soon in her young life. But she was confident that Gabrielle would make the right one.

At that moment, Bianca heard her mobile phone ringing. "I wonder who that might be?" she asked of her daughter, as she rose to her feet and picked up the phone from the top of the kitchen counter. Looking down at the face of her mobile phone, she immediately recognised the number of the caller.

"Oh, it's Felipe!" exclaimed an excited Bianca, as she pressed the answer icon on the screen. "Hello, Felipe, how wonderful to hear from you!"

She indicated to Gabrielle, by pointing, that she was going to take the call on the outside balcony and headed in that direction.

"Felipe is my uncle – Mother's brother," explained Gabrielle to Mai Thi, in her best Vietnamese, referring to her booklet.

Mai Thi responded with "Ah, *chú của bạn. Tôi hiểu.*" *Your uncle. Yes, I understand.* They both laughed at, and understood, each other at the same time. The laughter abated, as a glum-looking Bianca appeared back at the table a few seconds later.

"Oh, Gabbie," uttered her mother, "your Poppy is in hospital. We need to get back to Brazil as soon as we can!"

"What's happened, Mum?" queried Gabrielle, standing up from the table and rushing to embrace her mother. "Is he okay?"

"Can we talk in the bedroom?" Bianca asked her daughter.

Mai Thi looked on compassionately from the breakfast table, understanding that something was not right, but unsure what. She smiled at Bianca, as the two distressed women headed towards the sanctuary of Bianca's bedroom. Once inside, Bianca relayed the message from Felipe to her daughter, with all the information she had gleaned from her elder brother's rushed phone call.

"When will we know if the operation was successful? Did Felipe say how Poppy was feeling? Will he be okay, Mum?" questioned Gabrielle, now crying and looking frantically into her mother's eyes.

Bianca took a deep breath, stood up straight and put each of her hands onto her distraught daughter's shoulders. "Well, Gabbie, perhaps we should both get on the first plane back to Brazil. Or maybe I should go back alone. Felipe did mention that they would know more about Poppy's condition tomorrow, Brazilian time – it is nighttime at home now. The doctor, Dr Alma – he is a good friend of your Poppy – is looking after him at the Nova Serrana Hospital and he advised Felipe and Mateus that the operation went well. But time will tell. He will need a long period of convalescence now, according to the medics. I would understand if you wanted to stay here with Dai for a short while," offered Bianca to Gabrielle. "But I need to get back to Nova to look after Papa straight away. Your uncles and Aunty Clara will do all they can, but Papa will need me to be there for him."

"Let's wait until tonight and then ring Uncle Felipe or Mateus again to see how Poppy is getting on," responded Gabrielle, hugging her mother.

"We can ask Dai to organise flights, I am sure Tina will have someone at their travel agents who can get urgent tickets for us," Gabrielle continued, but then she seemed to have second thoughts, looking deep into her mother's eyes before saying: "I love Poppy with all my heart, you know that, Mother. But if I could get a few more days with Dai, well, that would mean the world to me. If we call Brazil tonight again and see what Poppy's position is, then if he is recovering, I could maybe follow you on a later flight. But I understand that you need to get back as soon as you possibly can to look after him and organise things. I am sure that Poppy would want to get this USA shipment organised and finalised as soon as we could. I can do that for you, Mum, with Dai's help."

"You're right, Gabbie. You are right. It will take us two days, almost, to get back home and we can ring later tonight to get an update from Felipe. That would put my mind at rest. We have only been here for less than a week and I agree that you need to spend more time with Dai. He is a good man and he would be devastated if you were gone so quickly. I was young once; I know how it feels, darling," replied Bianca, smiling through her tears and placing a soft kiss on her daughter's forehead.

"You'd better explain things to Mai Thi; she will be wondering what is happening. I will start packing right now. Then we'll get a taxi to Dai's work and explain everything to him and Dung Lam."

Within an hour Gabrielle had explained what had occurred to Mai Thi and had rung Dai to bring him up to speed. Bianca had speedily packed up her wardrobe of clothing, most of it unworn because of the truncated visit. The taxi was booked by Mai Thi and she offered to pray for Gabrielle's grandfather. She also genuinely consoled Bianca as the trio travelled the few minutes along the coffee-tree-lined road to the Lam Dong Factory.

Although Dai was exceedingly busy at the office finalising details of the USA airfreight of coffee beans, he was taken aback by the news of Luiz Almeida's illness. During his brief stay at the Nova Coffee Company headquarters, he had built up a strong relationship with Gabrielle's grandfather and had admired his qualities, both as a leader and as a man. Dai was now more comfortable with how things had turned out between the two coffee companies and was hoping and praying that Luiz would survive this terrible blow and once again take his place at the head of the Almeida household. He had briefed Tina to order a pair of first-class airline tickets back to Brazil for Bianca and Gabrielle, refining his request to book Bianca's ticket on the first available flight, but to make Gabrielle's booking flexible, so that she could make the trip later, if required. He had made this decision after discussing it with Dung Lam, directly after Gabrielle had phoned him from his mother's home.

By the time that Mai Thi, Bianca and Gabrielle had arrived at the Lam Dong Coffee offices, all the necessary work had been done on the robusta coffee bean order for Nova Coffee. The factory Inventory Manager had calculated that, even though a large amount of beans had been destroyed in the fire, there was ample stock of excellent quality robusta-style beans to fill the Nova order. The artwork of the Nova Coffee logo had arrived via email from Felipe and the bag-printing section of the Lam Dong factory had set up to produce the 200 specially printed bags required to pack the order. Dai had stipulated that the printing department should keep a digital version of the new artwork on file in their computer system, for use on possible future orders for Nova Coffee. All that was left to do was for Bianca or Gabrielle to check off all the relevant paperwork, so that the airfreight transaction could take place seamlessly and the delivery date could be booked in as soon as possible. Dung Lam and his Logistics Manager had ensured that, after production and packing was complete in Buon Ma Thuot, there would be enough time to road-freight the bags down to the commercial airport in Ho Chi Minh City and then onto the USA via DHL Air Freight, all in time to be delivered well within the specified date on Nova Coffee's Tender agreement. Bianca was suitably impressed with the way in which Lam Dong had handled the rushed order and, after checking the paperwork had all the relevant details correctly listed, she signed off the order. She then asked Tina to advise Mateus of the Lam Dong Coffee bank details via email, and request payment by digital bank transfer.

"It is the middle of the night over in Nova Serrana, Dai. But Mateus can forward payment details first thing in the morning, now I have sanctioned the transaction," stated a very businesslike Bianca to Dai, as they sat around the boardroom table next to his office.

"It is an absolute pleasure to do business with such a fine Brazilian company," replied Dai, with a huge smile and a cheeky wink to Gabrielle.

"We are all praying that Mr Almeida will have a speedy recovery from his operation – all of my family are very sorry for the bad news."

"Thank you, Dai. I must say that it has been a marvellous experience to visit your country, even though my visit is to be cut short, and so good to meet your charming parents," responded Bianca. "Your mother is beautiful and has made our stay here so comfortable. Your stepfather is a very impressive leader of this company and such a charming man. I very much hope that Nova and Lam Dong can indeed work together in the future on many more joint ventures.

"I would also like to say that, assuming my lovely daughter Gabrielle stays on in Vietnam for a while longer than me, I am sure that you will look after her well in my absence. Then maybe, just maybe, the Almeida family will see you, and hopefully your parents, over at Nova Coffee again, in the not-too-distant future."

With her little speech over, Bianca walked towards Dai, hugged him, and gave him a soft kiss on his cheek. Her daughter smiled and once again her legendary control of emotions failed as tears of joy trickled down her cheekbones. Bianca turned to her daughter and embraced her fondly. Tina then broke the atmosphere by rushing into Dai's office, waving two separate pieces of printed paper.

"Mr Phung, ladies... we have a response from Brazil from Mr Mateus, with an Official Purchase Order for the coffee, and our travel agent has some good news on a flight for Bianca. However, you will need to be at the Ho Chi Minh City airport by later tonight to catch the flight. Is that okay?"

Dai responded first, looking down at his watch. "If it is alright with you, Bianca, Gabrielle and I can drive you down to the airport this afternoon." Then turning to his secretary, he asked, "What is the latest boarding time for first-class passengers on the flight, Tina?"

She looked down at the flight schedule and read the details, "It is an Air France flight, Mr Phung. Flying out at 10pm, local time. So, you would need to have Bianca at the airport by 7pm or 8pm to give enough time to get her through Customs and Security. It is nearly 10am now, therefore you would need to leave here within the hour or so to be sure of getting there on time. Shall I confirm the booking?"

Dai looked at Gabrielle and Bianca to confirm his response.

"Yes," agreed Bianca. "I have done most of my packing already. So I could be ready to go by 11 o'clock, if that's okay with you and Gabrielle?"

"Are you sure, Mum?" piped up Gabrielle. "Are you okay for me to stay in Vietnam a little longer, until we find out how Poppy is?"

"Of course, darling. You and Dai need some more time together. I can look after your grandfather as soon as I get home. The sooner the better, I feel. We can phone and talk to your uncles back home on our trip to the airport, on my mobile," replied Bianca positively to her concerned daughter. "It will be fine. If Dai promises to look after my little darling, of course," she added, looking towards Dai with a smile.

"Of course, Bianca. You know I will," responded the happy young man. "So, Tina. Can you please confirm the flight for Bianca, and I will talk to Dung Lam to let him know what is happening?"

At this point, Mai Thi, who had been an interested onlooker during the conversation, broke her silence. "My son, can you please tell me what is going on? And what I can do to help you all?" she asked Dai in her local tongue. Dai explained to his mother all that had been said and a warm smile lit up her face. She offered to go home with her guests to help them both prepare for the trip and said that she would prepare some food for them all to eat on the way, to save time. Dai agreed to finish up at the office after he had seen his stepfather, and then go home to get a change of clothing and meet the girls at his mother's place in one hour's time. He explained this to Bianca and Gabrielle; it was agreeable to all concerned and Tina offered to order a taxi to take the trio back home again.

Bianca moved out to Tina's office to check that all the correct paperwork was ready for the shipment of coffee beans to proceed. This gave an opportunity for Dai to pull Gabrielle to one side and usher her across to the office window area, out of Bianca's earshot.

He planted a kiss on her willing lips, and she responded in kind. He then whispered to her, "Gabbie, I cannot wait to be with alone with you again, but we still have work to do before your mother leaves the country. I need you to arrange something for me. I asked Tina to give me one of her nearly empty perfume bottles, of which she has many. Earlier this morning I washed out the bottle and replaced the contents with your famous LDA–Lam Dong Antidote – in a ten times concentrated form. I asked Tina to gift-wrap it for me. I know you may think that my idea is weird, but you can tell your mother that your Aunty Clara asked you to bring back some exotic Vietnamese perfume for her, then she can take it back for Mateus, unknowingly, in her general luggage. You can ring Mateus once Bianca is on board the plane tonight and let him know our plan. He will then be able to perform a small spraying test on the coffee trees, once he has diluted it down. At least then he will know that the antidote works. Our scientists are currently making up a batch of 30 litres of the antidote, which we can ship safely to Brazil. Dung Lam has organised the delivery to be there within six days. According to Mateus' figures, that should be enough to do the trick on the leaf rust. What do you think?"

"The more I get to know you, Da Ca Phung, the more you amaze me!" shot back a smiling Gabrielle. "And the more I love you," she softly added.

"One more thing. Here is your Aunty Clara's 'gift'," He handed her a small, gift-wrapped package from the top drawer of his desk. "And also, pack an overnight bag for this evening. We won't be driving back until tomorrow morning," added Dai, just before Bianca burst into the room, catching them in another loving embrace.

"Okay, cut it out, you two. I haven't even left the country yet!" said Bianca, smiling broadly. "Tina and I have completed all that is needed to get this order over the line. So I am ready when you are, Gabrielle. I just need to go to Dung Lam's office to say my goodbyes to him. Then Mai Thi and I will meet you downstairs when the taxi gets here. See you later, Dai," finished her mother.

As Bianca sauntered out of the upstairs office, she turned to Tina, sitting at her desk, and farewelled her with a final quip: "If you ever get fed up with working for your Mr Phung, there will always be a job for you in Brazil at Nova Coffee, if you get the urge. See you on the email, Tina. Thank you for all your help."

On the Road Again

Around an hour later, Dai rolled up to his mother's house in his Range Rover, the petrol tank filled to capacity at the local service station and his trusty suit bag resting in the boot. Mai Thi had done a great job in packing a huge cool-bag full of sumptuous home-cooked food for the journey and Gabrielle had successfully sold the story of Aunty Clara's perfume gift to her distracted mother, before secreting the package into Bianca's general luggage. Gabrielle appeared first down the stairs, a sheepish look on her face and a small overnight bag tucked under her arm. She raced to the car and asked Dai to open the boot, so she could hide it before her mother came down to the car. Dai jumped out from behind the wheel, did as he was told, and then motioned for Gabrielle to sit in the front passenger seat, as he set off through the downstairs garage entrance to get Bianca's bulky luggage.

Bianca was saying her sad goodbye to Dai's mum on the outside balcony on the first floor of the house. "Oh, Mai Thi. I cannot thank you enough for looking after Gabrielle and me so wonderfully. It was an absolute pleasure to meet and get to know you both. You have an incredibly special son and I have a feeling that we shall be seeing each other sooner rather than later. I know that you will look after my Gabbie for me. Thank you for everything!" finished Bianca, as she put her arms around her hostess and kissed her goodbye.

Although not understanding most of what Bianca had said to her, Mai Thi certainly understood the emotion. Her response in very broken English brought Gabrielle's mother to tears. "I will pray for your father, Bianca, and I will look after Gabrielle like my own daughter. Safe journey."

With that Bianca pulled a handkerchief from her jacket pocket, wiped her moistened eyes, picked up her hand luggage, and headed off as Dai appeared next to her to transport her suitcases to the car. He kissed his mother and hugged her happily before saying goodbye, whispering that he would not be back that night.

Mai Thi gave her son a loving smile and a wink as he went downstairs. "Drive carefully!" she shouted from the top balcony, and Dai waved as he whisked his two guests off in his shining Range Rover. His mobile phone beeped to alert him of a text message, as he went through the gears and hit top speed on the motorway, heading south. As he glanced at the phone face, he smiled. It was a message from Tina that read, "Your booking is confirmed at the Park Hyatt Saigon. The champagne will be chilled on your arrival."

After the Operation

It was a beautiful 26 degrees Celsius in Nova Serrana. Around midday Mateus Almeida was steadily working on the production plan for the arabica coffee bean crop. He already had a third of the proposed order ready and packed to be containerised and then trucked down to the port of Santos, just south of São Paulo. They still used his mother's former family business, the Costa Export and Import Company, to look after their shipping requirements. Mateus had meticulously planned and booked his 40-foot containers to ship and carry the precious coffee beans up to the Port of New York and Jersey. From there, the local American coffee importers would organise trucking of the full containers of Nova Coffee beans to their various warehouses and roasting depots around the States. This shipment was the first of many to be delivered, in line with this Tender, and Mateus wanted to make sure that it all went off without a hitch.

He had received the Lam Dong Coffee banking details, along with an email from his sister, earlier that morning. Bianca explained to him that all was going to plan in Vietnam and that the airfreight delivery of robusta beans would be in America in plenty of time to make the Tender deadline date. She also told him that Gabrielle would advise him of exactly when the Lam Dong Antidote serum would be arriving at Nova Coffee, confirming that she thought it would be less than a week, in a concentrated form and they would be using DHL Express Air Freight. Mateus was extremely pleased with all this news and even more impressed with the results that

Bianca and Gabrielle had achieved in such a short time. Most importantly, she told Mateus that she was on her way home from Vietnam and would be home within 36 hours, but Gabrielle would be staying on with Dai and his family for a little longer. She asked about their father's situation and said that she would try to call her brothers via Facetime on their way to the airport. Mateus replied to the email, congratulating them on their efforts, whilst raising his concerns about Gabrielle being left on her own in a foreign land. He confirmed that he and Felipe would visit the Nova Serrana Hospital later that day and would update Bianca on the phone about their father's health status when she rang them.

He rang his brother's mobile number later that afternoon. "Hi, Felipe, any news from Papa's doctor?"

"Yes, sorry I haven't got back to you. Dr Alma did ring about 30 minutes ago; he was positive about Papa's recovery from the operation and suggested that we pop into the hospital around 6pm tonight," he answered. "Would you like me to drive this time? I can pick you up at your place around 5.45pm, if that's okay with you, Mat?"

"Yes, Felipe. Thanks, I should be ready by then. Oh, by the way, I also heard back from our sister. All has gone well over there and she is on her way back home, but not with Gabrielle, apparently. We'll talk about that in the car on the way to see Papa, eh?" responded Mateus. "See you soon."

Two hours later they had driven to see their father at the hospital and discussed all that had been going on in Vietnam on the way. Felipe wasn't that concerned about Gabrielle being left in Vietnam by her mother. He could understand that she would have wanted to see Dai for a longer time than the few days that they had so far been there for. He added that he had the confidence in their niece to know that she could look after herself. She had proved that during her time at university in the States, when she was even younger. Arriving at the hospital, they were confident on how the business was progressing without their father's strong influence. However, they were looking forward to seeing him after the gruelling operation and checking that he was feeling okay. The news from Vietnam would certainly make him a lot happier, they surmised.

Dr Alma was again waiting for them in the reception area when they walked in. He briefed them on their father's welfare, which was quite promising considering the seriousness of his condition, then led them through to the Recovery Unit. Luiz was, surprisingly, lying in a semi-upright position in his bed. His head was heavily bandaged with tubes inserted into his nostrils and mouth to help the breathing process. His eyes were initially closed as his sons walked into his private room, but they slowly opened when he detected that the doctor had entered the room. "Hey, doc, how am I doing?" he asked wearily, loosening his mouthpiece, as his good friend moved bedside and clutched his large right hand.

"You are doing remarkably well for an old guy, Luiz," Alma answered. "I have got some visitors for you, old friend. Your two sons, Felipe and Mateus."

"Oh, hello, boys," whispered Luiz, slightly awkwardly, due to the apparatus stuck in the corner of his mouth. "How are you getting on without me? Do we still have a coffee business?" he joked, struggling to fully open his eyes to see his sons clearly.

"It's all good news, Papa. The Vietnamese trip was successful for the girls. Gabrielle and Dai were successful in getting an antidote developed for our leaf rust and Bianca has sorted out a decent supply from Lam Dong Coffee for the quantity of robusta beans that we were short of for the first order. Bianca is on her way home now, as we speak. She wants to look after her dear old Papa," explained Mateus.

Luiz smiled and then paused for a moment and slightly raised his free left hand, before speaking. "But what about my little Gabrielle, is she coming home so soon as well?" asked their father.

Felipe responded to that question. "Well, it seems, Papa, that she is rather taken with Vietnam and of course with young Dai Ca Phung. She was desperate to know how you are feeling but has asked to stay over there a short while longer and Bianca agreed. I assume that our sister feels that Gabbie will be fine over there with Dai's family and will be back soon enough. They will be calling us later tonight to fill us in with the details… but both send their love to you."

" She is a tenacious young thing, your niece. That is great news, she has obviously hit it off with young Dai again, by the sound of it. Probably charmed the pants off his mother and father as well, knowing Gabbie. Yes, I think that's great news. And well done with the US order, boys, I'm enormously proud of all of you," replied Luiz, who was noticeably tiring.

David Alma squeezed his hand and told him to get some rest again. He advised the two boys that it was time to retire from the room and that maybe they could visit again tomorrow night. Their father had drifted off into sleep again, after the doctor had adjusted his breathing apparatus, so they both kissed him on the forehead and made their way silently outside the room.

Bye Bye, Bianca

Dai and his passengers had made good time on the car trip to the airport. After driving for almost three hours non-stop, he indicated to Gabrielle that he would need to pull over soon at the next service station. He desperately needed to use the men's room and to eat something, along with his obligatory strong coffee. Bianca had fallen into a deep sleep in the back seat of the Range Rover, much to the delight of her daughter, who had grown tired of her mother's constant advice streaming from the back compartment of the car. Dai pulled over at the next major service station and managed to park next to the amenities block without waking Bianca.

"Do you want coffee or a cold drink, Gabbie?" Dai asked, as he got stiffly out of his Range Rover and stretched.

"I'd love a cold bottle of water, please. I'll get the food out of the cold pack. I am starving!" she replied. "And, Dai, you had better get a black coffee with a couple of sugars in for Mum, please." Bianca was by now waking up in the rear of the car. He ambled off quickly to the toilet, giving Gabrielle the thumbs-up sign on his way.

"Oh, hi, honey," muttered a weary Bianca. "I must have fallen asleep, sorry, darling."

"That's okay, Mum, it has been a rather hectic morning. Dai and I had a lovely chat whilst you slept. Are you hungry?" she responded.

"I am, actually. Let's see what wonderful food Mai Thi has packed for us," Bianca replied with a smile.

A few minutes later, Dai returned to the car with a tray of two hot coffees and a bottle of water. Bianca and Gabrielle had already devoured much of the beautiful, packed lunch that his mother had prepared for the trip. He grabbed himself a savoury filled croissant from the bag and handed out the drinks to his fellow travellers.

"We might go to the toilets, Dai, before we head off again. If you don't mind?" asked Bianca, opening her door.

"Good idea mum," added her daughter following her.

Five minutes later the women returned and jumped back into the car.

"You keep eating, ladies, I will keep on driving. It is still around four hours yet until we reach the airport, so we'd better keep on going," said Dai, as the women returned.

"If you don't mind, Dai, I might get into the back seat now," said Gabbie. "We need to call Brazil on the way on Mum's mobile and I would like to speak to my uncles too. Is that okay?"

"No problem, Gabbie. I'll put some music on," Dai replied, as Gabrielle moved into the seat next to her mother in the back and clicked on her seatbelt.

Dai finished off the remainder of his coffee before heading off again along the QL14 Highway, heading south-west towards the Vietnamese capital. By 5pm, they were only an hour or so away from their destination. Gabrielle had calculated that it was around 7am over in Brazil, so she asked her mother to video call Mateus, who always started work earlier than Felipe. She could not wait to see her uncle's face again and find out how her Poppy was recovering from the operation. Bianca had fully charged her phone at Dai's mother's house before the trip to ensure she could use it without hassle on the trip, so she keyed in her brother's mobile number. Mateus picked up his phone immediately – he was already at his desk at the Nova Coffee office.

"Hey, little sister, how are you? Where are you now?" he questioned, as his image appeared on the screen of Bianca's phone.

"Hi Mat," replied Bianca excitedly. "Gabrielle and I are on our way to the airport. Dai is driving us there. We are about an hour or so away. How is Papa?" she asked nervously.

"As well as can be expected. It was a long and dangerous operation for him to endure, but he seemed surprisingly well when we saw him last night.

The doctor is still cautious about the outcome. But he said that Papa had done exceptionally well for a man of his age and thought that, after a lot of rest, he would recover quickly. Felipe and I told him that you were coming straight back from Vietnam and he seemed really pleased to hear that."

"Did you tell him that Gabrielle is staying on with Dai for a while?" asked Bianca, apprehensively.

"Yes, we did. He seemed to take that okay. Even said that it was great news that she was happy with Dai. We told him how well you had both done on your trip over there and he was grateful to you both and sent you his love. After that he became tired, so we were advised to leave his bedside," replied Mateus.

"Oh, that is so good, Mat. I am anxious to get back as quickly as I can, but also confident that Gabbie will be fine over here for a week or so before she returns home. Dai's parents are beautiful, Mat, and Gabrielle is incredibly happy. Here she is. I will pass my phone to her."

"Hi, Uncle Mat, thank you for looking after Poppy so well!" shouted an emotional Gabrielle to the phone, as she saw her uncle's face. "I will not be that long over here. But I need to stay a bit longer with Dai and he may need a bit of help from me at their lab. The tests went so well, and we managed to get the results we needed. I may talk to you a bit later today about that if you don't mind? Anyway, I will put you back to Mum and please, please, please give my love to Poppy when you see him again. Here's Mum," she said, passing the phone back to Bianca.

Bianca carried on her conversation with her youngest brother and promised him that she would look after their father once she was home. She also gave Mateus her flight details and asked if he could arrange an internal domestic flight from Rio to Nova Serrana, to help her get back home as soon as possible. He agreed and said his goodbyes, adding that he would personally pick up his sister from the local airport and take her straight to see Luiz, if he was fit enough to see her. He finally added that he would text her the Brazilian flight details he was booking as soon as he could, after checking the time that she was due into Rio from Paris.

By 6.45pm, a tired Dai had succeeded in getting Bianca to the international airport on time. He helped with Bianca's luggage and got her to the check-in counter for the first-class section. As Bianca booked her bulky luggage in, Dai and Gabrielle stood arm in arm, watching. Gabrielle gazed into Dai's almond-shaped eyes, smiled sweetly, and kissed him gently on the mouth.

"Thank you, Dai, for making all my dreams come true," she whispered to him. "As soon as Mum gets through the security section, we can go to our hotel. I am sure that she will want to get some Duty Free on the way through, so it should not be too long until we are alone. I can't wait."

"Me too, Gabbie," uttered Dai, once again returning her kiss.

It was fifteen minutes before Bianca had disposed of her luggage and acquired her boarding pass. She strode triumphantly towards the couple and threw her arms around them both at the same time.

"I am not going to keep you hanging around, my darlings. Let's have a quick goodbye drink at the bar out here. Then I can toddle off into Duty Free to do some last-minute shopping before I head to the first-class lounge at the boarding gate," she announced.

As promised, after only one drink at the bar, Bianca said a tearful goodbye to her daughter and Dai. She headed off in the direction of the Security gates, urging them to go.

"After all, my dears, you don't want to waste a minute of your time at the lovely hotel that Dai has organised for tonight, do you?" she said with a chuckle and a playful wink to her embarrassed daughter.

"Let me know when you arrive home safely, Mum. Call me. I love you, Mum!" said a coy Gabrielle. "Have a safe flight."

"And you, young man," said Bianca to Dai. "Make sure you look after my daughter; I know you will."

"Goodbye, Bianca. You know I will look after her. Thank you for everything," added Dai with a peck on her cheek as she left the bar. Looking back happily at them both, Bianca gave them a final wave, clutching onto her Louis Vuitton "Keepall" bag. Dai and Gabrielle stood there silently, as her slight figure disappeared into the thronging crowd on the concourse.

"Would you let me escort you to the beautiful Park Hyatt Saigon hotel, Gabbie? I believe that the champagne will be perfectly chilled by the time we arrive," said Dai, offering Gabrielle his arm and wearing a huge grin on his happy face. With a silent, affirmative nod of the head she took his arm, smiled and off they went.

"Don't forget, I have got to phone Uncle Mateus again and let him know about Aunty Clara's perfume present!" giggled Gabrielle, as they walked towards Dai's car.

"You can call him in the car on the way to the hotel. When we get there, you are all mine, so you won't have time!" replied Dai, smiling.

Once Bianca was out of sight of her daughter and through the security gates, she looked around for a quiet place inside the luxuriously appointed first-class lounge. She smiled confidently at the smart young lady who greeted her at the reception area, showed her boarding card and waltzed into the area of comfortable seating next to the well-stocked bar. She attracted a few admiring glances from the well-dressed men already there, who looked up from their books or tablets as she passed by. Approaching the bar, Bianca indicated to the barman that a glass of chilled champagne would be excellent. "I will be sitting over there, when you are ready," she announced, pointing to an empty table in the corner of the room. Although her somewhat arrogant demeanor was, outwardly, a sign of assured confidence, deep down she was anxious. She was worried about her father's health. Bianca's relationship with her father had started off rather awkwardly in her youth; Luiz had tended to think that she was too spoiled, especially by his wife Beatriz. But through the tragedies of Beatriz's early death and the breakup of both of Bianca's marriages, she had become much closer to her father. Luiz had become exceedingly dependent on his only daughter, both in his business and personally. Once Gabrielle had grown up and became more independent, her mother had gravitated towards her father and the two were now noticeably closer. The suddenness of Luiz's illness had shocked her more than she had shown to her daughter, so she decided to ring her eldest brother, Felipe, before she boarded the plane to check on her father's well-being. She knew that Felipe, the brother who she had always supported through some turbulent times in his life, would be more open and honest with her than Mateus about their father's condition. She needed to know the true situation. Even before she had made herself comfortable in her seat and pulled the phone from her Louis Vuitton shoulder bag, the young barman had appeared and placed her champagne on the table, along with a small bowl of savoury nibbles, and shot her a cheeky smile. Bianca still loved the attention, that would never change.

Alone at Last

Gabrielle had made the phone call to her Uncle Mateus on the way to the hotel from the airport. She laughingly advised him of their plan to secrete the small sample of the Lam Dong Antidote in the perfume container being carried by Bianca. Mateus appreciated the humour of the plan and thanked her for organising it. He also asked Gabrielle not to forget to bring back a real perfume for her Aunty Clara when she eventually arrived home in Brazil. She agreed and asked her uncle to pass on her love to all of his family, her Uncle Felipe, Eduardo and, of course, her Poppy.

A few minutes later, Dai pulled up at the entry to the five-star Park Hyatt Saigon.

"Wow, Dai, it looks so lovely," Gabrielle had gasped as they approached.

"Only the best for you, Gabbie," replied Dai, leaving the car keys in the ignition as he opened his door to get out.

Before Gabrielle had time to move, the passenger seat door was courteously opened by a smiling doorman, bedecked in a smart uniform. Noticing that she was of non-Asian appearance, the young man greeted her in English with, "Good evening, madam. Can I help you with your luggage?"

Dai had released the lock on the boot, and, on her positive response, the doorman quickly retrieved both bags from inside. Dai quietly said something to him in the local language, which the young man responded to with a bright smile, and he carried the bags inside. Another staff member, dressed in identical uniform, appeared and jumped into the car to valet park it in the underground car park.

Dai offered his hand to a delighted Gabrielle and they walked together to the flower-decorated reception desk inside the hotel foyer. As they arrived at the desk, the young couple were entranced by the beautiful sound of a sultry singer, emanating from the ground floor Lobby Bar, expertly accompanied by a man on a grand piano. The hotel itself was decorated in the French Colonial style, which did not please Dai. But its elegance impressed his young partner immensely and that was all that mattered. He quietly confirmed with the very helpful receptionist that the champagne had been delivered to his room and that it was on ice, before giving her his credit-card details and escorting Gabrielle towards their top-floor accommodation.

Gabrielle and Dai stood outside the door of their room on the sixth floor of the luxurious hotel. They had taken the ornate elevator up to the top level and were now waiting for the porter to unlock their door and transport their luggage inside. The young man smiled gratefully when Dai placed a substantial tip into the palm of his hand, after he had explained all the amenities of the room and offered to uncork the awaiting bottle. Dai dismissed his request. "No, thank you. I will open it myself, in a while," he responded with a smile. "Thank you for all your help."

"Oh my God, Dai. It's beautiful," gasped Gabrielle, as she entered the luxuriously appointed room and gazed out of the large window, looking down on the brightly lit area below. "What is that lovely building on the far side of the square?" she pondered.

"That is the famous Saigon Opera House, but it is not as lovely as you, Gabbie," replied Dai, as he gently placed his hands on her two shoulders from behind and kissed her bare neck. She slowly turned around to face him, draped her arms around his neck and kissed his awaiting lips passionately before breaking away.

"Let me have a quick shower, Dai. It's been a long day," she quietly whispered. "If you want to take the cork out of that lovely looking champagne in the ice-bucket, I will be back with you soon."

"It would be my pleasure, darling," replied a smiling Dai, as Gabrielle released her embrace, picked up her overnight bag and slipped into the bathroom.

Dai quickly unzipped his suit bag, pulling out a fresh shirt and his toiletries. It certainly had been a long day for him too; an early start at the office followed by a long, hard drive to the airport, and it was now close to 10pm. But he wanted to make the most of this special night and he wanted Gabrielle to be as happy as possible. After quickly stripping off the shirt he had travelled in, he quickly applied both deodorant and aftershave to his tired body, then slipped on and half-buttoned up his clean shirt before walking across to the chilled bottle of Veuve Clicquot, nestled in the melting ice of the silver bucket. After he had popped the cork out of the slender neck of the bottle and dimmed the lights in the room, he heard the bathroom door open. Without looking around, Dai selected two flutes from the cabinet above the sideboard where the ice-bucket had been placed and started to pour the chilled bubbly.

"I love the sound of popping champagne corks!" proclaimed Gabrielle, as she nestled in behind him. She placed a tender kiss on the nape of his neck and positioned her arms around his midriff. As her lips slowly left his neck, Dai felt the sensation of her warm, firm body pressing against his. He finished filling the second flute with champagne, picked up a glass in each hand, raised his arms slightly above his head and swivelled, still within Gabrielle's tight embrace. As he turned to face her, he slowly sought out her slightly opened mouth with his own eager lips and kissed her lovingly. He could feel her body through the silky dressing gown she had put on, still warm and moist from the hot shower. They disengaged from Gabrielle's hold, he handed her a glass of the champagne, took a sip of his own and led her to the foot of the bed. They silently sat down next to each other, looking intently into each other's eyes. She raised her glass to him, and he reciprocated.

"To us, my darling Dai," whispered Gabrielle, touching his glass gently then taking a long sip of the cool liquid.

Dai sipped his drink, then carefully placed his glass on the tiled floor. He smiled and looked deep into her jade eyes, took the almost empty glass from her, and placed it next to his. She pushed herself off the bed, got to her feet and stood facing him. As she bent forward to kiss Dai, he released the loose-fitting cord that fastened her gown. She eased herself out of the slippery garment and pressed against his body, feeling for the buttons of his shirt. Dai's head fell backwards onto the soft bed and she kissed him torridly. Slowly working her way down from his lips, she unbuttoned his shirt, slowly and deliberately pulling the garment from him. They kissed again, this time even more intensely. Gabrielle pushed herself off Dai's prostrate body, sat up on her knees, and admired his well-developed chest. A smile enveloped her beautiful face. She had worn nothing under her dressing gown and Dai looked up adoringly at her perfectly formed, tanned body. He smiled as she once again leaned forward and helped him out of the rest of his clothes, kissing his body passionately as she made her way up his torso and lay on top of him. Once again, their lips met and Dai rolled Gabrielle over onto her back, as she sighed with pure joy.

"I love you, Gabbie," exclaimed Dai.

"I love you too, Dai," gasped Gabrielle.

The next morning, after a lazy in-room breakfast followed by further tender lovemaking, Dai and Gabrielle drove back to Buon Ma Thuot. Dai rang Dung Lam just after they had started to head north on the highway, to let him know that they would be home by early evening and that he would see them tomorrow morning at work. The traffic was slightly heavier at this time of day, so the young lovers stopped two or three times along the way to eat, drink and fill the car up with petrol. They talked incessantly to each other. Life was good.

Back Home

Bianca's internal flight arrived at the local airport in Nova Serrana slightly later than scheduled, due to congestion on departing Rio. Her brother Mateus was already there to meet her, as promised. On the way back from the airport, Mateus planned to take her to see their father at the local hospital. According to Mateus, Luiz had progressed well since Bianca had spoken with Felipe, some 36 hours before, so Dr Alma had sanctioned a visit by Bianca on her return.

The drive to the hospital was only twenty minutes or so and Bianca had arrived well-rested after an excellent flight on the long leg of the journey back from Paris. She felt fresh and happy, and was keen to see her father and get back home to the Nova Coffee compound. As they arrived at the hospital, Bianca spoke to Mateus before they got out of the car.

"How is Papa looking after the operation, Mat? Has he got many scars?" queried his sister, wanting to prepare herself for any shocks.

"Surprisingly, sis, he was looking well when we saw him yesterday. His head is bandaged, but you can't see any scars or anything, so it shouldn't be too traumatic for you. He also has tubes poking into his nose and mouth to help his breathing. But apart from that he seems quite comfortable. He is excited to see you, Bianca. But he tires easily after five or ten minutes of conversation, so do not take it personally if he drifts off into a sleep. Dr Alma tells us that this happens quite regularly, so soon after the operation," answered Mateus. "Let's go, hey?"

"Thank you, Mat. That helps me. I can't wait to see him."

Luiz was half asleep as they entered his room, escorted by the head nurse. He lay with his eyes closed as they proceeded to take a seat on either side of his bed.

"Mr Almeida, your son and daughter are here to visit you, sir," announced the nurse, which alerted Luiz to flick his eyes open.

As he looked to his left, the sight of Bianca brought a smile to his face. Mateus gently held his father's right hand and whispered, "I've got a present from Vietnam for you, Papa."

"And what a marvellous present it is, Mat. Thank you. Hello, my darling, welcome home," said his father, as he accepted Bianca's kiss on his cheek.

"So good to see you, Papa. Looks like you have been in the wars whilst I have been away. But never mind, I am back home now, and I am here to look after you," she said, tears streaming from her eyes.

"Thank you, honey. It sure is good to see those beautiful eyes again. When did you get home from Vietnam?"

"I just arrived at from Rio in the last hour. Mateus brought me straight here," she responded, drying her tears with a tissue from a box next to his bed.

"The boys told me how well you and Gabbie did in Vietnam. I am so proud of how all of you have handled the whole USA order situation. Felipe and Mateus told me that it is basically sorted out now, Bianca. How did you enjoy being in Vietnam, and how is young Gabbie? I hear she needed to stay a little longer over there," asked Luiz.

"Well, Papa, I was impressed with the Lam Dong Coffee operation. Dai's parents are wonderful people and everybody at the company was so helpful. I think that we may have an interesting future with both Dai and his company. Gabrielle seems absolutely smitten with him and the more I got to know him, the more I liked him. The way he and his stepfather, who runs the company, work together is very impressive. They certainly pulled out all the stops to ensure that we could save our coffee crop, and they are going to supply the extra robusta-style beans that Mateus needs to complete the first order. It was a really successful trip, even if I say it myself, Papa," answered Bianca. "But that is not for you to worry about right now. Between us, we can look after Nova Coffee fine. Remember, you and Mum taught us how to do that. You need to get well, Papa. And I am the one who will make sure that happens!"

"Wow, what did your mother and I create?" chuckled a happy Luiz, holding both his children's hands tightly and smiling brightly. "It seems that I am in your hands, kids. Something that I will not argue with, I assure you."

With that, he again began to tire, and his eyes slowly closed, then flickered, as he struggled to keep awake. Mateus looked at his sister and gestured that it was time to go. Bianca nodded at her brother, kissed her father on the forehead and stood up to leave. Mateus put his hand onto his father's shoulder and whispered, "Goodbye, Papa. Sleep well."

As they left his side their father quietly whispered, "Goodbye, Mateus. Goodbye, Bianca. I love you." He then wandered into a deep sleep.

All's Well That Ends Well

Four days later, Mateus received the parcel that he was hoping for. The local courier pulled up at the Nova Coffee compound with his long-awaited supply of the Lam Dong Antidote from Dai's company in Vietnam. He had previously been given the disguised package from Bianca's luggage when he had dropped her home after their visit to Luiz in hospital.

His sister passed it on, with the glib remark, "Your niece asked me to pass this on to Clara, more perfume, I'm told. Can you give it on to her when you get home, please, Mateus?"

"Will do, sis, it will just add to her massive collection!" joked her brother, happy in the knowledge that his serum sample had arrived as planned.

That day he had watered down the concentrated liquid and sprayed a small section of the affected coffee crop, knowing that any result would take a few days to show. To his delight, the sprayed trees were showing a marked improvement in leaf cover after only three days.

"Maybe this Dai Ca Phung isn't too bad after all," he thought to himself as he looked skywards towards the precious canopy of trees.

Back in Vietnam

Tina Lei was typing up a report concerning the fire at the Lam Dong factory, required by Dung Lam for insurance purposes. He had dictated it into his smartphone and emailed it across to her the previous day. Dai had offered to let Tina do the job, as his stepfather's secretary was away on vacation. As she typed, a notification banner lit up on her screen, advising that an email had arrived from Nova Coffee. Knowing that Dai was keen to know when Mateus had received his shipment of the antidote, she clicked over to her inbox immediately. On seeing the content was positive, she forwarded the email to Da Ca Phung's laptop. She then called Dai on his phone line to advise that it had been received.

"Hi, Mr Phung, an email has just arrived from Brazil; I have forwarded it to you. I think you will be pleased," she chirped over the internal line.

"Thanks, Tina!" replied her boss, who was in his office with Gabrielle, door closed. "Wow, Gabbie. Mateus has got his delivery of the bulk Lam Dong Antidote and is confident of it working after he tested the 'perfume' you sent over to his wife. It seems he is happy that it will do the job," he informed Gabrielle.

"That is great, Dai, if Uncle Mat gets on with spraying the trees, he should be able to stop the spread of the virus and save his crop. How marvellous!" started his excited and happy girlfriend. "He'll be so pleased. He has worked so hard for the last 12 months to get those coffee beans ready in time for the big US order."

Dai walked across to her as she rose from her boardroom table chair, where she had been working on formulas for the Lam Dong laboratory. They embraced and Dai spoke to her quietly and deliberately. "Well, Gabbie. You have done so much towards this result. Your uncle should be so proud of you. The robusta beans should be arriving at the airport in the States very shortly. So, I would say that, all in all, Nova Coffee should be more than happy with what Lam Dong has produced for them. Hopefully, it will lead to more business in the future, for both of us."

"I know it will, Dai," affirmed Gabrielle, as they snuck in a kiss, well out of sight of the ever-alert Tina.

Back in Brazil

A month later, Gabrielle flew into Nova Serrana with Dai, after her epic trip to Vietnam. There to greet them were Mateus and Felipe.

Gabrielle had been in constant contact with her mother for the last four weeks, keeping her updated on the ever-blossoming love between herself and Dai. She was also always eager to hear about the health of her precious Poppy, whose progress had been superb under her mother's care. Bianca had secured Luiz's release from hospital and he was now comfortably convalescing in his own home. So much so that Bianca had urged Gabrielle to stay a little longer in Vietnam. As well as her daughter's budding relationship with Dai, Bianca had been made aware of the invaluable benefit that Gabrielle had brought to Dai's Lam Dong coffee company in the scientific and chemical laboratory area. The loss of Dr Chien had produced the opportunity for the young Brazilian to shine as the temporary head of the scientific department, a challenge that Gabrielle had taken in her stride and excelled at over the last four weeks.

In the meantime, Dai had also been getting on famously with Mateus, via email and Skype. Gabrielle's uncle had been successful in arresting the leaf rust in his crop and had also successfully supplied the first shipment of top-quality Nova Coffee arabica beans to the US. On time, and gratefully received by their northern neighbours. On Mateus' request Dai had brought with him a small amount of the latest Anti-Leaf Rust serum for

Nova Coffee to test and use. He also had the relevant paperwork to offer Nova Coffee first refusal on the exclusive distribution of Lam Dong's latest range of serums and spraying chemicals, carefully drafted by Dung Lam, for the whole of South America. It was an offer that Felipe had encouraged Mateus to look at very closely, as projected sales in the region were huge.

The two Brazilian brothers heartily welcomed their niece and her partner back to Brazil. They escorted them back to Mateus' truck, filled the boot with Gabrielle's luggage and Dai's smaller bags and drove towards the Nova Coffee compound. They all chatted incessantly about numerous subjects, including Luiz's latest health update, how well Bianca was performing her job as chief carer and the success of the initial order to the USA. Nevertheless, Mateus was still uncertain about the relationship he had with Dai. The doubts he had about why the outbreak of leaf rust had occurred in the first place still bugged him. Felipe, on the other hand, was effusive about the many opportunities that a commercial alliance between Nova and Lam Dong could bring. Gabrielle was still totally enamoured with her fresh and growing relationship with Dai and was enthusiastic about maybe returning to Vietnam in the future.

Dai sat in the back of the truck next to Gabbie, holding her hand. He was happy that he seemed to have developed a much better relationship with the whole of the Almeida family, and he was more than content with the way that things had turned out with Gabbie. However, even though he had navigated the successful turnaround of his poisoning of the Brazilian crop, his subconscious still harboured that nagging hatred for the Americans. As the chatter between Gabbie and her uncles continued all the way back to the Nova Coffee compound, Dai looked aimlessly out the window of Mateus' truck at the hot and dry Brazilian landscape passing by, his thoughts once again straying. He believed that he could not completely blot out the strong feelings that flooded his mind, fuelled by his family's past experiences. Dai confirmed, in his head, that he needed to fulfil his original quest to hurt the USA somehow. But next time it had to be more direct and, most definitely, not include the Almeida clan.

In less than five minutes Gabrielle would be reunited with her mother and her beloved grandfather. Dai could start talking with the Almeidas about his plans for a commercial future between Lam Dong and Nova before he jetted back to Vietnam in eight days' time. There was also a little bit of news that they both wanted to reveal to the whole Almeida clan. But that would have to wait until the timing was just right.

www.ingramcontent.com/pod-product-compliance
Lightning Source LLC
Chambersburg PA
CBHW020824260626
47169CB00003B/821